STRIFE & HARMONY

An International Anthology of Stories

Edited by Dixiane Hallaj and
D. J. Stevenson

S & H Publishing, Inc.
Purcellville, VA

Copyright © 2019 by S & H Publishing, Inc.

All rights reserved. No part of this publication may be reproduced, distributed or transmitted in any form or by any means, without the prior written permission of the publisher, except in the case of brief quotations embodied in critical reviews and certain other noncommercial uses permitted by copyright law. For permission requests, write to the publisher, addressed "Attention: Permissions Coordinator," at the address below.

Dixiane Hallaj/S & H Publishing, Inc.
P O Box 456
Purcellville, VA 20134
www.sandhpublishing.com

Publisher's Note: This is a work of fiction. Names, characters, places, and incidents are a product of the individual author's imagination. Locales and public names are sometimes used for atmospheric purposes. Any resemblance to actual people, living or dead, or to businesses, companies, events, institutions, or locales is completely coincidental.

Ordering Information:
Quantity sales. Special discounts are available on quantity purchases by corporations, associations, and others. For details, contact the "Special Sales Department" at the address above.

Strife & Harmony/Dixiane Hallaj and D. J. Stevenson, ed.
ISBN 978-1-63320-072-2
Ebook ISBN 978-1-63320-143-9

Previously published stories:
"The Big Drum" was published under the title "Birth of a Rebel" in *Forging Freedom: Volume II*, 2015, Freedom Forge Press, LLC.
"The Were Four" was previously published by Alliteration Ink: 2013.

STRIFE & HARMONY
An International Anthology of Stories

Table of Contents

(NOTE: Spelling and punctuation vary by country of origin)

NAMES IN A HAT 1
Diane Helentjaris

JADEN ROSE, GHOST TALKER 15
Lenora Rain-Lee Good

THE BIG DRUM 28
Dixiane Hallaj

SIPPY AND THE OLDER WOMAN 41
Erica Williams

JULY 17 51
Don Roberts

ABOVE RIO DE JANEIRO 62
Dian Stirn Groh

ME-ALITY.COM 72
David Boop

THE ACCOMMODATION 91
Margaret Pearce

CHARLIE'S WEEKEND 100
Ellen Barnes

TO PROTECT AND SERVE 114
John Peel

PASSAGE 127
Terry Korth Fischer

THE WERE FOUR 139
Alethea Kontis

FAR HORIZON 153
C. M Stucker

FOREVER GONE 163
Azure Avians

WONDER WOMAN 180
John Jeffire

THE WHOLE KITTEN CABOODLE............ 190
Patricia Powell

SYMBIOSIS 201
S. M. Kraftchak

MACHINATIONS IN THE MUSEUM 219
Madeleine McDonald

THREE WISHES 227
Robert Kibble

ALI 252
Liz Fyne

*A short story is a précis: an essential essence,
a sharp quality distilled from quantitative narrative.*

— *Richard Bunning*

NAMES IN A HAT

Diane Helentjaris

The white stallion's muscles moved rhythmically under her. His rumbling hooves stirred up the only breeze blowing across the harvested ground. As the fieldstone wall loomed up, sweat dripped down and burned Lydia's eyes. She knew the danger of jumping the stone wall but trusted the horse. There was freedom in being airborne, no matter how short-lived. Pegasus, neglected since Colonel Thornton's death two days earlier, hankered for the jump as much as she did. Neither the enslaved, busy at work, nor the master's family crying over the Colonel's open grave would know. She and Pegasus craved this. They jumped.

As Lydia neck-reined the white stallion back for another go at the wall, a distant hunting horn rasped its warning blare. While waiting back at the stable, Caesar must have seen the funeral party cresting the hill.

"Just once more, Pegasus," she whispered, her bare feet goading him forward for their final flight.

As Lydia and Pegasus reached the stable door, bandy-legged Caesar ran up, his legs see-sawing with the effort. Caesar snatched Pegasus' halter.

"You best git them britches off and git back into your dress, girl. You know Miz Thornton don't 'prove of you wearin' pants. And now the Colonel's passed..."

Lydia scurried off to an empty stall where a bright green dress hung from the hay rack. The loudly-colored fabric blared her enslaved status as surely as Mrs. Thornton's understated silks whispered of wealth. A few months earlier she'd turned fifteen and switched from the short shifts of girlhood to long dresses. Her passage to womanhood signaled by the change in clothing, she soon would be expected to start bearing children. Lydia peeled off the homespun britches she'd found in the ragbag, stuffing them behind some buckets. Hoping she didn't smell too "horsey," she tied a purple head cloth over her coppery ringlets and strode off to the summer kitchen to help.

Set back from Chestnut Grove's main house, the small summer kitchen buzzed with activity. Aunty pulled a perfectly browned apple pie out of the oven. Golden juice bubbled up from the vent holes cut in the crust. Wartime shortages could not dampen the Colonel's funeral meal.

"Lydia, take that platter in and put it on the sideboard… and where have you been?" sputtered Aunty Beebee. Aunty Beebee pointed to the rough-hewn oak table. There sat a blue and white porcelain platter heaped with buttermilk biscuits slathered with butter. Thin slices of salty ham, cured in the plantation's own sheds, peeked out of each one.

Lydia picked it up. Walking along the flagstone path to the house, she slipped three of the ham biscuits into her pocket. Even with the war, Virginia was bounteous in October.

No noise came from the big stone house. Chestnut Grove was one of the largest plantations in Albemarle County. Colonel Thornton had often bragged about Thomas Jefferson himself riding over from nearby Monticello to sample Chestnut Grove's hospitality. Matter of fact, "pass along" seeds from Jefferson's orchard had flourished at Chestnut Grove, producing the Spitzenburg apples in today's fragrant pie.

From the back of the hall Lydia could see straight through to the front door. One of the enslaved workers had propped it open with a brick in the hope of enticing a breeze into the house. Turning right, she entered the shadowed dining room. A black swag hung along the top of the Thornton family portrait which ruled the room from above the mantle. After Lydia carefully placed the biscuits on the mahogany sideboard, she paused before the oil painting.

In the middle reigned the stern-eyed Colonel, his wife Jane and their children arrayed around him like planets circling the sun. And there in the background, balancing a tray with a decanter of wine, stood Lydia's mother, Sabine. Only fifteen, Sabine, dressed in a saffron yellow gown, lit the painting with her beauty. Her curly hair peeped from a vibrant green and purple head wrap. She was clearly a Thornton, her face a darker version of her half-sisters and brothers. Lydia loved to look at her mother's face. She thanked God for whatever urge drove the Colonel years ago to include his enslaved child in this family portrait. In the painting, an African cowrie shell dangled from Sabine's neck. Now, just as the Colonel's dimple dented Lydia's chin, the cowrie shell nestled between Lydia's small breasts.

The Colonel had always been kind to her, almost tender. She would miss his calm presence. Lydia had never known her father. Others enslaved at Chestnut Grove claimed he was Jane Thornton's brother and had died in a duel. But it made little difference who her father was. Lydia knew, under Virginia law, a mother's status cast her children's fortunes. Children of free women were free at birth; babies of enslaved women were born enslaved.

That afternoon, the Colonel's heirs gathered in the sitting room for the reading of his will. The Thorntons, tired from their trip to the graveyard, stomachs stuffed from the funeral dinner, perched and perspired, awaiting the lawyer Sam Chase. The ladies futilely fanned themselves. Newly widowed Jane Thornton stared out the window. Her youngest child, twenty-two-year-old Eliza, held her hand. Mrs. Thornton's other daughter Abigail, with a middle softly thickened by early pregnancy, whispered to her husband, Jeremiah Linville.

Lydia quietly carried a tray of glasses filled with lemonade from one to another. Passing Mrs. Thornton, she overheard Eliza whispering to her mother.

"I hope the twenty-mile wagon trip on Three Chopt Road didn't harm the baby. I don't know why Jeremiah has to keep Abigail with child year after year. Surely…"

"Hush, Eliza. Not now. Have some respect," Mrs. Thornton cut her youngest daughter off in mid-sentence. The widow turned to her son Randolph's wife, Emmaline.

"Emmaline, dear, what news do you have? Our last letter had Randolph near Fredericksburg," said Mrs. Thornton to her daughter-in-law.

Lydia, her tray empty, left for the summer kitchen and didn't linger to hear the reply.

Outside, the tangy scent of the English box hedge filled the warm air. Lydia pretended not to see Caesar huddled on a bare patch beneath the sitting room window. An accomplished eavesdropper, Caesar often used the bower to listen in on the Thorntons. Today the other enslaved men and women were counting on him to hear and share the will's content. As with many illiterates, he had prodigious memorization skills. The contents of the will would spread fast among Chestnut Grove's enslaved. Even those rented out to work on Richmond's defenses would get the news quickly. Caesar had often bragged to Lydia of the Colonel's hints of future freedom. She said a short prayer for Caesar, hoping he'd gain his freedom. A wasp, attracted to the sugary drops of lemonade on Lydia's tray, droned around her hands. She flapped the tray and it angrily buzzed off toward Caesar. The sound of a man clearing his throat and rattling papers drowned out the wasp. Mr. Chase, the lawyer, began to speak and Lydia could not help but listen.

"And as for my slaves, I am directing Samuel Chase to write down the name of each one on a chit of paper. These chits are to be placed in a hat and my heirs are to draw out the number of chits as listed here. Each heir will become the rightful owner of the slaves whose name they draw…"

There would be no emancipation for those men, women and children held in slavery by the Colonel. Lydia, hot tears dripping onto her tray, heard Caesar's strangled sob. Her heart broke.

Around midnight, a lone cricket chirped amongst the summer kitchen's stored provisions. Aunty Beebee sat on a sawed-off log in front of the empty fireplace, her ample silhouette outlined by moonlight, her voice firm and low.

"You got to go, Lydia. You got to go now, tonight. Else Master Linville will take you away to Goochland tomorrow. We talked about th'other day, what we'd do if the Colonel sent us elsewhere. You're a young girl. You can grab your freedom. A girl lookin' like you won't be safe from a master like Jeremiah, especially now Abigail's with child again. You got to go."

"What about you and Caesar? I don't want to go without you. Where will I go up north? How will I live? Can't I stay here?" pleaded Lydia.

"Caesar and I will be fine. We're stayin' here with Master Randolph and Ms. Jane. We're both too old to go, but you got to go now. Just remember…never trust a white person except maybe a Union soldier, even if they say they want to help you. You may have blue eyes, but you're still

African. Freed Black people will help you. Union soldiers or freed Black people. That's it. Anyone else, be on guard. We're not too far from Pennsylvania..." Aunty Beebee went on. "Just keep the big mountains to your left. You should reach those freedmen in Orange tomorrow and after that, you'll be on the Carolina Road."

Lydia trod gingerly in the grass along the side of the moonlit road leading away from Chestnut Grove. She hoped the trees lining the stone fence rows would hide her. Aunty Beebee's cloth poke hung from her waist, heavy with food, a little money, and scrounged-up clothes. The dress and shawl in the poke looked more like a white person's clothing than Lydia's gaudy dress. She'd change clothes when she got further north. For now, if stopped by a patrol, she'd use her old permission slip. She'd claim she was being rented out to Jane Thornton's sister to help with the autumn harvest. Farther along, once she was north of the large Albemarle plantations, she planned to pass as white. Whispering a little prayer, she picked up her pace.

Hours later, Lydia's homemade shoes were proving no match for the road's stones and holes. She was sure she would find a blister if she took her left shoe off, but she didn't have any time to waste.

"I sorely miss you, Pegasus. Sorely!" she joked. Looking right, the sky was definitely starting to lighten. In the last little bit of time, the birdsong had changed from an occasional hunting owl's hoot to the soft calls of mourning doves. Soon the road would beckon to travelers who wanted to avoid the midday heat. She'd been walking the rolling hills all night. She would speed up and walk fast as she could on the downslopes. Next, she would slow down a little on the gentle upslopes to catch her breath. Surely, she must be near Orange. Lydia's only trip to the little town before this had been when she was twelve. She'd been sent along with Aunty Beebee to help with a wedding. She couldn't remember the terrain, but according to Aunty, the freed Blacks lived in the southeast quadrant of Orange. The prevailing northwest winds blew the entire town's chimney smoke toward their little collection of small cottages and cabins, making it the sootiest, cheapest, and least desirable neighborhood.

The creak of a wheel silenced the doves. A dilapidated old wagon was cresting the hill behind her. With no time to hide, Lydia forced herself to keep on walking.

In her mind, she went over her story: "I'm just going to Arrow Wood to help with the harvest. My owner couldn't spare more than one slave."

As the wagon drew near, she turned and let her breath out. The driver was Black. The man stopped his wagon beside her and tipped his hat. "Morning' Miss. Where you goin' all by yourself?"

"Orange, Sir," Lydia said.

"Well, climb on up. You don't want to be wanderin' around by your lonesome. Orange is jest a hill or two more ahead. Who you seein' in Orange?"

Lydia looked the older man over. There was no smell of alcohol about him. His work clothes were worn, but clean. A smile lit his calm mahogany face. He glanced at her poke.

"I think I know where you belong, Miss. Don't worry. My name's Elisha Martin. I'm a free man, a carpenter, livin' just outside Orange. I'll git you where you're headin'."

Lydia smiled, clambered in and covered herself with the horse blanket and empty feed sacks in the back of the wagon. She must have dozed off as it seemed no time at all before she was furtively hustled into a small log house by an elderly Black woman.

Once in the door, the tiny-boned lady introduced herself as "Miz Smith" and shooed her up a wooden ladder.

Broken chairs, ratty baskets, a broom, and sacks of provisions were strewn about. In one corner of the attic, a large wooden chest partially blocked a window. Following the old woman, Lydia saw a pile of old clothes on the floor snugged between the chest and window. Finger to lips, Miz Smith pantomimed to Lydia to rest on the pile and go to sleep. Lydia was only too glad to get off her aching feet.

She slept through the day at Miz Smith's cabin, tucked up under the eaves, out of sight. Lydia woke up in the gloaming. The aroma of frying chicken filled her nose and made her stomach gurgle.

With a crash, the weight came down on her. She wasn't on her way to help a neighboring plantation owner with his harvest. She was illegally fleeing slavery, according to the law. By now, Jeremiah Linville had certainly figured out she had fled. He might be in Charlottesville right this minute putting a notice in the newspaper with a reward for her return. If she were caught, she'd certainly be beaten at the very least and maybe worse. She may have feared he'd treat her poorly before now. By running away, she'd guaranteed punishment if she were ever caught. Lydia took a gulp, sent up a prayer for protection, and edged over to where the ladder poked into the attic. Down below, Miz Smith hummed a hymn as she stirred up cornmeal batter. A pot of greens bubbled on the wood stove right beside an iron skillet of frying chicken. Miz Smith looked up at Lydia. She put a finger to her lips, cutting off any conversation for now, a wide grin splitting her diamond-shaped face. A palm out hand let Lydia know she needed to stay upstairs.

Once full darkness fell, the light from downstairs changed. Miz Smith had lit a lantern and pulled shut the flour sack curtains.

Only then did she whisper up to Lydia, "Supper."

Lydia clambered down the narrow ladder, bringing her

poke with her. Over the tasty meal of chicken, cornbread and seasoned greens, the two chattered like old friends. Miz Smith had scrimped and saved and bought her freedom years ago, marrying a freedman, Jonas Smith. Now, she was a widow. She supported herself scrubbing laundry and sewing. Miz Smith had two grown sons in town and three grandchildren. She kept busy with her work, but things were hard with the war. Still, she made out okay and considered herself fortunate. Lydia was safe in this part of town, but Miz Smith still liked to be cautious. She'd put up others fleeing slavery and wanted to be able to keep on doing so. Lydia helped her clear the table and wash the chipped dishes.

"The next part of the trip will be both easier and harder," Miz Smith said. "Easier because the road's flat, but harder because there's not many freedmen to help you. You'll be on your own till you get to the Quakers in Loudoun County. You can trust them. You look like a strong girl and I know God will keep you. Just find a good hiding place during the day to sleep."

"But my aunty said not to trust any white people getting north except Army men. Aren't Quakers white?" said Lydia.

"You can trust the ones on Goose Creek. No one else. Tomorrow you should reach Culpeper. After Culpeper, you'll need to change your clothes and try to pass as white. You'll be too far from Albemarle County for anyone to believe you're being rented out," answered Miz Smith.

Miz Smith stuffed Lydia's poke with apples, cornbread dodgers. and fried chicken wrapped in greased paper. It was midnight. The air held the crispness only felt in the fall. A horse snorted and rattled its harness outside the cabin. With a hug and a kiss for Lydia, Miz Smith opened her back door to reveal Elisha Martin sitting atop his wagon.

"I can give you a head start, Miss. Just crawl back under the blanket like you did this morning. I'll git you a few miles out of town. Save you an hour's walkin.' My home's out that a way so's no one thinks twice seein' me on the road," said Elisha.

Lydia climbed in. Elisha's horse snuffled. With a screech, the wagon rumbled north in the cool night.

Journeying from Miz Smith's house had been easier than the first leg of her trip, just as the old lady had promised. Although the Blue Ridge Mountains were still to her left as she traveled north, their peaks in this part of Virginia were further off from the road, lower and not as dramatic as they had been in Albemarle County. The Carolina Road in this part of Virginia followed a flattened pathway.

Even so, Lydia was exhausted by the time she saw the chimney smoke from Culpeper's homes. She'd had a couple of little crying fits towards the end of her walk, her thoughts flying back to Chestnut Grove. But, then, she reminded herself that Chestnut Grove would never be what it had been. The Colonel was dead, and, with his demise, his protection evaporated. The enslaved of Chestnut Grove by now were all divvied up, split amongst the Colonel's heirs. Still, she yearned for Aunty and Caesar especially. She certainly didn't miss scrubbing the Thornton's iron skillets and emptying their chamber pots without so much as a "thank you" sent her way. Now, she had hope. If she could get up north to Pennsylvania and maybe on to Canada, she could be whatever she wanted to be. She'd be free. She wasn't sure how she'd earn her bread, but she'd be the one to profit from her work, not some so-called owner. Maybe she'd be a seamstress like Miz Smith. Lydia loved horses. Maybe she'd run a livery. She'd scrimp and save and get enough money to buy Aunty Beebee and

Caesar's liberty so they could all live together again. Only better, because they'd all be free. Pondering the opportunities of freedom cheered her up and made her lonely day bearable.

By dawn, a little abandoned shed had beckoned her, offering respite. Situated at a burned-out farm site, Lydia figured no one would bother her if she slept here. With a quick prayer, she tumbled into a deep sleep.

Aunty Beebee sat at the wooden table in the summer kitchen, chopping apples with her favorite kitchen knife. Lydia nudged the fruit she had peeled toward Aunty, doing her best to keep the older woman's pile of fruit stoked. The heady aroma set her stomach to growling. Aunty looked up from her work, worry in her light brown eyes.

"*Lydia be careful! Pay attention!*"

A rumble of thunder rolled out, wakening Lydia from her dream. Narrow spokes of light poked between the shed's dilapidated gray boards. Lydia peeked out through a crack in the walls.

That's funny. Not a cloud in the sky, yet it's thundering.

Digging into her poke, Lydia pulled out a misshapen apple she had picked on her walk. She ate a chicken leg, worried since only two wings remained. Remembering Miz Smith's recommendation and feeling ill at ease by Aunty's dream warning, she pulled out the brown calico dress and rust jacket.

Might as well just leave this slave dress here. That way I won't have to carry it. Lydia stuffed the cheap cotton dress and purple head scarf into a corner, covering them with rotten wood and straw. She reached back, plaiting her copper curls and tucked them into a crocheted snood Aunty had stuffed into the poke. Her blood-crusted left foot caught her eye. Her shoe had torn in the early morning hours. Lydia's shoes were straight-last; each one fitting either foot. She put the torn shoe on her right foot and tucked a square of linen over the scraped bloody side of her left foot.

That's the best I can do, for now. Maybe my feet'll toughen up soon. She was ready to walk.

From a distance Lydia's white heritage could shield her. By passing as a full-blooded Caucasian, she hoped to gain the liberties granted the race in Virginia. She knew few white girls had her height but couldn't change her tallness. Lydia planned on following Aunty's recommendation. She'd avoid contact with anyone and make herself scarce as she traveled toward freedom. She had never been so lonesome.

Venus twinkled in the early twilight, yet the thunder continued and grew louder as Lydia drew near the Rapidan River.

Must be raining the other side of the mountains. She could see a line of trees snaking through the grain fields ahead, marking a river path. Maybe they'll be some pawpaws by the river. Her mouth started to water just thinking about the rich custardy fruit. Drawing closer, a dank smell hit her.

"That water stinks. And no pawpaws." Disappointed, she moved on to look for a spring up the road.

A thrumming sound and the crack of gunfire joined the thunder.

"That's cannons, not thunder!"

Lydia rushed toward the river, looking to hide in the brush along the banks if need be. She spied some blue cloth in the brambles at the side of the road; drawing closer, Lydia gasped. The pile of cloth was a Union soldier, his blue cap blown five feet away from his disfigured face. He was clearly dead. His saddled bay mount, white-eyed and skittery, reins caught in brambles, gave a snort. The girl approached quietly, unsure.

"Whoa, girl. Shh…You'll be all right." She gently took the reins, patting the mare on the nose. The big horse quieted at her touch. Lydia reached into the cloth bag, pulling out her last apple and offered it with an open, flat hand. Soft lips accepted the gift. The horse, at least, was fine. Lydia looked down at the dead soldier.

The man's red hair shone in a beam of light from the setting sun. His feet were shod in new-looking leather boots. Lydia glanced at her feet, then his.

"I am so sorry, Sir, but I need your boots. I truly do. You won't need them to walk around heaven, but I have to make it north."

She thought for a minute or two, then tied the horse up and set to work. When she was done, the soldier was in his skivvies and she was now in full Union regalia, with a mount to boot. Aunty would be proud. She said a short prayer over the dead man after closing his eyes. Engrossed in her tasks and distracted by the sounds of battle, she didn't hear the Union officer's horse until he was ten yards away.

"Halt! What're you up to, soldier? Who's that in the ditch? What the….?" A stern-faced man astride a barrel-chested gray horse glared down at Lydia.

Her borrowed clothes were askew. She had missed a button in her haste.

"You're not a soldier! Who are you? Are you a secessionist trying to probe our lines? Speak up," he barked.

Startled, Lydia stepped back, caught her borrowed boots on a root and fell, dislodging her cap. Long braids of hair tumbled loose.

"Why, you're a girl… What in tarnation are you doing in that uniform?" said the Union officer.

Lydia stood up straight.

"I'm sorry, Sir, but I just have to get myself north. I've been walking and walking for days and my feet are so sore and my clothes so cumbersome and he doesn't need them anymore. Please, Sir, don't hurt me. Just let me have these shoes and go on my way. I can give you back the other clothes if you want. But I have to get north, and I need the boots. Can you help me, please?" Lydia said.

The soldier just stared.

"Where's your family? There's a war going on here and it's no place for a girl. I can't spend all day talking."

Lydia quickly explained. Her parents were dead, and she had been enslaved and was heading north to be free. She'd been told she could trust the Union Army. Couldn't he help?

Begrudgingly the man agreed.

"Quick. Get over here. We've got to cut off them plaits. You'll be safer kitted out as a soldier than as a girl. The Colonel can figure out the rest. Just let me do the talking and remember, your name is 'George Washington Smith' no matter what. Mine is Silas Green," said the soldier.

An hour later two Union soldiers trotted north along the moon-brightened Carolina Road. Silas sat atop the grey like a sack of potatoes. His slender companion rode her bay with rare grace. A soft smile playing on her face, Lydia reached up and tapped the cowrie shell through her uniform shirt.

"North," she whispered, "to freedom."

Writer and photographer Diane Helentjaris often combines her love of the gorgeous Blue Ridge Piedmont with her love of women's history to produce fascinating stories and photos. Find her at dianehelentjaris.com and see many of her photographs at dianehelentjaris.zenfolio.com.

JADEN ROSE, GHOST TALKER

Lenora Rain-Lee Good

5:03 pm on a Friday in April.
Computer: off. Desk: cleared. Coat: on. Light: off. Just as I pulled the door closed to lock it, the phone rang. It had that insistent quality and after a two-ring hesitation, I turned on the light and walked to my desk.

"Jaden Rose speaking."

The voice on the other end hesitated a moment, "Uh, is there any chance Jaden Rose is still in the office? I'd really like to talk to her."

Don't people listen? I smiled, and hoped the irritation wouldn't show in my voice. Why did I answer the phone?

"This is Jaden Rose. How may I help you?"

"Uh, Ms. Rose, I'm Elizabeth Dunlap, in Bacon Springs, Oregon. And I think we have a ghost problem."

"Oh? You *think* you have a ghost problem? What makes you think so?" Usually people know if they have a ghost, so this definitely piqued my curiosity. A little.

"It's Emma. We think. Emma Anthony. She came over the Oregon Trail in 1847, and drowned in the river, the Bacon Springs River. It was always assumed, though there was no proof, that Jacob Peek killed her."

"I see. Miss Dunlap, it's Friday evening, and I'm on my way home."

"Yes, ma'am. I understand, but, well, I need to tell you this. The story goes that Jacob was one of the first settlers of Bacon Springs. He came over with the first wagon train in 1843 and homesteaded here, with a few other hardy souls.

Anyhow, the wagon train that Emma Anthony was on with her parents and brother, came through in 1847 and stayed over a few days to rest and then to look for and bury poor Emma. Jacob said they could bury her near his cabin and he'd take care of the grave. His cabin is now the cornerstone of our museum." She paused. I didn't say anything, and she soon continued. I wasn't being uber polite, but she seemed to be uber nervous. And if I encouraged it, I feared she'd go on and on and on. Frankly, I feared she'd do it anyhow.

"He married a couple years later and quit leaving flowers on Emma's grave. Legend says that's when his haunting began. On his wedding night. Someone dribbled water on him while he slept. From then on, his shoes were always filled with water, and he began to lose his mind. He, of course, blamed his wife, and she ran off with someone else, said he did it to himself. Anyhow, she was long gone, and it continued until he died, a very old man. Nuttier than a squirrel's lunch, but harmless. Kind of added character to this place, the old-timers said. Others could see the water, but not how it got there. It stopped when he died."

"I see. And now it's started again?"

"Yes, and we're not sure what to do about it."

"Before we go any further, and I put you on the clock, let me ask you a couple of questions. Have you, or anyone tried talking to Emma, explaining the situation? Asking her to leave?"

"Well, uh, no. I didn't know we could do that."

"Anyone can talk to a ghost. Of course, it helps if someone can see them, so you're facing them when you're talking to them, and not the wrong corner of the room. They do like it when they're respected."

"Really? I didn't know that."

"A lot of people can see ghosts. A few of us can hear

them when they talk to us. That's where I come in. I'm one of the few who can actually carry on a conversation with them. I suggest you, or someone, try talking to Emma and tell her, gently, but firmly, that she's dead, that Jacob is dead, and that she really should consider moving on. If that doesn't happen, send me all the information you have on Emma and Jacob, and a check for $50.00. The $50.00 is non-refundable and covers my time to read the file. If I decide to take the case after reading the file, *if* is the operative word here, I'll contact you, and the money will be applied to your final bill. Be sure to have all the relevant contact information enclosed with the check. Any questions?"

"Uh, no. I guess not. At least not now. Thank you."

"You're welcome. Have a good weekend, Ms. Dunlap."

"Uh, yeah. You, too. 'Bye."

I hung up the phone and got the hell out of there before I got stuck trying to talk to another bimbo-sounding blonde. Which is not a fair assumption, I know, so don't start with the letters and emails and tweets. And, just so you know, I'm a blonde.

Two weeks later an overnight packet arrived from Ms. Elizabeth Dunlap of Bacon Springs, Oregon, with two neatly typed, single-spaced sheets about Jacob and Emma, a cashier's check for $50.00, and a note in large, loopy handwriting telling me three of them had gone to the little museum and talked to Emma, telling her the water was damaging things, and they'd really appreciate it if she'd move on. They weren't sure she was there, but the next day the floor was flooded. Fortunately, there was no damage. I took the packet home, poured myself a glass of a local vintner's red wine (Patrick Hood's Malbec if you want to know), and read about Emma and Jacob.

According to what I read, Jacob had the hots for Emma, who did not reciprocate. She had just turned fifteen and was not interested in marriage. She wanted to reach the fabled lands of Oregon City in the Willamette Valley. Jacob, according to some source not cited, feared he'd sleep cold until the following year when the next wagon train came through. But before the train moved on, Emma disappeared. Her body was found the next day, face down in the Bacon Springs River. Jacob, who had considered moving on with the train to stay close to his beloved, decided, instead, to stay near the burial site of his one true love. And apparently went insane.

There are ways to get rid of ghosts. The easiest is to explain the situation to them and ask them to leave. Often, they leave on their own once they understand they are dead. Next is to perform a ritual banishing them. This often works, but creates hard feelings, and costs a great deal more money. And if the ghost is adamant about staying, they can come back. Mostly, I just listen to the ghosts, see what they want, and if possible oblige them. That's the best all around. I am one of the few who can hear them *and* understand what they say. They do not always speak the same way we do; their speech is often slow, though occasionally it's faster. Pitch can be different; syntax can be off. I earn my money.

After reading the packet, and doing some research, I contacted Ms. Dunlap, told her my fee, and prepared to drive to Bacon Springs, Oregon, so named because of the springs that bubbled up fresh water that emptied into the aptly named river. It seems when Mr. Jacob Peek arrived in 1843, he had a small herd of pigs he brought overland. They smelled the water and, sure they were dying of thirst, stampeded into the springs and drowned.

While packing my bag for an overnight at the Bacon Springs Bed and Breakfast, my old friend and college roommate called.

"Why, Doctor Allyson Heath, how are you?"

"Mostly, I'm fine. Haven't heard from you in a while, just curious what's going on, and are we still on for next weekend?

"Next weekend?" My mind went totally blank as I searched for my calendar.

"You forgot, didn't you? You're coming down to Tim's ball game."

"Yes, I forgot. But yes, I'll be there. It's on my calendar at work; however, it's a good thing you called to remind me. I'm heading down to Bacon Springs as soon as we hang up. They have a ghost problem; I'll just take care of business there, and come early. What can I bring?"

"Bacon Springs? They got a hog haunting them?"

"No, it seems some gal who came over on one of the wagon trains in 1847 died there, and she's haunting them. An Emma Anthony."

"Really. Wonder if she's related to the Oregon City Anthonys?"

"Could be. Anyhow, it seems she's haunting the old Jacob Peek place."

"Jacob Peek? I remember reading about him. Something about being under suspicion of murder and going around wetting himself. Yeah. I remember. We studied him in one of our psych classes."

"One and the same, I think. Okay, now that I'm taken care of, what's with the 'mostly fine' bit?"

"Oh, I've let one of my clients get to me. I do pretty well at putting up that wall, ya know? But every so often, one of them finds a crack and slithers through."

"Want to talk about it? I've got the time."

"A young gal, here in Oregon City, who has severe eating disorder. She self-medicates on her thyroid medication, and anything else she can find."

"Ouch."

"Yeah. Ouch. She won't eat, and when she does, she barfs it back. Jaden, I don't think this gal will live out the month if something isn't done, and I'm damned if I can figure it out. Right now, she's in the hospital, but these gals, and it is mostly gals, are sneaky little manipulators. Her doctor has tried everything she can think of, the hospitalist has tried, and I've tried. I'm just feeling such gawd-awful defeat right now."

"I can understand. Hang in there, girlfriend. You've been known to work the now-and-then miracle. You'll come up with something. I just know you will."

"I appreciate your trust. See you this weekend."

10:20 am, on a Wednesday in June, in the dry and dusty town of Bacon Springs, Oregon.

I stood in the door of the museum and watched a woman dust the shelves. A towel was spread out over a damp spot on the floor. "Ms. Dunlap? I'm Jaden Rose. Is this the haunted building?" It was a rhetorical question. I could tell, as soon as I pulled into the parking lot, it was haunted.

"Oh, yes. To both questions. I'm Ms. Dunlap, and as you can see by the dampness, over here next to the bed, it's also the site of the haunting." She walked over to the towel and picked it up.

Ms. Dunlap was a fairly nondescript person; just what one would expect to find in a dusty museum in a dusty part of the world. Faded would be the kindest word I'd use to describe her to the police, if I had to. Faded hair (blonde, by the way), faded clothing, faded skin. Faded personality. But she was alive, and most live people look some faded to me. Ghosts, on the other hand, are often vibrant.

I looked around. There was one car in the parking lot. Mine. There was no Emma. From the dust on Ms. Elizabeth

Dunlap's shoes, I assumed she walked to work. "Ms. Dunlap, where was Emma's body found, and where is she buried? And where did Jacob die, and where is he buried?" She walked to the door, gave a feeble and somewhat faded smile and stood next to me. Even her perfume smelled faded. She pointed out the areas and offered to show them to me.

"Thank you. If you don't mind, I'd like to check those places out. Alone." The little bit of eagerness fell from her face. She obviously wanted to go along, but I need aloneness for first contact.

I walked to the burial plot, looked it over, saw two fairly new headstones, placed by the Bacon Springs Historical Society, and enjoyed the shade. Someone had fenced the plots and planted cottonwood trees to offer shade from the summer sun.

The walk to the river was short and cool. Trees and sagebrush vied for water along the banks. There was a wooden walkway down to the water, and a plaque stating "The body of Emma Anthony was discovered here in 1847."

"They're wrong, you know. I warn't found here, I was over yon, on t'other side. But they didn't want to make a bridge for the folks who come by."

"Hello, Emma. May I call you Emma? Or do you prefer something else?"

"You can hear me? Can you see me?" Shock and excitement colored her voice.

I turned toward her and saw a young girl, wearing a wet yellow prairie dress with green leaves printed on it sitting on the bank in the shade. She was watching me. Her pink sunbonnet tied under her chin rested on her back. Her long dishwater-blond hair fell below her shoulders, in wet, scraggly strings. Her sad pixie face watched me with a hint of curiosity. Hope and a smile played at her mouth. "Yes. I can hear you, and I can see you, too." I smiled. "May I join you?"

"I need joining? Am I coming apart?" She frantically began to look at the bodice of her dress.

"No, I meant, may I sit with you?"

"Oh. Yes. But not too close, or you'll get wet. I declare, it's been such a spell since anyone could see me, and hear me, I'm not much used to conversing." She motioned to a nearby log for me to sit on. "I used to yell and scream at Jacob, but he never heard me. I'd sing to the animals, but I don't think they heard me, either."

"Emma, may I call you Emma?"

"What else would you call me? It's my name."

I smiled at her. She really was a beautiful young lady. "You might prefer I call you Miss Anthony."

"Oh. No, I think it's nice to hear my name again. Anthony was my daddy's name and onct I married, it'd change. But Emma.... Emma is *my* name."

"Emma, why did you haunt Jacob?"

"Oh, I guess because I could. And it bothered him some. You know he kilt me? I didn't want to marry him. I wanted to go on to Oregon City, but he wanted me to stay and cook for him, and clean his little house, and have his children."

She paused, and I finally broke the silence. "Did you want to get married and have children?"

"Oh, yes. I wanted a husband and children. I wanted my own home and to cook and clean. Just not Mr. Peek's. Now I'll never have the chance. I loved to cook, and was the best baker on the train. People brought me their flour and fat to bake their bread. They really liked my bread. I had the touch, you know."

"That's quite a touch to have. I've never been able to bake a decent loaf of bread. Why didn't you want to marry

Mr. Peek?"

"Well, you see, I had just turned fifteen, and I know lots of girls that age was married and even mommas, but Papa told me I didn't have to get married if'n I didn't want to. I didn't want to. Not then. Not to dusty old Mr. Peek. Besides, there was a young man in the train that smiled at me and looked much more interesting than dusty old Jacob. And he was nicer. His name was Earl." Lost in her reverie, she stopped and smiled as she thought of Earl. Her voice was slow, but mostly at the speed and syntax of her day. Shaking her head, she went on:

"Anyhow, the last night we was goin' to be here, Mr. Peek, he asked my Papa and me if he could take me for a walk. He had something to show me. Papa said yes, I could go, but to be back early as we was leavin' the next day."

"And where did Mr. Peek take you?"

"Oh, he took me to his cabin and showed me how nice it was and showed me his bed. He… he pushed me onto it and had his way with me, even though I said not to. I fought, but to no good end. I would have screamed, but he covered my mouth. He said I had to marry him because no other man would have me. I ran from him soon's I could, told him I'd tell my daddy what he done, but he come after and caught me by my arm. I tried to get away. He doubled his fist and hit me in the stomach and threw me into the river. I couldn't breathe, and the water was so cold, when I hit it, I breathed it in instead a air, and I drowned."

She stopped, and this time I waited for her to break the silence. It was several minutes before she did. Ghost Talkers develop a lot of patience. Sometimes we break the silence, but it's a fine line we have to learn. I felt she needed to think, quietly, for now.

"The next day, someone found me, but it was too late. And when I tried to tell them what happened, no one could hear me. Mr. Peek said I was fine when he saw me last, that he'd walked me back to the train after a walk by the river. Maybe, he said, I went back to the river? He said I told him I liked the river. That war a lie. It's ugly. They believed him."

She stopped talking, and after what I hoped was an appropriate length of time, one can never be sure with the deceased as time runs very different for them, anyhow, I responded. "That was a terrible thing he did to you. I'm sorry no one heard your side of the story."

"He offered to bury me near his home, and promised to keep it clean, and plant trees by it, and told my parents they could come any time. They agreed, and the day after my burial, the wagon train went on without me. He would come out and talk to me, tell me how sorry he was, but that it was my fault, that if I'd only listened to reason and married him, none a it would a happened. And he put flowers on my grave."

"Abusers often blame their victims. It was not your fault, Emma."

"It warn't?"

"No. It was his fault. Most assuredly his fault."

"I thought so. And it took a while afore I could really hant him. But when he convinced another girl to marry him, he stopped putting flowers on my grave and quit coming to talk to me. I became both angry, and skairt for her. I heard him mumble about how if she didn't obey him he'd teach her, just like he teached me. And on their wedding night, she was a tiny thing and some skairt a him, I stood on his side of the bed and dripped water on him. He accused her, of course, but I had only dripped on the side away from her. She convinced him it was a leaky roof." She giggled, and then said, "It war raining." There was a long pause before she began speaking again, "The next night, when he got into bed, his side was wet, where I'd laid down. He accused her of doing it, raised his fist to hit her, but she had enough backbone to run to a neighbor's afore he could. After that night, his bed was usually wet. She refused to return to him. She told everyone he'd wet himself and then blamed her. A man come down, out of the mountains, and she went back with him. It took old Jacob a time afore he realized it was me wetting his bed. Sometimes, I'd stand next to him, before he slept, and drip on his face. Sometimes, if his feet war bare, I'd drip on them. Sometimes, I'd go back to the river to stay a while."

"Emma. Do you know what year it is?"

"No. Should I?"

I smiled at her. "No. But you've been dead for many, many years. Jacob is dead, too. In fact, they buried him next to you."

"He's dead? Well, that explains why he's not in his bed. I guess the last time I came to the river and stayed..."

"Yes, he's dead. And his house is now a museum."

"A what?"

"A place where people come to see how people of your time lived."

"It's changed? Nobody lives there now?"

"No one lives there now. It's changed very much. It's now a museum people come to visit."

She looked at me, then at the river, and appeared to think about this.

"Emma, I've been asked to come and to talk to you, to see if I can convince you to leave. To move on. You're disrupting people and causing damage to the museum. It's your history, Emma, and our history and people are fascinated by it."

"I'd rip it down, if'n I could." There was petulancy to her voice that hadn't been there before.

"You'd rip Jacob's home down if you could? But, Emma, it is no longer his."

"I'm never to be a mother now, am I? Or eat another cake? Or see the fabled Oregon City? It's not fair! It's just not fair!" She stood and threw a mild tantrum; complete with stomping her tiny bare foot, and water flew away from her to splatter everything close by. Even me. Teens are teens are teens, no matter what year they lived in.

"No, Emma. It isn't fair. But you really do need to move on. It's time to go. I can force you, but I don't want to resort to force. It's much better for you and for everyone else, if you go on your own."

We talked for a while longer, bargaining, if you will, and finally, I agreed to try to meet her request. It wasn't such a big thing, but I didn't know if I could do it. However, she agreed to stay out of the museum, at least until I returned the next week with an answer; one-way or the other.

Her last words haunted me all the way to Oregon City. She so wanted to eat and taste, just one more time, real bread hot from the oven, a cake, and food of any sort.

Two years later, 4:25 pm, on a Monday, my office
A young woman, in the pink of life, carrying an alert and seemingly healthy child, I guessed to be about 6 weeks old, entered my office. "Jaden Rose?" she asked, somewhat hesitantly. She looked familiar but I couldn't place her.

"Yes, I'm Jaden Rose. May I help you?"

She smiled a wide and beautiful smile, "Oh, no, ma'am. We just wanted to meet you and thank you. You don't recognize us, do you?"

"You do look familiar, but no, I'm afraid I don't recognize you."

"We aren't surprised. I'm Sally. You introduced me to Emma a couple years ago in Bacon Springs. I was, literally, at death's door."

"Sally?" I stood and looked at her. I had, indeed, taken her to meet Emma. She was anorexic, on some kind of thyroid and diet pills (too many and not prescribed), and her therapist, my good friend, Dr. Allyson Heath, in Oregon City, told me she probably had less than two weeks to live — if that.

She laughed. "Yes. It's us. Emma is still with, in, me."

She held up her hand as I'm sure the anger I felt crossed my face. "It's all right. Really. Once you introduced us, and she, uh, moved in so to speak, I began to change, and for the good. She made me mark the calendar and at the end of two weeks, after eating more than I'd eaten in years, she started to leave, to move on as she put it, per your agreement, but I told her to stay. Actually, I begged her to stay. I ate more, enjoyed life more, and began teaching her about all the new things that have happened since her death. I married my high school sweetheart and we had a baby. Emma says she'll leave, any time, but Ms. Rose, I don't want her to leave. Besides, she has to help raise our little girl, Jaden Emma Anthony. Yes, we married an Anthony, a descendent of her brother. Isn't that just too much?"

She began to laugh, and I looked into her eyes, and saw Emma laughing, too.

―――

Lenora lives in the high desert of Washington State where she writes poems, novels, and radio plays. When not writing, she reads, quilts, makes jam, and takes road trips. Her novel, Madame Dorion: Her Journey to the Oregon Country, *is published by S&H Publishing, Inc. Her most recent novel,* Jibutu: Daughter of the Desert, *is published by Silver Sage Press, an imprint of S&H Publishing.*

THE BIG DRUM

Dixiane Hallaj

Boom! Boom! Boom! The steady beat of the drum echoed across the valley. Nadeem's hand froze with a fig halfway to his mouth, and his heart started thudding like a faster echo of the big drum.

"Do you hear it, Nadeem? They've come." The rustling of the thick foliage overhead accompanied his brother's voice. "Come on, let's go." Soon a bare foot poked through the broad leaves of the huge fig tree, followed by Amer. He wiped his sleeve across his mouth, but it did little to erase the signs of eating as many figs as he'd put in the bag.

Nadeem scrubbed at his own mouth with his shirttail. "I'm not going."

"You have to, silly. Everyone has to go. The Turks don't ask—they give orders. Isn't it exciting? If they take us, we'll get to see the whole world. We'll go places no one's ever been."

"Not no one. There's people there or the soldiers wouldn't go."

"But they're not people like us. They talk gibberish, and I heard they have tails, and…" Nadeem didn't hear the rest because the tone of their mother's call started them racing to the house. Nadeem worried when he saw how pale Mama's face was, but Amer was too excited to notice.

"The Turks are coming, Mama. We heard the drum from the fig tree. We're going, aren't we, Mama?"

"Yes, we're going." Amer ran and hugged his mother, so

he didn't see the tears in her eyes.

Nadeem saw the tears, and his fear grew to a lump in his stomach. "Can I stay home with Hala?"

"No. Hala already left with Papa. No one can stay home. The soldiers will ride all over the valley. If they find anyone in a house, they burn it down."

"What about Grandmother? She can't walk to the village. Will they burn her house?"

"Papa took the donkey. He'll get Grandmother and meet us at the village."

Papa always thought of everything. Hala was too little to walk all the way to the village, and Mama was too big with child to carry her that far. Mama was shoving bread, cheese, olives, and other kitchen things into a bag. "I don't know how long we'll be gone. Nadeem, you carry this. Amer, get some warm clothes in case we have to stay all night."

Mama hurried them out the door in front of her. They hadn't walked any farther than the almond tree when she told them to wait a minute. She ran back to the house for "one more thing."

Amer hadn't stopped talking about the Turks. "Have you ever seen their uniforms? They're wool with bright brass buttons. They'll keep you really warm in the winter. And they give everyone boots to keep their feet warm, too. Great shiny leather boots."

"And in the summer, you'll cook inside that wool uniform and melt right into those leather boots that raise blisters on your feet."

"It's only just starting autumn. By summer the war'll be over, and we'll come home."

"They also give you a sword and a gun."

"Yeah. Isn't it great?"

"No. They expect you to use them."

"Yeah. They'll teach us to shoot—we'll have our own guns."

"Amer." Nadeem stamped his foot. His brother could be so aggravating. "You'll have to shoot other people—and they'll be shooting at you. You could get killed."

"They won't be people like us. They'll be those funny people with tails and maybe even horns. It'll be like killing a chicken." The loud squawk of a frightened chicken made both boys laugh.

Mama was back, tying a sack closed. "We might need more food." A muffled squawk from the sack protested. "We can bring her back if we don't need her."

Half a mile toward the village, they saw Papa. He was leading the donkey with Grandmother and Hala on top. Papa waved and waited for them. The family walked another two miles, joining the trickle of families walking toward the village. Papa walked with his arm around Mama, and they talked in low tones. Nadeem thought Mama was crying, but when he tried to get close enough to hear, Grandmother grabbed his sleeve and made him walk next to her. Amer had already run ahead.

"Grandmother, how come the Turks can tell us what to do? Even the village mokhtar doesn't do that. He settles arguments and stuff, but he doesn't order us around."

"Sometimes he does."

"That's only when he's collecting taxes, and that's for the Ottomans, too." Grandmother was quiet so long that Nadeem started talking again. "Amer said killing people in the war would be like killing chickens because they aren't like us."

Grandmother gave such a big sigh that Nadeem looked to see if she was having trouble breathing, like she did last year. No, it was just a sigh. "That's at the bottom of it all, child. The Turks are pretty good to us as long as we pay the taxes, but in the end—we aren't Turks."

Nadeem took a couple of minutes to think about that. "So they're the Turks and we're the chickens." He scuffed up dust from the dirt road. It probably wouldn't rain until next month. "I think Amer wants to be a Turk."

Grandmother chuckled. "Amer's a very stubborn youngster. If he wants it badly enough, who knows? He might find a Turkish wife to help him along." She reached out and tousled Nadeem's wavy black hair. "And what about you? Do you want to be a Turk?"

"No. I want to stay and help Papa with the farm. He'll need more help when the new baby comes." Nadeem watched the small puffs of dust that swirled around the donkey's hooves. Life without Amer wouldn't be as much fun. Hala was too little to climb trees, and she was just a girl anyway. "Grandmother, Amer'll still be Palestinian, won't he? Even if he puts on a Turkish uniform, he'll always be Palestinian."

"Palestinian, Greater Syrian, Arab. He can't change his blood."

"So he'll always be my brother."

"Of course."

Satisfied, Nadeem skipped ahead. There was a mulberry tree just around the bend. If they were lucky, there might still be some ripe mulberries to pick. As Nadeem hoisted himself onto a low branch, Amer's voice above him said, "Don't bother. The mulberries are all gone."

"I should've known you'd be here," said Nadeem with a laugh as he dropped out of the tree to the purple-stained dirt beneath it. Amer landed next to him, and they waited for the family to catch up.

The drum beat was louder now.

When they entered the village, the first house they passed belonged to the widow Um Tariq. The boys were surprised to see half a dozen horses standing in the yard. Um Tariq was shouting, "Just keep those horses away from my spinach patch." They could hear men laughing inside the house. Um Tariq waved at them to stop. She ran over and asked if she could stay with Grandmother. "There won't be anything left by the time they leave, but I can't stay in the house with those louts."

Another group of soldiers stood in the road, blocking their progress. They ordered the women to go off to the left, and the men to go straight. Nadeem was leading the donkey, and he started to the left. The soldier grabbed the back of his shirt and pointed in the other direction. Nadeem passed the reins to Mama and grabbed Papa's hand. Amer already had the other hand. Together they walked toward the center of the village.

It looked very different from the quiet village Nadeem had known all his life. It was noisy with men shouting over the sound of the drum and horses snorting and stamping—more horses than Nadeem had ever seen.

The three joined a group of men and boys from the village. The group got larger as the day moved toward afternoon. Nadeem's head throbbed in time to the incessant drum beat, and his stomach growled in counterpoint. Even Amer's excitement faded.

The drum stopped, and Nadeem thought for a moment that he'd gone deaf. Then he heard the horses again, and a baby cried in the distance. Amer elbowed him and pointed to the mokhtar's house. Standing in the doorway was a tall Turkish soldier, resplendent in a uniform with gleaming brass buttons and gold braid on his epaulets. Shiny black boots reached his knees, and a helmet with a brass ornament on top added even more inches to his frame. He studied the crowd from beneath his dark bushy eyebrows as he turned his stern face with the thick moustache from one side to the other. He looked very grand with his bandoliers across his chest.

"See?" whispered Amer. "I told you they had nice boots."

"But only the Pasha Effendi gets to wear them. Look at everyone else."

Amer ignored his words.

The officer nodded at his men. He took a slender stick from his belt and held it against the wall of the mokhtar's house. One of the soldiers ran up with a half-burned branch. Using the charred end, the soldier drew a line on the house where the officer's stick pointed. A sound like a hive of angry bees arose from the village men, and the soldiers moved a little closer. No one said anything out loud. Papa put an arm around the shoulder of each of his boys and pulled them close. Nadeem wanted to ask what was happening, but it didn't seem the right time to talk.

The officer gave an order, and the soldier standing next to him shouted, "All you men form a single line," in strangely accented Arabic. Other soldiers began pushing and shoving the men into line. The mokhtar brought a chair and small table out to the yard, and the officer sat and crossed his legs. The mokhtar went back in the house and came out with a tray holding a brass coffee pot and a small cup. He placed these on the table next to the officer before going back inside.

Nadeem watched as the men were marched, one by one, past the line on the wall. Only a few boys were pulled out of line and sent to join the women. It didn't take long for Nadeem to understand that only the boys shorter than the mark on the wall were sent away. He clutched his father's shirt. "Everyone?" He forced the word past lips paralyzed with fear. They couldn't take everyone—what would the village do? Everyone meant Papa, too. He looked at the

THE BIG DRUM/HALLAJ

men around him and the boys some of them held close. He knew almost all of them by name. What would their families do without them? What would Mama do? How would Grandmother live all alone?

Old Abu-Mustafa reached the front of the line, leaning on his stick. The soldier snatched the cap off his head and showed his nearly bald head with its fringe of white hair. Then he made him open his mouth. The officer frowned, and the soldiers sent Abu-Mustafa away like the small boys.

Soon it would be their turn. Nadeem tried to swallow. He couldn't slouch low enough to get below the mark. Neither could Amer, but Amer didn't want to. If they took Papa and Amer, there would be no one to help Mama. He had to get away from the soldiers and stay with Mama. But how could he? There were soldiers everywhere.

A shot rang out behind them. Had the soldiers shot someone? The officer shouted orders and everyone, soldiers and villagers alike, started toward the shot. This was his chance. He could run faster than anyone in the village. Maybe he could run and hide until they left. He had to try.

He slipped out from his father's arm and started running. He ran past the mokhtar's house. He ran past the next house and turned away from the road. It was a full six seconds before he heard a shout behind him. He ran behind the next house and he heard more shouts and the pounding of boots. He looked around wildly for a place to hide. They'd find him in no time if he hid in a house. There were no trees he could climb, nothing he could hide behind.

Then he spotted the well. He could hide in the well until the soldiers were gone. The pounding boots were getting closer. He moved the heavy wooden cover aside just enough to squeeze through. He lowered himself into the well, feeling for toe holds in the cracks between the stones lining the well. His heart, already pounding, stepped up the beat as voices approached. He had to get out of sight.

His toes finally worked their way between stones and he reached up with one arm to slide the cover back in place. It didn't budge. His breath came in short gasps of sheer terror. His toes protested holding his weight, but he had no choice. He needed both arms for the job. Exerting all of his strength, he managed to slide it almost closed. He used all of his strength for one last desperate effort, and the lid dropped into place. The sudden movement shifted his weight and one of the stones beneath his toes moved.

Then the unthinkable happened—his foot slipped, and he plunged down through the darkness. The shock of the icy water cut his scream short. Fear turned his arms into windmills. He choked and sputtered as he flailed in the inky wet prison of the well. What had he done? He'd surely drown. He'd never been in water deeper than Mama's washtub. He'd traded one death for another.

Pain lanced up his leg as his kicking foot hit the side of the well. Sobered by the intensity of the pain from his probably broken toe, Nadeem stopped flailing. Kicking and bobbing, he felt for cracks in the walls. It may have been minutes, but it felt like hours before he discovered that the water didn't quite cover his head. It had been a long, dry summer. If he stood on the tips of his toes, he could breathe. Except for the pain in his toe, he managed to stand quite easily by resting one hand on the wall.

Nadeem's heart skipped a beat when he heard the cover scrape against the stones overhead. The sunlight was blinding after so long in complete darkness, but it showed the outline of a Turkish army headdress. Nadeem tried to call for help. Even the Turkish army would be better than a slow death in the freezing water of the well. He drew in breath to holler for help, but the cover slammed back in place before a sound escaped.

Seconds ticked into minutes, and possibly hours. Nadeem had no way of measuring time. Cold occupied his thoughts. The cold water seemed to be pulling all the warmth from his body. He was sure if the soldiers opened the lid again, they'd hear his teeth chattering before he called for help.

He explored his prison by feel. The stones had been fitted together with expertise, allowing few cracks large enough for fingers or toes. The walls were rough, except below the water line where they felt a little slimy. The well was narrower down here, too. He could brace his feet against one wall and his back against the other. That relieved him from having to stand on tiptoes to breathe.

It had been past lunchtime when the soldiers lined them up. Nadeem figured he had already missed another meal. It must be dark outside. Could he climb out of the well? Would it be safe to try? Maybe not. He'd wait.

Nadeem tried to count minutes, but not only was that boring, but he kept losing track of how many minutes he counted. How long would the soldiers stay? Mama had packed food and brought a chicken in case they stayed longer. How long could he wait without food? He could starve to death.

Hours passed, at least Nadeem thought that hours had passed. His hands and feet were losing feeling. If he was going to climb out, he'd better do it while he could still feel the cracks between the stones. He started up, feeling carefully for the best places for his fingers. His sore toe still hurt, but it worked as well as the others. Slowly he inched his way up the sheer wall of the well. It was a lot harder than climbing a tree, especially in the dark. The rough stones scraped the skin off his fingers. Moving one hand

and then one foot at a time was slow work. His arms ached and a painful cramp in one foot made him stop for several minutes, supported by the other foot and hanging by the tips of his fingers.

How high was he? How much farther did he have to climb? It was too dark to see anything. He prayed he'd reach the top soon. His fingertips were getting numb with cold, and the ache in his arms turned to agony. He put the fingers of one hand in his mouth to warm it and get the feeling back. It tasted of blood. Without warning, the stone beneath one foot came out of the wall, leaving him hanging by one hand and his injured foot. Before he could find a crack for the other hand, another stone moved and he fell back into the water.

Back on the bottom, Nadeem tried to restore feeling to his bleeding fingers. Maybe he could go up keeping his back on one wall and his feet on the other. His hands could help him slide his back up the wall an inch at a time, while his feet kept him steady. He hadn't gone far when his leg muscles began shaking with fatigue. Not long after that, as he put all his weight on his feet to move his body upward, the muscles refused to hold his weight, dumping him once more to the bottom of the well. This time he got a nasty bump on his head before landing.

That's when the tears started. With nobody to witness his humiliation, there was no sense in keeping them bottled up anymore. He was going to die down here in the dark. It didn't matter if he cried like a little baby, or screamed like a girl. No one could hear him. He cried until he thought he'd run out of tears. His sobs gradually faded away, leaving him exhausted.

He was hungry, cold, and so tired he wouldn't have been able to stand on his own feet without the water making him lighter. What if he fell asleep? He'd probably drown. Would he die of hunger first? He wondered how long it would take him to die. He was a total fool. If there'd been any chance of escape, the older men would've run away.

He jerked his head up with a start, coughing and choking on water. He must have dozed off. His eyes must have closed without him noticing. After all, it didn't make a lot of difference if they were open or closed in the bottom of the dark well.

No one knew where he was. No one would think of looking in here. He wondered if Mama knew he hadn't gone with the Turks. Were the Turks gone yet? Papa must be really sad. He knew Papa didn't want to go and leave Mama alone.

Yeah, that's why he'd run in the first place. He couldn't give up now and leave the family without anyone to take care of them. Now at least they'd have him to lean on. He thought about the other families, the ones without older boys. What would they do? How could the village survive?

He had to stay awake. Someone was bound to come for water. Once the Turks left, people would move back to their houses, and someone would need water. All he had to do was stay awake.

He sang songs; he told himself scary stories of jinn and efreet, but he couldn't make up stories as scary as the Turks coming and taking away all the men in the village. He hollered for help until his throat was raw. His voice got quieter and quieter, but he kept going. He had to keep going for Mama and the village. He pounded the walls to warm his hands and the pain of the rough stone kept him from sleeping. The more he thought about the village and what the Turks were doing outside his well, the angrier he got. He'd never forget this day and what the Turks did to them, and he'd never forgive the Ottomans. All he had to do was stay awake.

And then, it happened. Blinding sunlight poured into the well before it was partially blocked by a bucket. The bucket landed in front of him, and it took all of his strength to grab it. His arms didn't want to move, and his hands were dead things with no feeling.

"Help. Help me, please." He wasn't sure his weak cries could be heard from the top of the well, but he hung on to the bucket as hard as he could. He heard a sound, and then nothing. Had the person been frightened and run away? Tears threatened, but he held them back. "Help me." He tried again.

"Who's down there?" A man's deep voice echoed down the well.

Did that mean the Turks were still here? No matter, he couldn't hold on any longer. "It's me, Nadeem."

"Can you hold on to the bucket?"

"I'll try." He couldn't. His arms gave out and he dropped back down before they'd pulled him halfway up.

The man came back with a rope with a loop on the end. "Put this under your arms. We'll go slow." Despite their best efforts, Nadeem got a few more bumps and bruises on his way up, but he didn't mind. Hands lifted him over the edge of the well, and he had a fleeting thought of how wonderful it was to be in the sun before he lost consciousness.

Nadeem woke up wrapped in a blanket. He didn't know whose house he was in, but it looked like a village house, and he didn't see any soldiers. He sat on the edge of the bed and clutched the blanket as he realized he wasn't wearing anything under it. "Is anyone here?"

"Oh, glad to see you're up. Hungry?"

"Abu Khalid! How come you're still here?" The man held up his right hand, swathed in thick bandages.

"I shot myself in the hand."

"That was the shot we heard?"

"Yes. I told them that I was running to enlist, and bringing my own gun to help when I tripped." Abu Khalid gave a deep hearty laugh. "They decided the army would be better off without me."

Nadeem tried to stand up, and fell back on the bed. His legs wouldn't hold his weight, and the room started spinning around him. "I have to get home."

"Not until you can walk. You've been two days in that cold water without food. You're lucky to be alive."

Abu Khalid brought him a bowl of bread soaked in hot sweet tea. "Sorry there's no milk. The Turks ate our goat before they left."

"I had to stay alive, for Mama and the village. I think it was anger that kept me alive. I'll never forgive them for taking Papa and the others."

"You're a plucky resourceful kid, Nadeem. Who knows, someday you might even lead the rebellion that rids us of the Turks."

AUTHOR'S NOTE: This tale is based on a true story. An old man in a small village in Palestine told us why he called World War I the Big Drum, and he related his memory of how the Turks conscripted the men of his village. His story of the man who hid in a well for two days did not end well. Ironically, the man died of pneumonia soon after his rescue.

Dixiane Hallaj lives quietly in Northern Virginia — when she's not gallivanting off to see more of this wonderful world. Find Dixie on her blog, DixieHelpsWriters.wordpress.com where she posts when the spirit moves her, or on her much-neglected website, DixianeHallaj.com.

SIPPY AND THE OLDER WOMAN

Erica Williams

Sippy's husband was cheating on her with an older woman. An older woman who wore a red velvet jumpsuit and matching gloves, and danced the Lindy Hop with a grace that was unnatural, and frankly unseemly, in a woman of seventy-four years.

Something had been awoken in her husband Algernon at his retirement party last month, some social rebirth had taken hold of him. It was like the shedding of his regular workday schedule had rearranged his entire outlook on life, as though now every day was a holiday, and each night a Friday night. He looked so *alive* all the time, and it was sticking in Sippy's craw, not that Sippy would admit to either the feeling, or to ever having anything resembling a craw.

This was not what Sippy Moynihan had had in mind when Algernon finally retired. She had expected him to be underfoot and in her way, a constant reminder of how Algernon was like a child, and needed her direction in life. When he'd worked, she'd kept him clothed, fed and watered. She'd managed their social calendar, penciled in the bridge nights, and the symphony concerts, the opera benefits and the neighborhood barbecues. All he had to do was show up and be polite. She'd assumed this would continue into retirement. She had been counting on her continued indispensability.

But Algernon resisted. He said that he was retired from everything now, including social obligations. Now, his only job in life was to enjoy himself. Sippy, who'd thought that these activities were things they both liked to do, was dumbfounded.

"Oh, surely you could tell I didn't like those things." Algernon said one morning after she'd suggested they renew their opera subscription. Then he shocked her by pulling her close to his chest with one arm in an extravagant display of happiness or freedom, like they were in a scene of some romantic comedy and gave her a silly little kiss.

She didn't like how buoyant he was these days; it seemed a rebuke against their entire married life.

She shrugged him off. "No, I couldn't tell. You were always very nice and companionable, and smiled to everyone there."

"That was my schmooze face!" he cried and twirled away to fling open the closet doors in their bedroom. "A face I don't ever have to make anymore." He began pulling suits off the rack and tossing them into a messy pile onto their marital bed, the bedspread of which Sippy had spent a good few minutes smoothing wrinkle free just the hour before.

Sippy, who'd liked that schmooze face, had built a life around that schmooze face, asked him what he was doing.

"Donating the suits. I don't need them anymore."

"What do you mean, you don't need them anymore?" She pulled the clothing into her arms, getting draped in happily flung ties for her efforts. "When we go out to functions—"

"No more functions!" Algernon trilled, and then dress shoes started to ping into the room, narrowly missing the antique desk Sippy had spent years searching for and finally found at, of all places, the Shack o'Antiques just down the street.

"Watch the furniture!" She tried to pick up more clothing, but pieces were coming out thick and fast and she was quickly overwhelmed. Shirts slipped to the floor in crumpled heaps and Sippy twitched at the sight of them. "What on earth are you going to do with your time?" she asked. And, more disturbingly, she thought, what was his retirement wardrobe going to consist of? Sweatpants and T-shirts? Board shorts and knee-hi socks?

Algernon stopped what he was doing, the mauled hangers clanging noisily in his wake as he turned to the laptop still open on his bedside table. "This." He turned the screen to her, and Sippy looked on in wary apprehension. She had no idea what to expect, but it certainly wasn't this: a World War II enthusiast re-enactment group.

And that's how his love affair began. Algernon traded in his work suits for World War II air force officer suits, anointed with medals he collected on shopping jaunts with his newfound friends. Algernon would be gone for whole weekends at a time, off to camp reenactments and shows. She was a World War II widow seventy years after the fact.

One day, a WWII era jeep suddenly popped up in their driveway, much to Sippy's chagrin. Algernon, still giddy with the rush of an expensive purchase, had insisted it would be a lark, a "neighborhood talking point" if they kept it parked in front of the house, blocking the view of Sippy's prized perennial garden, she couldn't help but notice. Sippy, who had no desire to be a "talking point" in anyone's house, had immediately ordered it cloistered into the shed.

Sippy did go to one show, once, after much urging by Algernon, and was horrified by what she saw. Algernon and his friends were dressed up in their regalia, walking around the grounds, answering questions of the public, staging earnest battle reenactments complete with tinny sound effects.

It was worse than community theater.

And then there were the swing dances, where the "officers" would get together with the ladies. A woman named Tabitha was at the center of it all. She, in her red velvet jumpsuit and victory rolled hair, hands clad in dainty matching gloves, would get whipped around strong male shoulders and over balding heads like she was weightless as a puff pastry. Tabitha laughed at it all, positively giggled like a schoolgirl. How Sippy envied her straight back, and limber joints, points of issue for Sippy who was fearing the beginning of a dowager's hump and occasionally had problems reaching the zip on her dress. This unaccustomed envy sat in Sippy and festered because she didn't know how to get rid of it, or what to do with it. Sippy was used to being the envied one in the relationship, the one Algernon would lavish with attention. It had been that way since the start of their relationship: Sippy was the one on the pedestal.

When people asked how they first met, Algernon liked to tell the story of how he'd spotted her across the crowded university dining hall, sitting by herself, in profile, head bent over her books, twisting a lock of that luscious raven hair. How he'd worked himself up to go over and talk to her, the regal beauty known across campus for turning down all the men who'd tried to date her. And for some reason, she'd chosen him, and wasn't he the luckiest man on earth? Their audience would say "Awww", and Sippy would smile demurely and know she was loved.

The fact was, Sippy had gone to university for one thing: to find a suitable husband. Nowadays, of course, it was practically a sin to admit to such a lowly goal as a husband and a family. But there was something to be said for making a lifetime of companionship and love a priority. Sippy had seen Algernon Moynihan sitting day after day by himself in that one corner of the cafeteria, intent on his notes, and she had kept her ears open to hear what was said about him: that he had a good head on his shoulders, but wasn't full of himself, that he was well liked and smart, that he would go far. But she also knew she needed someone who would be amenable to her steering, and something in his open face spoke of a lack of artifice, and she knew he was the one. So she'd planned her outfit for the day, timed it so she would be all alone, and sat exactly where he could see her to her most advantageous (her left profile). She'd staged the whole thing. *She* had been the great instigator of their love affair, not Algernon. Algernon knew none of this.

All of this ran through her mind as she watched the dancers, Algernon looking so happy in Tabitha's arms. Sippy began to feel a terrible sadness, at herself, that deepened into a determined dislike of Algernon's entire enterprise. She was the one who loved him more, it wasn't the other way around like she'd always thought. Or maybe it had been, but life had a way of unbalancing things, shifting weight from one side to another in a stealthy way. It scared her that he had found something apart from her that he loved, that showed that he in fact could live without her, could have an enjoyable life when she was not around.

"What did you think of the dance? Did you like it?" Algernon asked, coming over to her, sweaty and glowing in his separateness.

"No," she said primly. "I did not. Could you take me home now, please?" He looked hurt, but she chose to ignore it. She knew it didn't matter what she said. He had made it clear he didn't need her approval. Not anymore. Algernon, after all these years together, had moved beyond her. Couldn't he see how this made her feel? Or did he only have eyes for that Tabitha now?

Tabitha was a whole nine years older than Algernon, twelve years older than Sippy. When Sippy was young, people in their sixties and seventies had just been interchangeable, all wrinkled and white-haired, but when oneself was in the thick of those decades, well the difference between them was vast. The seventies were definitely the old aged, on the fast track to elderly, while someone in their sixties could still be considered late middle age, these days. Yet her husband preferred an older woman to her.

It was incredibly humiliating.

At first she tried to ignore the whole issue, treat it like a spring cold, a minor inconvenience that would pass with the persistence of time. But Algernon didn't seem to notice her remove, didn't seem bothered at all, so entranced was he with his newfound life and his newfound friends. Sippy felt the sting of being forgotten for the first time in their marriage, and at the unexpected imbalance of power.

* * *

One night, Sippy made her *croquettes de saumon*, one of her most prized dishes and Algernon's favorite, for dinner. He'd made his usual appreciative noises, but was it her imagination or was there a little less enthusiasm than usual?

After dinner he took his Churchill biography to sit in his hideous faux leather recliner that Sippy had banished to the back porch when it had shown up for delivery one ghastly day right after the retirement party. She'd not recognized it at the time, but perhaps that had been a portent of things to come.

Normally she'd busy herself on the phone with her friends, going over the day's gossip, but today she felt like she didn't really want their chatter in her ears. That maybe it was time to figure things out. So she sat across from Algernon, smoothing her skirt over her knees, a little drink of brandy clutched in her other hand.

Sippy could not fathom what it was that drew her husband to this venture of his. It was a celebration of death and horror as far as she could see, a romanticization of tragedy by those who were too young to have experienced it.

"It's the last great war," he explained over his gin and tonic when she asked. "It's probably the last war that was so clearly right versus wrong. What would our world have been if evil had won? The men and women who sacrificed so much deserve our gratitude forever. We can't forget, we can only celebrate."

And Sippy suddenly felt silly and small, though she knew that wasn't her husband's intention. She murmured something benign and said she was feeling tired. She was half hoping that he would look up in alarm, ask her if she was all right, or offer to accompany her upstairs. But he just said, "Okay, darling" his eyes back on his book. "I'll be up soon."

She took her time changing into her matching pinstriped pajamas, and nestled under the covers.

No husband.

She went to the kitchen for some water for her noisily announced dry throat.

No husband.

She made a few unnecessary movements of furniture, normally something that would bring him right to attention with a rushed, "Now, now, let me take care of that for you, honey."

But still, no husband.

Sippy got back into bed and pulled the covers up again in a minor huff. She plucked up the television remote control, finger jabbing the channel up button so quickly she could barely see what was on. But then something caught her eye, and she went back. *Grease* was airing on The Classics channel.

Sippy was a secret lover of musicals. Musical theater was, admittedly, a bit of a ridiculous passion to have, its song and dance numbers more suited to polite contempt than any sort of high art appreciation. But darn it, if that music didn't just fill her head with frothy fantasy. Sippy had a secret DVD collection of all the musicals, and would watch them when Algernon was off on his trips.

So she stopped on the channel, pulling her knees up into a childlike embrace. She watched, enthralled, as good girl Sandy won back bad boy Danny, and the beginnings of a plan emerged in Sippy's brain.

* * *

It was a good thing she knew no one at these World War II do's, Sippy thought as she watched the dance from the darkened doorway of the airplane hangar. A swing band was on a stage at one end, little tables were scattered about, cigarette girls flaunted their wares, and the dance floor was packed. The overall atmosphere was one of heady perspiration.

It had been quite a simple task, in the end, to find a 1940's polka dot dress thanks to the internet. The little cap with lace veil was hairpinned on her Veronica Lake waves (Sippy had always been a dab hand at hairstyles). It had been quite fun, actually, getting ready. She had almost forgotten the night's objective, so caught up was she in the curling of lashes, and the slicking on of red lipstick. She had gotten a few appraising looks from men as she'd entered the dance hall, something she hadn't experienced in years. Sippy looked like a vixen and she knew it. And it felt so very different, yet so very good.

Now, as she huddled in the corner of the full hangar-cum-dance hall, she was afraid she was beginning to lose her nerve. She preferred to be the sensible one who maintained the decorum in the place, kept things under control.

Then she spotted Algernon out in the center, under a spotlight, dancing with that Tabitha again. This time the woman was dressed in a peacock blue number that was cookie monster bright, with matching shoes that made her ankles look thick. Sippy prided herself on her thin and shapely ankles and often chose to enhance them with tea-length skirts. But Algernon looked good, she had to admit. He had been taking dance lessons and he and Tabitha were causing quite a stir on the dance floor. Well, Sippy had a few tricks up her sleeve too. One couldn't watch musicals all one's life and not have tried a few moves oneself, now could one?

Sippy strengthened her resolve with a deep breath and a smoothing hand over her raven waves. She turned to the man standing next to her, an eighty-year-old if he was a day, and said, "Let's dance," then took his arm and led him to the dance floor. The man looked positively delighted.

Algernon didn't see her at first, so engrossed was he in his dance with Tabitha. But it was hard to ignore the whisperings that were arising about the new couple on the dance floor, the murmurs that rippled through the room, the people parting to give Sippy and her partner more space.

Sippy was enjoying herself. She shimmied and shook all around her partner, whose name she hadn't thought to get. He didn't add much to the partnership anyway, except for the look of delight and good fortune that lit up his wrinkles. Sippy drank it in, slaking a thirst she hadn't even known she had. Everyone was admiring her, looking at her, she was the center of attention, and it felt good.

And then, he cut in, like a man from a movie musical, her husband of forty years. He swooped in and scooped her up and twirled her off, and she giggled into his ear as she saw Tabitha melting into the background.

"What are you doing here?" Algernon asked, delighted, his breath warm in her ear.

'I've come to take you back, to make you remember me, to make you see me again.' Sippy could have said any of these things, but instead, she said, "To tell you I love you."

Algernon smiled and said, "I love you too." And he kissed her long and hard, and Sippy didn't care who looked.

―――

Erica Williams is a physician-author who writes lighthearted fiction. Her stories are often centered on the imaginary town of West Hamm. See the map and meet more characters at www.westhamm.com. Other stories have appeared in Edify Fiction Journal and Thema Literary Journal.

JULY 17

Don Roberts

Willie, just ten years old, knew one thing for sure. He knew when he would die—the exact day, but not the year. Well, not die exactly the way ordinary people die. The spacemen would come back to get him and take him into the night sky on the exact anniversary of their first visit. His hillbilly granny told him so, and he trusted her to be truthful.

Willie always looked forward to her summer visits. This time there was something different. Sure, she still dipped snuff, and her can of Chattanooga Chew was deep in her apron pocket. Like always, her calico sunbonnet covered her wispy gray hair. While the tobacco-juice spitting and "I'm from the hills" hat irritated Willie's mother, the three boys thought she was cool with a capital C.

The difference was that, this time, she paid way more attention to Willie than his brothers. It started the very first day. Almost as soon as she walked through their front door, she asked him, and only him, to go picking dandelions with her. "I can unpack later. Willie, let's you and me go do some picking in that big open field across town." He grabbed an old gunnysack and away they went, leaving his brothers looking disappointed at being ignored.

Before they started to pick the golden-headed weeds, she lowered her skinny self down onto a shady bit of grass. "Sit by me for a spell. I've got a lot to say. Mind, it's for your ears only. I know things you need to know."

"What do you mean? Is it a secret or something?"

"Willie, them shiny metal men came for me just like they did you."

"You, too? Wait a minute, who told you about them coming for me? Nobody was supposed to say a thing about it to anyone, not even kinfolk."

"Listen and learn. Your old granny knows lots of stuff."

She leaned closer. "It happened to me way back on the first Armistice Day celebration after the Great War." Willie watched as her weatherworn face lost its hard edges. Even her eyes got a dreamy, far-away look.

"That day we went into Dyersburg for the parade. I remember like it was only yesterday. There was some fool dancing and prancing around in the flag-lined street. It was like he was the devil himself, dressed in red flannel long johns. He was supposed to be the king of Germany, or some such person. We had a grand time hooting and hollering at him. There was lots of speech-a-fying and waving of Old Glory. We didn't get back to the cabin 'til nearly dark.

"Pa said I could sleep on the porch since it was such a fine evening. Sometime during the night, those metal creatures came and claimed me. There was nary a face on any of them. Antennas was sticking every which-a-ways and poking me to distraction. I was paralyzed, struck deaf and dumb. I was."

"What did they say?"

"They said not a word, but I got this powerful feeling that they would let me stay at home for now. Then they would come back for me on the self-same day, way in the future. I figure they put that thought in my head. It's clear as a bell to me, even now. The exact date it happened was November 11, 1919.

"Willie, the next morning I told Ma and she didn't believe a word of it. Told me to keep my yap shut, or people would think I was titched in the head. She was right. Once I wrote a little story about it, and the teacher told me to not write lies. Then she read every single word to the whole class, and everyone, including her, laughed their fool heads off. For a time, kids called me Spacey Gracie. That was it. I never told a living soul about it again 'til now."

The little hairs on the back of Willie's neck rose up and he shivered — excited and scared at the same time. Way back then, nobody believed his Granny. He sure as heck didn't want to be called Spacey or Mars Boy. "Jeez, Granny! Is there more stuff I need to know?"

"Those metal creatures tell me what I need to know. You'll hear from them, too. Every once in a great while I get a powerful thought and the little scar behind my ear tingles to beat the band. That's when they talk to me — like they're finding out about how Earth people live through me. I guess they read my mind or something. That's how I learned they will protect me against harm until the end."

"What do you mean, Granny? Until the end."

"Willie, hold on. I'll get to that soon enough.

"Even though Ma warned me to watch what I said about those creatures from afar, I got a reputation for being titched in the head anyway. It was because I sort of passed out when those spacemen was a talking to me. I mean I always got real quiet and went sort of limp. After those metal men was finished jibber-jabbering at me, I perked right up. If my eyes was rolled up in my head, they got normal again. Here's a piece of good advice for you, Willie. If you think they gonna start talking to you, go off by yourself."

Without saying more, she gently bent Willie's head toward his shoulder. Her bony fingers flipped his ear toward his face. "Just as I thought. They put their mark on you, like they did to me. If you don't believe me, stand in front of a wall mirror with a little hand mirror to show the back of your head. You'll see their handiwork as plain as day.

"As the years flew on by, I figured out that they would come again on November 11. Every year on that day that's when my little scar starts to ache a little. You just watch and see, that's when they'll come for me and I'll sort of die, least ways, I'll go away forever. You best remember July 17. Your Ma told me on the phone that was when you had a terrible nightmare. So, that's when they came for you. That's your day."

Willie could hardly believe his ears. The exact selfsame thing had happened to her way back in 1919. There was another reason he believed her. She showed him the little scar behind her right ear. The next day when he used a hand mirror to see his, it was exactly like hers—a tiny number 8 lying on its side.

He was sure he never had it until after the spacemen left him. If he had, his Ma would have noticed every time she shampooed his hair. She spotted it soon after the thingamajigs from space got ahold of him. "Willie, I declare you must of got a deep cut behind your ear from playing all those rough and tumble games with the village idiots. It's a funny-looking scar, that's for sure." He didn't give it another thought at the time, figuring it was what she said it was—just a battle scar from play. Now, he knew better.

His old grandma wasn't finished talking about the funny-looking, sideways-lying scar. "Willie, there's more to know." She cleared her throat, spat a stream of tobacco juice off into the weeds, and got real stern looking.

"This is real important. Pay close attention to any tingling you get from that scar. That means they is about to do something. Another thing: best take heed if your scar gets hot to the touch and your head starts to feel like it's gonna explode. That's a warning."

"Does it mean I'm about to up and die?"

"No, not by a long shot. You won't even be sick—nothing like that. It's their way of telling that danger is coming your way. Back off if you're about to cross a bridge, or take a car ride way up in the Blue Ridge, or do anything dangerous. Those spacemen want to keep you alive until they're ready to take you up amongst the stars."

"Why?"

"I don't rightly know. I guess they're using us to study Earth people, so they need to keep us alive. That warning has helped me many-a-time. When my head's throbbing I just flat out refuse to do anything dangerous. Then something happens. and people say I must be a witch or something to escape the tragic accident. I'm no witch, but I am something special—now you is, too.

"That's another thing. No need to worry about Heaven or Hell. You ain't going there. We're going to a different place, a better place. We'll be like heroes to them space folks."

Willie was starting to like the idea of being so special. "Granny, did you start hearing those voices as soon as those spacemen finished poking and prodding you?"

"It ain't every day. It's only now and then. The last ones I heard was about you. They told me they latched upon you like they picked me. That's why I came to visit. I'll still get back to the hills before Armistice Day." Granny stood and dusted herself off. "Well, that's that. I do what the voices say. I told you everything—'specially the stuff they didn't get to say 'cause they had to leave in a hurry. That way you'll know what to expect. They want people to treat you like you're a regular kid."

Just then Bobby Ray, trailed by little Henry, came racing into the field. "Ma says if we're going to have a mess of greens for supper, she needs to get them pronto. We're gonna help you pick those dandelions."

Supper seemed to take forever. Bobby Ray kept going on and on, telling his grandma about how he almost single-handedly won the last football game of the school year. Then, little Henry kept jabbering about starting first grade. Willie said little, preoccupied as he was with being special.

Not long after supper Granny asked him to take a little walk with her. "Lord knows, I need to walk off that mighty fine supper your Ma made." As soon as they got round the corner, she peppered him with questions.

"Now, tell me what you remember about July 17."

"Us kids like to sleep on the porch in the summer. I was on that old sofa bed tucked up against the front window, almost asleep. From the snoring sounds I could tell Bobby Ray and little Henry was fast asleep at the other end of our big old porch."

"It was pretty much the same for me, Willie, except I was out on our porch alone. How did it commence?"

"All of a sudden I saw a bright, bright light coming out of the night sky right towards our front yard. In a couple of seconds, it dropped straight down, near the porch.

"Was it a different kind of bright?"

"It was shiny as the noonday sun, but the brightness didn't spread out, sort of like the beam of a flashlight."

"That's exactly how it was when they came to claim me. Was their spaceship little?"

"It wasn't a ship exactly. It was an egg-shaped ball of light that looked smaller than the metal guys that got out of it. I know that don't make sense, but it's true. In my confused mind, I wasn't scared yet, just puzzled."

"Now that I recollect, it was like that. What did you do?"

"I raised up on my elbow to get a better look, and saw a bunch of them metal thingamajigs coming right towards me. I tried to yell across to wake up Bobby Ray and Henry, but suddenly the words wouldn't come. My mouth moved, but I made not a sound."

"It's terrible bad to be so scared, Willie. I'm ashamed to admit it, but I wet my pants that night—couldn't help it. I bet you felt trapped. I surely did."

"Granny, they pinned me down on my back. They poked me from my head to my toes and back again. Then, they flipped me over then poked me some more. It didn't hurt, but it was scary. The last thing they did was grab ahold of my head. I figure that's when they branded me with that scar."

"Didn't they do or say anything else?"

"They didn't get a chance to 'cause Bobby Ray woke up, and started screaming for ma and pa. Until then I knew what was going on, but I couldn't talk."

"Did they turn tail and run?"

"Quick as a flash they got back to that shining thing in the yard. It didn't take them more than a few seconds to disappear along with the ball of light. Their hold on me was broke so I started to yell bloody murder. I was so scared. Ma had to hold me down to keep me from jumping up and running in circles. I think she was afraid I would wake the neighbors. After a while I calmed down, but I didn't sleep a wink that night.

"Next morning Daddy tried to get me to believe it was only a bad dream. Bobby Ray tried to get the truth out, but Daddy said he was walking in his sleep, like he'd done before. Nobody argues with Daddy when he's riled up, so Bobby Ray was sleepwalking, and I had a nightmare."

Bobby Ray's advice to Willie was short and to the point: "No one's going to believe us. That's just the way it is. Forget about it. Ma said we was to keep our traps shut. The neighbors wasn't to think they was living next to some crazy no-account hillbillies."

"You don't have to tell me how hard-headed your Daddy is. I raised him. And your Ma shouldn't worry about what the neighbors think. It don't matter a whit."

"Granny, I don't want to get you mad, but I still have a couple of questions."

"Out with it, boy."

"You said you would die or go away on November 11. Will it be this fall?"

She stopped smack in the middle of the street, turned, and put both her hands on his shoulders. A good thing there was no traffic. At first Willie thought she was getting riled up, like she did sometimes. It wasn't that at all.

"That's right sharp of you to ask. You know, I think it will. My scar has been acting up like it never did before. Here it is, only August, and it's tingling to beat the band. Don't have no headache, and it ain't hot to the touch so it must be something else. November 11 is just around the corner. I think they're letting me know I won't have any more birthdays."

Willie swallowed hard and asked what he most wanted and feared to know at the same time. "How do you think it will happen?"

"Well, I think I know where it will happen—on the front porch of the old cabin where they visited the first time. Of course, I'm not certain, but I've got a powerful urge to go back there. It's empty and there's no nearby neighbors. I'm going to sit there that evening and wait for them. Don't tell no one. It's our secret. When it's your time, remember what I've said. To tell the truth, I'm looking forward to it as much as those Holy Rollers yearning for Heaven."

Their evening stroll ended back where they started. Nobody was on the front porch. "Willie, let's sit a spell and catch some of the cool evening breezes."

Rocking back and forth on the porch swing Granny crooned some of her favorite hill folk tunes. Willie fell asleep in the cocoon of her encircling arms.

A few days later she announced that she was going back to the Tennessee hills. That morning she had mysteriously put a small sack on the kitchen table. "I've got something for everyone."

She pulled out her Pa's pocket watch for Daddy and some smelly lavender sachets for Ma. Next, she slid her battered old harmonica toward a grinning Bobby Ray. It took hardly a second for Little Henry to untie his sack of penny candy. Finally, looking hard at Willie, "Here's something real special, my wild songbird whistle. It'll help you think of me."

Willie begged her extra hard not to leave, but her mind was made up. She left a couple of days later. Sure enough, they got word that she had disappeared on November 11, just like she said she would. The Tennessee authorities sent a search party out, but, as they said, she was old and tended to wander around those hills. She could have tumbled over a cliff or fallen in the swift-moving creek. Her body was never found. Willie grieved, but kept his silence, just like he'd promised.

* * *

In the town's library he saw Albert Einstein's head on a *Life* magazine cover. Those lying down figure 8s were whirling around his head under the title, "Infinity Explained." Willie read the story a couple of times trying to understand it. The C- grade on his famous scientist report was proof that he never quite got the hang of it, not entirely. The only thing he learned for sure was that infinity has something to do with time never ending. The brainy spacemen must have known what they were doing when they picked that infinity symbol.

As he grew up none of his friends, or anyone else for that matter, suspected he was destined for space travel. Paying heed to his Granny's advice, he abruptly took off when he needed to be alone to hear them telling him stuff. More often than not, he blew his treasured silver songbird whistle when he felt lonely and different. After a few years Willie decided that living in a humdrum town wasn't so great. That's when he joined the army.

In boot camp the barber shaved his head down to the skin, exposing the scar behind his ear. He was nervous, but no one noticed. Willie liked army life and reenlisted, becoming a career soldier stationed stateside. When he had a chance, he became a camp barber. Were there others with that infinity mark? He did see a few — a total of four — over the next twenty-five years. All of these young Army recruits had one thing in common — no interest in talking to him about it. "That's an interesting looking scar behind your ear," was always followed by dead silence.

Upon retirement he returned to his old hometown and married a childless widow. When his parents moved back South, he bought his old home. After his wife died, Willie spent more and more time alone. Strange as it might seem, he secretly anticipated and feared space travel at the same time.

On the evening of July 16, he placed his old granny's favorite rocking chair on the porch near the window. As soon as he sat down, he pulled out the silver songbird whistle. Softly blowing it, he brought her sun-bonneted image into mind and it comforted him. He was ready to face what was coming. His scar was buzzing like crazy. It was time.

* * *

Oh, Infinite One. Our study of compatible worlds is now complete. We have made contact with beings on the third planet from the small orb in the Milky Way Galaxy known to Earthlings as the Sun. We selected and studied certain genetic strains of beings along with a descendent from each. The results are conclusive.

They do not merit further consideration. Earthlings are a quarrelsome lot. Turmoil is constant with new wars breaking out as the flames of old ones flicker. Individuals have not yet evolved from their physical bodies nor are they close to creating significant robotic enhancements. These primitives continue to suffer from the maladies of physical illnesses. Their thinking capacity is minimal. Emotions run rampant with the limbic system, rather than logic, playing the dominant role in their behavior. Simply put, Earthlings are not suitable candidates for infinite life nor are they evolved enough to be used as replacement parts for our enslaved populations on nearby planets.

The test subjects may be examined, if you desire. They are mounted and identified in the Intergalactic Hall of Curiosities."

―――

Don Roberts is a self-proclaimed country boy with a strong streak of Wanderlust. He met his wife in Venezuela, and during his thirty years as a teacher in Pittsburgh's inner city, he led People-to-People delegations to Europe, the Soviet Union, Australia and New Zealand. He has not yet managed inter-stellar travel. His coming-of-age novel, Echoes From the Hollow *was published in 2019 by S & H Publishing, Inc.*
Find Don at https://www.facebook.com/don.roberts.3154

ABOVE RIO DE JANEIRO

Dian Stirn Groh

"What? Say that again. I'm going to Rio de Janeiro, Brazil? Are you kidding? My second trip out of the pool and I get a five-day trip to Brazil? Of course, I can be at the airport in an hour! I'm going to love this job! Thank you so much."

I carefully wrote down everything the Pan Am Miami Crew Scheduler said. Departure time was ten-thirty PM but I had to report to the briefing office an hour before that. When I hung up the black rotary dial telephone, I started screaming with joy and excitement as I ran to throw on the uniform that was one of the reasons I had chosen Pan Am rather than Braniff, TWA or Delta in 1969. The beige Evan Picone jumper over a crisp white cotton blouse with matching ascot tie made me feel professional and fashionable.

My grin spread from one ear to the other. Nobody was there to see. Even tugging on pantyhose in Florida's sticky climate didn't dampen my spirits. So glad I had applied make-up earlier. Halfway through dressing, I ran back to the phone to call a cab. Beige bowler hat on my bobbed hair and white gloves on my hands, I threw my regulation brown purse over my shoulder, grabbed my packed red American Tourister Weekender in one hand, a regulation navy tote bag in the other. Out the door of the Miami Springs apartment fifteen minutes after receiving the call.

* * *

As the cabbie dropped me off at international departures, I floated through the terminal to the crew lounge, signing-in for briefing. Being the youngest stewardess, I sat quietly while Herman Black, the graying distinguished looking male purser, assigned us positions on the Boeing 707. The others all had been working together the whole month and had their favorite jobs, I got the leftover first-class cabin. Herman said, "Don't worry about the service. We'll help you out."

Maybe he could tell I was a bit apprehensive about handling the elaborate meal services for which Pan American was known. Boarding, even the cabin demonstration and take off were fine. I sat at the front entrance on the pull-down jump seat of the Boeing 707 next to dashing purser Marc Valdez. Much younger than the other man, he chatted with me and put me at ease. Finally, we reached the top of our climb. We all sprang into action. Removing hat and gloves, I donned the white butcher apron and tied the strings around my waist. Who thought of white for the plane anyway? I was sure mine would be a mess by the end of the flight.

Although I handed out the fancy menus, with such a late departure, most of the ten first class passengers didn't want the full seven courses. Champagne or Mimosas before departure, cocktails and hot canapes after the thirty-minute climb to the initial cruising altitude, they were asleep. The man in Seat 2B was the exception. Drinking cognac in the curved lounge opposite the galley, Mr. Rui, a tall, swarthy gentleman wearing a dark cotton blend suit with a white shirt and tie, read palms as a hobby. He said, "It's an excuse to hold hands with pretty girls." I blushed.

He asked, "Which hand do you write with?"

I said, "The right. Why?"

"The opposite is your original life plan so I will read the

right, the path you are on."

Staring at my two palms, I realized he was correct in one thing. They didn't match. On my left the top crease, supposedly my love line, started at the edge of my hand and ran deeply ending below my index finger. Twisting my hand with my thumb out, there was one deep crease on the edge below where my little finger attached.

As he held my right hand, he explained, "While I don't necessarily believe all of this, your hand tells me your life will be long, you will have three children."

Sure enough, I had three lines on the edge of my right hand where there was only one on the other one. Since I didn't have a boyfriend at age twenty-two, the number of children was insignificant to me. I had my whole life in front of me, a brand-new world to explore. Children were not on my mind in the least.

Eventually, even Mr. Rui vacated the lounge, returned to his seat and closed his eyes apparently drifting off. It was time for the galley girl, Donna, and me to take a break. As we sat on the jump seat away from passenger view, she mentioned she was married to Marc. I asked, "Did you meet on the airplane?"

"Heavens, no! But it did happen after I joined Pan Am. I grew up on the Caribbean island of Trinidad. Have you been there yet?"

"No." I laughed. "This is only my second flight. Can't you tell?"

"Not at all. You're a natural."

What a gem. I knew we'd be friends forever.

"So, tell me how you met."

"I was fresh out of training and hadn't even taken my first flight. My hair was in rollers, no make-up, just wearing a short T-shirt when my roommate, who was supposed to babysit for Marc's three little kids, called in a panic saying she couldn't make it. I'd have to go in her place. Turned out she'd met a pilot from British West Indies Air and wanted to go out with him. But she didn't tell me that part."

"Anyway, I went in her place. I saw those blue eyes, great smile and dark hair through the jalousie kitchen door, with the three kids in tow, my heart missed many beats. After that we had one date and that was it!"

"Wow, you had an instant family!"

"Actually, they live with their mother. We only have them occasionally. They're adorable, great kids!"

With that Marc came to say it was time to prepare for breakfast. Donna dashed to the galley, turned on the ovens, placed the towel tray inside the warmer, shoved a coffee pillow pack in the plastic holder while pushing the brew button and began organizing the service. We set up the rolling cart with white linens and fresh fruit. I went through the cabin dangling steaming towels from silver tongs. The passengers were grateful. If they had to wake up at 3:30 AM, at least the towels made it less traumatic. I took orders of how each person wanted his eggs prepared: soft-boiled, fried, over-easy or scrambled. Eggs to order. Donna was a whiz in the galley. Everything was beautiful and delicious.

In no time at all we were descending at Galeao Airport, Rio de Janeiro. Although traffic was heavy leaving the terminal and it took an hour to reach Copacabana, it was well worth the drive. As we cleared the tunnel, Sugarloaf, a treeless towering mountain resembling brown sugar rising from the azure sea, was directly in front of us. Incredible. Suddenly, I was wide awake. I simply couldn't believe I was really in Rio. Sensory overload. Creamy sand stretching to the ocean in a subtle crescent on my left side, rows of majestic old hotels extending behind wide mosaic black and white patterned sidewalks on the right hugging the same shape. I didn't know which way to look.

Gaping like a yawning animal, I followed the crew as we checked into the hotel. In addition to the key for the room, we were given Cruzeiros, Brazilian local currency, as per diem while we were on layover. Pan Am paid for our rooms but meals were another matter. Donna explained many girls went shopping with that money rather than eat at the hotel. Not being a compulsive shopper, I realized I was hungry.

Marc said, "After the porter delivers your bags to the room, take a quick shower to lose the smoky airplane smell, put your uniform in the hall in a laundry bag and meet us in the second-floor dining room for a Brazilian breakfast. By the way, here the second floor is number one on the elevator. You will have the room to yourself because Donna will be with me."

Although my room didn't face the water, I could hear the waves crashing into the sugary shore through the open windows. I thought I was quick to change, but actually I was the last one to the table. The guys all stood when I walked onto the terrace overlooking the view. As the neophyte, they allowed me to face the magnificent sea. A major sacrifice for the guys because they couldn't watch the slender bodies in microscopic bikinis as they played expert volleyball on the powdery courts. Their eyes did wander that way occasionally, but nobody turned completely around to stare. Guess they were all used to the exotic scenery.

After filling our tummies, fatigue began to set in. Time for a nap. Advised not to sleep all day, I set my alarm for three hours. When I moseyed down to the lobby, the two other stewardesses who worked the economy cabin, Tone, a blonde Norwegian, and Julie, a red-headed American, took me under their wings so I didn't have to tag along with Marc and Donna the entire layover. They led me to an open-air flea market several blocks behind the hotel to look at tie-dyed panels depicting church scenes, framed neon blue butterflies with a six-inch wing spread on a white background, gemstones attached to miniature spoon collections, embroidered placemats and tablecloths. They shopped, I browsed. At dinner we ate feijoada, a rich black bean stew made with salted, smoked and fresh pork served over rice with a lemon juice, tomato, onion and cilantro salsa. *Deliciousa.*

The entire layover was filled with exciting discoveries for me. A trip to a jewelry store led us to a day-tour of a quartz mine several hours from Rio. Not much of a consumer or wearer of jewelry, but already thinking about Christmas gifts, I was interested in learning about them. Who knew that Brazil was the producer of the largest variety of semi-precious stones? Taking the elevator far below the earth, I felt like a prospector searching for gems. Although we were restricted from poking or digging, they did allow us to take small souvenir bags of rough chips with us from the gift shop. Among the most spectacular stones found in Brazil were aquamarine, diamond, and emerald. I never did find a garnet, my birthstone, though I discovered a new field of knowledge. Of course, when I asked about the garnet, the salesman said, "No *problema.* I can get it for next time you come."

As miraculous as walking along the sparkling beach and touring a mine were, the most awe-inspiring adventure was the tour to the colossal Art Deco Christ the Redeemer statue standing almost one hundred feet tall two thousand three hundred twenty-six feet above Rio on Corcovado Mountain. To reach the humpback peak, we traveled through the lush Tijuca Forest, so dense the sun did not shine through. Upward the road twisted and turned on scary switchbacks near the pinnacle. Finally, we walked what felt like straight up to the pedestal. It was almost impossible to photograph the entire statue without leaning back at an uncomfortable angle. And to consider how they must have constructed it between 1921 and 1932 on the remote top of the crag was phenomenal. I was thrilled with my decision to leave my home state of Ohio seeking a hiatus from learning, planning to fly for two years until I decided what I wanted to be when I grew up. Although I had crammed many experiences into my three days, layovers do not last forever.

Again, the flight was a late-night departure. The crew bus picked us up at the hotel. The six of us, back in regulation uniforms, certainly looked different from the previous casual days. With a totally new cockpit crew, off we went.

For some reason we only had fifty passengers in the economy cabin where Marc, Donna and I worked this time. Again, Donna worked the galley while I served the passengers. Because of the light load, Marc said I could sit in the last row to see the lighted Redeemer as we took off. My assigned position was on the pull-down rear jump seat with him, but the small window in the exit door was too high and positioned for upward viewing ramp service when they came to open the door; therefore, we couldn't see out of when seated.

In the last row I was next to the window with a perfect view as we circled the statue on our ascent. It was a lovely clear night. I held my breath and marveled at man's artistic ingenuity and major engineering feat. However, once the statue was out of sight, bright orange fireflies began shooting from the number two engine. Concerned, I whispered back to Marc, "There are sparks flying out of the engine."

Marc calmly explained the situation to the cockpit using the interphone, which looked like a normal telephone, different than the intercom microphone. The First Officer said, "It's probably a rich mixture of fuel. It'll burn off by the time we reach our cruising altitude. But we'll send someone back to take a look."

Sure enough the relief engineer, good-looking and fairly young for a Pan Am crew member, bent down to stare at the offending engine. He assured the passengers, "Don't be alarmed. It's simply a rich mixture of fuel. Nothing to worry about. Sit back, relax and enjoy your flight."

The plane continued to climb and the sparks continued to fly. After about twenty minutes, the usual time it took to level off, Marc whispered. "Is it still emitting? If so, I should notify the cockpit."

As I prepared to reply, the sparks suddenly ignited into a huge glowing fireball similar to a harvest moon only brighter, more intense, so terrifying. "Yes, it's on fire!"

I jumped from the window seat to the aisle as if I could get away from it. My eyes must have been the size of half dollars.

Thank goodness Marc jerked the phone from its cradle and relayed the word to the pilots. The engineer immediately cut off the fuel. Then, all we saw was black sky. The captain came on the public address system and made the announcement there was nothing to worry about, but we would dump fuel and return to Rio. "Free cocktails for everyone."

Still wearing our hats and jackets, we stewardesses jumped up to walk through the cabin offering beverages and magazines. Attempting to keep the passengers calm, I was not frightened. I thought only what I needed to do to for others. One man traveling with his young children nearly lost it.

He raged, "This is preposterous. I'm going to sue Pan Am because my kids will never see their grandparents. My thoughts were was he going to sacrifice his children and save himself? Otherwise his statement was ridiculous. It reminded me of a stewardess saying: People sometimes do check their brains with their bags"

Well, a few complimentary drinks and everyone relaxed for the hour it took to disperse nine hours of fuel, dissipating long before it reached the jungle or the ground. We conversed with the travelers to lessen their fears and one or two even felt so comfortable, they actually dozed off.

Not knowing what would happen on landing, we had to prepare the cabin and passengers for the worst if there was fire or an emergency landing. They were relocated forward and aft of the wings as a precaution. We briefed everyone on how to use the slides at each door. Once the rubber exit ramps inflated, they were to jump, slide down and quickly walk away from the plane as far as possible.

Feeling the plane descend, I straightened my hat, put jacket and gloves on once again and walked through the cabin to make one last check on the passengers. All were staring out the windows with blank looks on their faces. When anyone turned toward the aisle, I smiled warmly. All was ready. I sat blindly on the jump seat; belt cinched as tight as possible. Proper evacuation procedures flashed through my mind.

Spoilers whirred as the flaps were lowered. The plane flared. I held my breath. Floating before we roared to the runway, it touched down smoothly. Whew! Better than my previous landings. The taxi toward the terminal seemed long. When the captain applied the brakes, steel portable stairs were driven to the front and a ground agent opened the door from the outside. Fresh air. No slides were necessary. Relieved passengers rushed to deplane. Crew members gathered belongings and followed. Only as we walked by the number two engine with a hole in the cowling the size of a softball, did I consider what could have occurred. How could I have been so naïve? I turned to the first officer, an irreverent chap who wore a baseball cap downline instead of his Pan Am military hat. My knees buckled, but I regained my balance. I said, "Yikes! I just realized we could have been killed."

"Naw! We had everything under control. You know a 707 with four engines can fly on only one, don't you? Come on. Let's go back to the hotel. This plane's not going anywhere soon. The sun's up. It's time for breakfast"

It dawned on me that the initial emergency training and drills had worked. I was proud and relieved that the hectic and stressful week of aiming fire extinguishers, memorizing locations of equipment on four different aircraft, practicing all types of incidents in mock-ups, jumping out a plane into a chute, even inflating a life raft and successfully swimming to it resulted in my remaining calm, confident and in control.

―――――

Dian's planned two-year aviation stint extended to seventeen flying out of four bases: Miami, New York, Honolulu and Los Angeles. She traveled the world, became a purser, recruiter, instructor and grooming coordinator at the training academy. From that training assignment, her "real job" developed into a career in education as an English as a Second Language teacher, college faculty member, private tutor and author. She currently lives in Texas.

ME-ALITY.COM
General Release Version 1.0

David Boop

Clicking my mouse may change reality, but I don't change.
I won't.
Not now.
Not ever.

* * *

Earth #1134.0

I lean back on my ergonomic chair and poke my head out of my cubicle. Looking left then right at my fellow wage slaves who are hunchbacked, ringing church bells as if they're IT Quasimodos. I wonder if they're actually resolving customer issues, or doing exactly what I'm about to?

Wheeling forward until I block my monitor, I log in. Me-ality.com released twenty new realities last night, but I'll review them at home. I already know which earth I want. She gets online at this same time every day, and I need to talk to her.

It's Earth #789, but Me-ality users give each world a nickname. "Moonless" is a reality where we never traveled to the moon. The space race got so heated, it nearly started WWIII. Earth's governments formed a pact making the moon off limits to human exploration.

Her icon lights up. I send a video chat request and maximize the window until she fills the whole screen.

"Hi, Mom."

She looks disappointed. "Ned. You know I'm Kate, not Katherine. Your mother died over a year ago. I won't accept any more chat requests from you if you keep doing that."

I internally scream *No!* "Sorry, slip of the tongue, Kate." I shift subjects quickly. "How are you today?" We exchange niceties for a few minutes. Kate cleans her glasses, cursing at the scratches; scratch-resistant glass was developed due to the space race. That and Tang.

"So...Haley left me," I admit.

"Oh, Ned, Neddy. I'm so sorry. What happened?"

"What always happens? She wanted the bigger, better deal. I'm never what women want." I plead, "What's so wrong with me, Kate? Seriously."

Kate muses. "Well, Ned, I can't say for sure. I couldn't have kids, as you know. You seem like a great person. Makes me wish I had adopted or something. Maybe you try too hard. I bet if you stopped looking, the right one will show up."

Ah, one of the old adages people use to comfort the unlovable.

She just wasn't the right one.

It isn't your time, yet.

She'll show up when you're least expecting her.

Kate's words don't salve my wounds. She's a good lady, but not a mother. Certainly not mine.

We agree to talk again, but I resign myself to finding another Katherine, one more like my mom. Alt-Real Inc. has released 2132 realities so far. Somewhere there has to be one where *my* mom didn't die.

Before I log off, I get a chat request: Nora Waters from Earth #238, dubbed "Seattle." My alt-daughter will keep pinging me if I don't accept. She's been my guide to the alt-nets, but her teenage drama wears on me. I have my own

ME-ALITY.COM/BOOP

pain to contend with.

I bring Nora's window up. Behind her, rains cascade down her window. It's always raining on #238. Not just in Seattle or London. Everywhere.

"He's such a MOSSHEAD!" the sixteen-year-old screams, and I'm forced to turn the volume down. Nora wears the latest emerald green latex hair. Hair mildews quickly there, so it's trendy to go bald and don faux follicles.

"Hi, Nora."

"Why does he have to be an asshat?"

"How should I know?"

"Well, you're him, right? I mean, like a different planet, but you're him. You should understand his assholeness better than anyone."

I raise an eyebrow. "Nora, did you just call me an asshole?"

She cocks her head like I've missed the obvious point. "No. Duh. You're like easy to talk to. Not a mosshead like him. Well, not all the time."

Gee, thanks.

* * *

Some telecom tech discovered alternate realities by crossing a zero with a one. He connected with a version of his wife who had married his brother instead of him. His company patented over two hundred uses for the revolutionary innovation overnight and rebranded it Alt-Real Inc. Their biggest success has been Me-ality.com, the social network of string theory.

I'd considered the idea ridiculous, at first. Life sucked enough as it was. How could looking at another Earth have any appeal? Mind you, some realities were much worse. Like Earth #451 where the Nazis won WWII or #452 where China did. Then there's #897 where a solar flare drove humanity underground.

Alt-real Inc. exists in one form or another on all of them, monitoring the alt-waves. I tried running Me-ality's code once. I was a toddler playing hide and seek with the Higgs Boson. I started surfing the alt-waves after the first anniversary of mom's death. Despite warnings from my therapist, I had to know if another Katherine Waters existed out there.

My first foray had netted me "Kitty," a drug-addicted online porn "star." Taffy cheeks hung under cesspool eye sockets. She'd lost her version of me to social services, but five of his brothers and sisters somehow went unnoticed. Kitty asked me for money. I blinked, dumbfounded. There's no way to physically bridge realities to loan her the requested $200 until payday, but then reality wasn't really her thing.

Next came "Rin," the artist. My mom had taken sculpting in college where she met my sperm-donor dad. Rin's tryst with him hadn't knocked her up, so she instead devoted her life to the pursuit of creative impulses. A promelanomian (even cancer has a right to live), she made her money doing murals in the rechristened "Enlightened Co-Op of Amerizen." She detested my pain and asked me never to contact her again.

I almost gave up after Earth #333, where Dad *had* stuck around. Adult to adult, I could see what features I'd gained from him: strong nose, weak chin, robin-egg blue eyes. He shoved "Kay" back from the monitor.

"What did I tell you about logging on to that crap? You gonna waste money talking to people that don't really exist? Goddamn slut! So, who's this dirtbag?" Alt-dad plopped himself in front of the camera. "You want her to show you her tits or something?"

"Fuck no. I'm her son. I mean—"

Alt-dad showed off his teeth like rotten fence posts in

ME-ALITY.COM/BOOP

front of an abandoned house. "I know what you mean, idiot. Why you talking to my Kay? Bet your mom thinks you're pathetic? You look pathetic. Glad my wife miscarried you."

"What?"

"Kay had a little 'accident' while pregnant with our first. 'Cause you're a fucking clutz, right, Kay? Anyway, we only had daughters after that. Your mom only had girls, too, huh?"

I disconnected cutting off his laughing fit.

Maybe raising me on her own had been hard, but that dickhead would have made mom's life unbearable. We'd stuck together through everything. She was my best friend and confidant. I was her unwavering caregiver until the very end — the only one at her side when she died.

Horribly. Painfully. Slowly.

Were all the alternate Katherine Waters funhouse reflections? Dark, distorted, wanting?

I had sworn off Me-ality for two weeks until Kate sought *me* out. She wondered what life would have been like if she hadn't developed uterine cancer in her teens. I reveled in her face, so much like mom's. We wept as I recalled the years of mom valiantly fighting brain cancer, especially those final few days; a mix of seizures and hallucinations. Kate put her hand on the monitor, tried to comfort me. However, I understand now that she doesn't have the life experience I need. I want a reality where my Katherine Waters didn't die, but maybe I did. Then, we'd be two sides of a coin, able to help each other through anything, even if we were realities apart. Me-ality has shown me anything is possible.

Anything.

* * *

At home, I scroll through the newly connected Earths. Altusers post viral vids of their reality as enticements for others log on.

Well…where not punishable by law.

Not all realities have welcomed the technology in the past, and some users have taken it underground. The most watched recording on the alt-web is from #445 as a rebel surfer is discovered and executed by the Luddite Regime ruling the world. We couldn't do anything but watch.

The twenty additional realities released today don't hold promise of me finding a match. The only Katherine I find has a mustache. On Earth #2119, dubbed "Tickler," everyone has one. Men, women and children. Something in their version of the Bible forbids cutting hair.

I switch off the feed, and sit in the dark trying to decide what to do with my evening. Turning on a lamp will light the spots where mom used to be.

Since I'm still dressed anyway, I grab a coat and leave.

Me-ality has turned imaginative souls into millionaires overnight; people whose alt-versions had invented a thing on one world that another world hasn't yet. Since its release, my reality has conquered space-travel, anti-gravity, and sentient androids. We're in a renaissance of technology. Yet, every world, *every* world has cancer. It binds us all together, this inescapable plague. That and Alt-Real Inc.

God allows us sex-bots, but not happily ever-afters.

Alt-restaurants are the biggest growth market. Tom 222's is my regular joint. The cuisine is based on Earth #222's vegetarian world. They've perfected fruit dishes that taste superior to our meaty contemporaries.

Tom's is sparse of patrons, so I'm able to grab a booth. I order a blueberry beer and apple burger with grape fries. Comfort food.

"Ah! Neddy!" Tom calls out from the kitchen, "I think that is your order and it is."

ME-ALITY.COM/BOOP

He waves to me through the window. Soon enough, he pops out from the back. I don't feel like socializing, but Tom takes good care of me, so I suck it up.

Tom towers over my booth. He wipes swarthy hands on his apron before offering me one. Tom is Romanian. He and his wife owned a bakery before opening Tom's 222. Their plancakes–pancakes made with plantain–are the talk of the town.

"How's the Sunday buffet, Tom?"

"Out to the corner. We have waiting list three weeks back. You think they never ate good food before Veggilot came along." Veggilot is Earth 222's nickname. Tom's been alt-surfing since launch day.

"They ate, but they never tasted." I finish his oft-repeated phrase.

Noticing I'm flying solo, Tom inquires, "Where is Haley? Why you not bring your lady?"

I don't want this conversation again, but as I struggle for an answer, Tom pieces it together.

"What? She see herself in another reality with different man? Think she will be happier? Cats. All women cats. Miauuu!" He makes clawing motions with his hands.

A string of curses come from the kitchen where Tom's wife is working. Tom shrugs in a "See what I have to deal with?" way.

"Nah," I lie, "she just wasn't the one. I'll find someone when I'm not looking."

He laughs. "Oau! I go make healing meal for you. Tomorrow, right girl will show up. Bring her here, and we open bottle of carrot wine together. She will be smitten!"

If the fruit farts didn't scare her away first.

* * *

My drapes are drawn to block out the world–all the worlds–from my mind, but I'm not ready for bed yet. Any sleep I get is a gift. Mostly, the nightmares wake me.

Memories of mom's soul-ripping last days. The sound of her rasping breaths shows up even in sex dreams. They come with twisted visions of her: her as a vampire, a zombie, a ghost. She's no benign spirit offering words of blessing from the grave. She calls me to join her. I accept in varied ways, sometimes by her hand, usually by my own.

My cell phone's Me-ality app vibrates. Resigned to my fate, I roll over. It's Nora, the alt-spawn. More drama, I'm sure. I click "Ignore." She pings again. By her third IM, she's added a 511 to the text–their version of 911.

Nora, adorned in a gold wig, is not angry. She's jubilant.

"You're so not fucking going to believe this!"

"What?" I yawn the cobwebs from my brain.

"#2147 has a time travel mod!"

I stick a finger in my ear and wiggle it. Did I hear her right? Time travel? And how'd she get #2147 already? Alt-Real Inc. just released through #2132 and won't unveil any other new worlds for a month.

"Huh? How do you know?"

She gives me the cat-eating-canary grin. "I got friends."

"You mean hackers. Didn't I—I mean your dad, tell you to stop hanging with that crowd? If you and your 'friends' keep playing with the code, Alt-Real Inc. will block your IP."

"As if. Anyway, it's not like actual time travel, but they found a way to go forward or back in the alt-streams. You can talk to a younger version of yourself. It's totally *sunny*!"

"You've done this?"

"An older version of me has. Turns out I was going to this killer *wave* Saturday night and, due to a series of events waaay beyond my control," Nora holds up her hand as if swearing on the Bible, "I get home after my curfew. Dad tells me he's not giving me a hydrofoil for graduation, after

ME-ALITY.COM/BOOP

all. Well, when the older me got the time travel mod, she IM'd to warn me, so I skipped the wave. Problem solved. I want the 'foil more."

"So, that's what it takes for you to behave? A new car?"

Nora rolled her eyes. "Not just any car, but a Mitsubishi Manta!"

Time travel changes everything. Nora keeps talking, but my mind races. What could I tell my younger self that would help mom? I suddenly had new options.

"Nora, can you show me how to hack into these new realities?"

There were many chemos that drained mom's life and didn't slow down the cancer's progress. If I can tell my younger self what to avoid, I could extend mom's life... or even save it!

I split screen with Nora and shadow her through a backdoor into my own world's Me-ality network. We go to the master reality list, and there are billions of unreleased realities.

"Don't let it freak you out. Most realities aren't that different. Alt-Real Inc. sorts them into major and minor realities. Major ones are like #600, where pets are banned and minor ones are like #239800317 where some dude chose not to wash his hands and gave some other dude a cold. Only major realities get released. They're in a subdirectory over here."

She clicks and a different list pops down. There are hundreds of Earths than haven't been announced yet.

"Why don't they release them all?"

Nora sighs as if giving a puppy a lecture on driving a car. "Beeecause, they have to screen the worlds first." Nora giggles. "There's a reality on the master list where no one wears clothes. All the boys go there. It's really no fun for girls. Once you've seen one..."

"Nora!"

She blushes. "Float, dude. You're the one that wanted this."

I grumble something about if I was her father, then I see #2147.

"That's weird."

"What?" Nora asks.

"See that plus sign? Only a few other worlds have it."

It indicates that world #2147 has a subdirectory. I click on it and another list drops down, starting with 2147.1. Under it is 2147.2, 2134.3 and so forth. I move the slide bar down until it reaches the bottom, 2147.1078. New numbers pop up faster than I can track.

I scroll to Nora's world, #238. It has the same plus sign. I open it. There are nearly a dozen versions of her world. "Every time you talk to someone in the past, it creates a subloop, like a spin-off of your own world."

"So, changes in the past don't roll forward to us?"

"Nah. I'm going to contact my younger selves, show them how to outthink dad. Maybe they'll get an even better car. Good karma and all that."

That meant even if I changed the past, *I'd* never benefit from it. Was that good enough for me?

After a moment of contemplation, I came to a decision. I wanted *my* mom to live, even if it's in another reality. I could still talk to the *real* her, not a mirror universe knockoff. A mom that would know everything about me.

"Teach me how this time travel mod works, kiddo."

* * *

During Me-ality's launch, I'd been focused on mom's fight, so I wouldn't be on the alt-streams while mom was alive. That meant convincing a younger Tom of Tom 222's to track me down. I picked a date shortly after mom's diagnosis. It wasn't the easiest conversation, but I did finally convince Tom I was legit. I knew he would have an even harder time convincing the younger Ned to get on Me-ality. I revealed a lot about myself to Tom, who was practically a stranger to me, and a total stranger to my younger self.

I, he, shows up a couple days later.

This isn't like the other worlds. The man across the screen isn't someone whose reality is based on a completely different set of rules. This *is* me, just a couple years ago. I look haggard.

"How?" younger me asks.

"I don't have a lot of time. This time stream mod takes a toll on PCs. They're not designed for it yet. I gave Tom a list of treatments that won't work on her. Do whatever you can to persuade the doctors away from those ones. Move on to others, even holistic if you have to. If nothing works, you'll be right here where I am. Go back to a younger you, and start the process over."

Ned Jr. turns ashen and his jaw slackens. Tears form at the edges of bloodshot eyes. "You mean, there's no hope? She's going to die?"

The stream lags and, when Ned Jr. returns, he's been pounding the monitor.

"Chill, bro. Right now, she only dies in my timeline. She might not in yours. Keep a log to pass on to the next me–us–down the line. We can do this."

Ned Jr. nods, and his face reveals the hope of possibilities unexplored; something I lost somewhere along the way.

I open Me-ality's master list. My Earth, #1134, has a plus next to it.

* * *

There are now one-hundred and twelve versions of my timeline. I open a chat request with my most recent contemporary. It's like a mirror, I'm very much like... me. He waited until our timelines coincided.

"You're the prime, right?" Ned.112 asks.

"Yeah. Any luck?"

"So far, no. We've managed to keep her alive a few more months, but there have been just as many sudden deaths from heart attacks or liver failure. Those versions of us hate you."

"They shouldn't. It's a mercy. I should tell them."

"Some of us have. There have been other twists in the timeline." Ned looks pensive. "Mom's died in accidents, too. Falls down stairs, car wrecks. Us, too. Sometimes with her. Sometimes just us, leaving mom to die alone. The Toms in those cases have stepped up to help her until the end, but when we die, she dies quicker."

It's difficult to digest it all. What holy hells have I unleashed on my alt-selves? My alt-moms?

"Tom? Why Tom?"

"We've become close through this. He's got a large family and adopted each version of us like we were long-lost cousins or something. His sense of humor is, y'know, a lot like ours used to be. On the days I miss her the most, Tom's there to bring me a smile. Oh, and free grape fries."

Tom and I? BFFs? Who would have thought it?

"Should we give up?" I ask, "Did you? You're the latest on my drop down."

"I haven't decided. I'm glad you logged on. What do you think?"

"We've kept her alive a little longer, right?"

Ned nods. Then there's still a possibility one of us will get it right. If we do, mom might have a thousand Neds waiting to chat with her.

"It's a slim chance, but it's our mom, right?" Ned.112 agrees. A resigned smile graces both our faces as one. "Go ahead and contact #113."

ME-ALITY.COM/BOOP

***

I'm eating lunch in my cubical, waiting for the latest update from my alt-selves, when I get an IM request from Nora. She doesn't have her latex wig on; her eyes jotting back and forth between monitors. Nora's cheeks are smeared with tear-washed mascara.

"You have to stop! Stop time traveling right now!" Nora tells me in a panic.

"We can't stop yet. Mom keeps dying. What? Did you get busted?"

"No, you mosshead! You have to stop or…" Her tears flow like the rain outside her window. She can barely speak. "Or it's over…all over."

"What? What's over, hun?"

"McFly is gone."

The kids dubbed #2147 "McFly."

"Gone? What do you mean gone? Like off the network?"

"No, like gone, gone! They changed their past somehow and wiped themselves out."

"Holy fuck! How's that even possible?"

Nora draws a breath to get the words out. "Every reality that #2147…shared their time travel mod with. Reality can only split…so much before it implodes. The more people use it…the faster their reality ends."

The implication hits like an iceberg. "Tell me you've stopped, Nora. Please tell me." I want her to say she's a mess because she's not going to get her Manta at graduation.

She doesn't. "I've shared it with too many friends…and then they shared with others. Our numbers, they're where McFly's were when they vanished…down the drain…we…we're circling."

I click into the backdoor. My heart slips from my chest to my ass as I watch Nora's earth drop down from 35 subloops, to 34, to 33. When I last viewed her list, she was nearing 3000. I click on my own submenu. I'm still growing. My stream goes up from 178 to 179.

"I'm scared," Nora confesses. "I don't want to die."

I put my hand to the monitor. "It's okay, sweetheart. It's going to be okay." My eye darts to the numbers.

238.12.

238.11.

Nora lays her hand opposite mine. "I just wanted to know if my dad was as big an asshole as he pretended to be. I should've known better."

"Why?" I can feel my own tears forming.

238.3.

238.2

"Because you aren't."

238.1

And then she's gone.

My hand presses a blank screen until it forms a fist.

I wail.

For Nora.

For mom.

I watched them both die right in front of me. Everything comes back; the helplessness, and the guilt, and the anger, making me nauseous.

I can never save my mom no matter how many earths I sacrifice.

I become a tornado. Red creeps in from the corners of my eyes. I tear pictures from the fabric cubical walls. Stapler, books, pens sail out the cube eliciting cries of surprise and alarm from my peers. Eventually only one object is left for my rage. I close my laptop hard and hurl it to the floor. I get to my knees and take it by the edges; slamming it over and over. I get a sense of accomplishment when chunks of plastic fly off of it. The lid flaps open, and I see bits of green and silver from the circuit boards. Drops of noxious liquid splatter on my face as the LCD screen shatters.

My co-workers try to calm me down. I can't hear them over the roaring in my ears, but they eventually reach some non-animalistic part of me. Realization of what I'm doing creeps slowly into my awareness. I give up, my body spent.

I drop my laptop to the carpet and stare at the cuts on my hands. Snot runs from my nose and mingles with tears before slipping past my lips. I reach for a tissue before remembering I threw them somewhere. I wish I was dead.

"Oh, shit."

I get up. I have to stop my past selves from more time travel. Nora told me the end comes faster the more the prime time line diverges. So far, it's only me with the time travel tech. We haven't divided as much as Nora's or the others have.

I can still stop this. I have to try.

I race from the office. If I use Tom's computer to contact the other mes, maybe I can stop our reality from imploding. I make a call in route — the last call I thought I'd ever make. The truth is, I'm gambling with reality, and I need backup.

Tom doesn't question me as I dash to the computer in his office. I connect with #1134.179. My younger counterpart picks up.

"Hey, Ned prime. I was just about to—"

"STOP!"

* * *

I feel this should be easier, contacting 178 realities and dissuading them from using the mod. I win over most. They wipe the hack from their laptops and reinstall an untampered with Me-ality. I mean, who would want to destroy all reality?

Ned.42 doesn't answer. It takes a dozen requests before

he does.

I know he's me, but not the best me. Dark circles raccoon his eyes. Tattoos graffiti his shirtless chest. His pallor skin hangs limply from his bones as if he has meth for breakfast. My alt-clone chose to let grief consume him. He's everything I've worried I would become.

"No," He says to my request to stop. "I won't delete it. In fact, you've given me an idea. Thanks, Ned."

He starts typing.

Panicking, I shake the monitor. "Ned? What are you going to do? This isn't just about you. We're talking our whole reality!"

He won't look at me. "You say we don't do it, right? We don't save her? Then what's the point?" He reaches for a cigarette. He drags it long and hard, as if it's the last one he'll ever smoke. "No reason we need to stick around."

Because he's my mirror self, he makes sense. These have been my thoughts, too, on those dark nights of the soul.

If we end it all, don't we take away everyone's pain, not just ours?

Then I think of a Nora; the girl who wanted nothing more than to understand her dad. Understand why he seemed like such a dick and yet planned to buy her the car she dreamed about for graduation. She'd never get her Manta. Never realize, as kids who transition to adults do; that their parents sacrifice everything, including being their friend, because they love them.

As their children, shouldn't we sacrifice for them?

"What do we have?" I ask. "We have hope."

Ned.42 looks at me disbelievingly. "Huh?"

I hide the movement of my thumb dialing my cell below the screen. "We have one more day, Ned. Mom didn't. Her time ran out. All those realities that have collapsed in on themselves? They ran out of time, too. But we haven't. Not yet."

The more I talk, the more confident I feel about what I'm saying. "We can make a difference. Not in mom's life. That ship has sailed. But in ours and others. Mom wanted us to be happy. Can't we do that? Live *for* her, even if it's not *with* her?"

My alt-self isn't becoming a convert. I give him time to make the right choice.

Ned.42 — the last holdout.

He takes another long drag.

"No. Fuck you. Fuck you and your hope."

He reaches for the keyboard, and I shout "Go!"

Ned.42's front door shatters. Shards of wood shoot toward him like daggers. Armored men follow the projectiles through, their Alt-Real Inc. logos lighting the room. The guns they wield look nothing like the ones on my world, but I don't doubt their effectiveness. The company acquires the highest-end technology from a billion realities.

There's a knock behind me. I tell them it's open. I'm still too shaky to get up. The suit that walks in is accompanied by only one security person. Tom's office door stays intact.

"Mr. Waters?"

I can't turn away from the monitor. "I wish it hadn't come to this, you know that? Still, I appreciate you letting me at least *try* it my way."

He smiles without emotion. "Of course, Mr. Waters. All versions of you have been customers in good standing. This minor hiccup needed resolution in the best manner possible. It's unfortunate so many others that downloaded the illegal modification didn't care as much as about reality as you do."

The suit walks over to the desk, pulling papers from a binder as he does. His muscle radios someone. I hear an echo from the monitor speakers. He's communicating with his alt-self on #1134.42.

"Sign here and here," the lawyer says.

I do.

"So, that's it? We're all blocked? Every Ned?"

"For a period of a year, yes. That should give us enough time to close this loophole in our programming."

Ned.42 is being dragged away in restraints on the screen; his face awash of fury and fear. How could I betray myself? He screams. How could I not understand him?

I do understand him, and me, too well.

I click the mouse and his world goes away.

I'm left to face mine.

* * *

The pain gnaws at the edges of us all. Where once there was just me alone, now 179 Neds exist, missing their moms every day. But it's better than oblivion, or so Jessica reminds me. I met her at Tom's #222.2, his second location. I'm no cook, but I do a decent job managing the place for him. And…the crowds love my first addition to the menu, coconacon–coconut bacon.

Ned.112 was right. Tommy and I do make great friends, brothers even. His family showers me with love, food, and Ouzo every Saturday afternoon at dinner.

I asked legal eagle from Alt-Real Inc. how many realities had disappeared off the master list.

"Twelve."

Alt-Real Inc's acquisition of alt-worlds returned to its normal progression with the release of Me-ality 2.0. And though I have my access back, I don't get on that much anymore. From Earth #2201, a Katherine Waters sends me friend request. She's a cancer survivor who lost her son Ned in a car accident a couple years earlier. I don't accept. I have *my* mom with me in every action, every decision. And I'm okay with that.

I do, however, contact a Nora Waters on #2213. Cute kid with cat-like ears and whiskers. And, get this…

It turns out her mom's name is Jessica.

―――

David Boop is a prolific Denver-based speculative fiction author & editor with novels, novellas, countless short stories to his credit as well as being an award-winning essayist, and screenwriter. Before turning to fiction, David worked as a DJ, film critic, journalist, and actor. You can find out more at Davidboop.com, Facebook.com/dboop.updates or Twitter @david_boop.

THE ACCOMMODATION

Margaret Pearce

We had been anticipating and dreading their breakup for years.

When Dad, an anal obsessive rigidly tidy freak, fell in love with Mum, a warm hearted and untidy lover of the universe, a certain lack of harmony could be expected. Mum was an earth mother type, a practicing Buddhist and a hopelessly impractical mystic.

Dad at last moved out. Despite being more legally with it than Mum, it still took him two years to gain custody of Jenny and me.

There was sufficient evidence of her slapdash attitudes to cleanliness and order, especially with the stray animals she rescued around the district and nursed in the house. Also being an earth mother type, the procession of improvident young men she housed and nurtured was looked upon with some suspicion by more conventional friends and Dad.

He had descended to unnecessary depths of bitterness during it all, claiming that she was an incompetent housewife, and a morally unsuitable person to raise us. What surprised me was that he was believed ahead of Mum.

When we were taken by court order, Mum shrugged and walked out of the family home. She had decided to join some Ashram overseas. We had been given permission to see her off at the airport.

"I hold no bitterness towards your father," she had assured us, bending to kiss us goodbye. "It is his karma to be his own worst and destructive enemy. Take heed of these lessons life gives you."

"Won't we see you again?" my sister Jenny begged, tears rolling down her face.

"I'll return whenever you need me," Mum assured us, enveloping us in one last warm incense scented hug. "All things in life are transient, and soon pass."

"You had no right to let Dad have custody," I accused.

I felt resentful. She could have shown some backbone and fought Dad more fiercely for custody. Our mother was warmhearted and caring. She had fed and cared for us as well as any other mother in the street. The fact that there were always stray cats, dogs, and birds with broken wings around, not to mention all the homeless young men she had housed, hadn't meant that she wasn't a good mother. Being too easy going and having a dislike of unpleasantness was also a fault.

"Now Billy boy," she said gently. "It is not in me to descend to your father's level and be so spiritually impoverished. Everything will work out. The universe is on our side."

She left. Jenny snuffled all the way back to the sterile environment of the clean flat where we now lived with Dad. I patted her absently. Kids don't have much control over their own lives. We had told the social workers and court people over and over again that we preferred living with Mum, but somehow Dad had ended up triumphant.

With Dad being so efficient, most of the flat was already packed up by the time we had arrived back. Dad had cancelled the lease of the flat. We were going to shift back home. The next morning, the removal van turned up with two brisk helpers for the shift.

"Wouldn't it be better to wait to check out the house first in case you want to get it cleaned?" I asked, remembering about Dad's obsessive cleanliness and the last few years of Mum's casual attitudes to dirt and debris.

"Waste of time, money and the lease of the flat," Dad said. "We'll shift back and clean up as we go."

Dad's triumph dimmed a little when we reached the house. Mum had an extensive herb garden in the backyard. I seem to remember the homeless young men being very helpful about nurturing the herbs grown there. In the front, the lawns and shrubs were overgrown. One of the side fences was falling down, and everything looked shabby and run down.

"Filth!" Dad exclaimed, brushing away the spider webs as he unlocked the front door. "What a disgusting stench!"

I didn't think it smelled that bad. The cat urine was a bit overpowering through the carpet, and there were unemptied litter trays in the long passageway. In the bathroom the bath was still half filled with birdseed from when Mum had nursed the parrot with the broken wing. A stray cat sprawled among the birdseed with a fresh litter of kittens.

The aromatic, pungent incense smell lingered in all the curtains and cushions. The removalists sniffed, sneaked a look at each other, dumped all the furniture in the big family room and fled.

Jenny and I ran straight to our bedrooms. They were a bit dusty but unchanged. Our shelves still had our favourite books and toys neatly stacked on them. The floors had polished boards and our hammocks still swung in their usual places. I breathed a sigh of relief.

When I came out again, Dad was yelling into his mobile phone. He wanted a dumpster bin delivered that afternoon. He wanted to throw out everything that was broken and germy and immediately!

He took the next week off. We thankfully went back to our usual schools. Dad pulled the carpets out and had the floors sanded and polished. He got carpenters in to replace all the rotten weatherboards and floorboards. The painters painted inside and out. A new double garage was built. Although he disliked gardening, he immediately got stuck into Mum's herb garden and pulled a lot of the lovely healthy fronded plants out by the roots and shoved them in the compost bin with lots of lime.

He decided that we could keep our hammocks. He put our unwanted beds in one of the back rooms. He then hinted about another mother and stepbrothers. Jenny and I looked at each other. This was something we hadn't heard before!

"Sneaky!" Jenny whispered. "He's had another lady all the time."

Every afternoon we came home from school to something new. There was a magnificent new refrigerator, a new stove, lots of extra electrical appliances and a new microwave.

"Don't know how your mother didn't poison you all," he grumbled. "That microwave was dangerous, the way it was leaking so badly. And it's probably been leaking for years. Not to mention being festooned in cobwebs as well. Ugh!"

"Mum didn't have any spare money to get anything repaired," Jenny pointed out.

"Nonsense!" Dad said. "She milked me for maintenance for you kids. She should have gone back to work."

I nudged Jenny to shut up. Dad paid as little maintenance as he could get away with. Mum made sure we never went short of anything despite of the shortage of money. She did work sometimes, but when she had bad sessions with her arthritis she had to stay home.

Dad had taken the mother cat and the kittens to an animal shelter. A few days later the invasion started. As there were no animals around to keep them down, we had a plague of mice and then rats. Dad left traps and poison, grouching about how abnormally large all the vermin were.

"Even the cockroaches are huge," he grumbled. "Haven't seen any that large outside the tropics."

The rats or something kept chewing holes in all the walls. Dad kept getting carpenters in to replace the boards they had chewed.

"Surprised that you kids hadn't been bitten by vermin or gone down with plague when you lived here with your mother," he grumbled.

"Our bedrooms were always clear of any vermin," I explained. "Although Mum didn't believe in killing anything live because she was a Buddhist."

"She said she had an accompaniment with all other living things," Jenny piped up.

"Accommodation," I corrected.

"Whatever, so they wouldn't hurt or annoy us," Jenny explained.

"Stuff and nonsense!" Dad snarled. "Stupid superstitious rubbish!"

He had cleaned or mostly replaced the drapes, curtains and cushions, so the place didn't smell of incense any more. It now smelled of cleaners, disinfectants and insect repellants. Despite all this, spider webs appeared every morning in the house. Every morning Dad cleaned them down with an irrational fury.

The only good thing about Dad's battle with the vermin around the house was that he was so busy cleaning and laying traps and poisons and getting pest exterminators in, that we didn't hear any more about a new stepmother or step brothers. Guess he had no intention of bringing a new bride or family into the house until it was spotlessly vermin free to his satisfaction. In which case, because of his high standards, it never would be.

There were never any spiders to be seen, but the webs themselves were large, sticky and clinging, draped from the ceiling down across the refrigerator, microwave and divider. Every morning Dad swept and washed down the walls. When he arrived home from work every night they were back up again.

I don't remember noticing spiders in the house before. Mum had never worried about the spider webs as they never seemed to have spiders in them.

"All living things are entitled to live," she always said.

Perhaps the incense smell had kept the spiders out. Although why would they come in to spin their webs?

Mum had explained that the webs were only to catch the flies in the house and the spiders then took them outside. Anyway, the new webs were never spun in mine nor Jenny's bedroom, just the passage, lounge, kitchen and Dad's bedroom.

The holes kept appearing in the walls. Dad kept getting carpenters in to block them up. There was a real persistent one in the kitchen wall near the ceiling. No matter how often it was blocked up or nailed or plastered over, it was always chewed through the next day.

We always sat at the kitchen table every afternoon doing our homework. When Mum was home the kitchen was the warm heart of the house. I started to sense something behind the blackness of the persistently opened hole in the wall. It felt like something intelligent was watching us. It somehow had a comforting feel, as if someone who really cared for us was keeping a watchful eye on us.

"Guess Mum's accompaniment with the spiders is still

working," Jenny whispered. She also sensed our invisible watcher.

"Accommodation," I corrected. "Good old Mum. Wish she could come back though."

"I miss her so much," Jenny said. Then she put her head down and started howling. "I want my Mum back. It isn't fair! I hate Dad! He's always picking on us and bad mouthing Mum."

"Mum promised things will work out," I soothed. "And she is going to come back when we need her."

"I need her right now," Jenny howled.

I shushed her. I was scared of Dad coming in and seeing her crying. It would only make him more rigid, more bullying and more hateful than ever. After a while Jenny settled down, and we got on with our homework in silence.

It was the next Saturday morning that I found Dad unconscious on the floor. I rang the ambulance and they rushed him to hospital. He didn't regain consciousness and died that afternoon.

Eventually they worked out that he had died of some spider bite. This puzzled everyone as there were no spider webs in the house when they collected him. Dad must have cleaned them all away that morning, as he usually did, before he was bitten.

Mum flew in at midnight. "Had a feeling things weren't going well," she said as she was let inside and rushed over to hug us. We had been sleeping at one of the neighbours. "I was on the first plane out."

"When did you get news of the death?" a puzzled policeman asked the next day.

"I didn't have any news. I just had a feeling about the kids," Mum explained.

"It won't be safe to move back in the house until it is cleared of any spiders," the policeman warned. "The experts seemed to think it was an Ajax Robusta bite."

"My ex-husband was probably outside clearing away some rubbish, got bitten and staggered back inside to phone before he collapsed," Mum said. "He had this habit of not wearing protective gloves when he was working."

After the funeral, everything sort of settled down. Mum moved back home again with us. She was thrilled about all the new furniture and appliances and the new double garage which meant there was somewhere outside to keep the strays. Her health improved a lot as well. Also Dad had left the house and money in trust for our schooling, so everything money wise was now comfortable.

For some reason, after Dad's death, the vermin stayed missing. Of course Mum managed to find the mother cat and the kittens. The spider webs didn't appear in the house any more either. Everyone said wasn't it wonderful that our Dad had finally got rid of the infestations, and wasn't it a pity that he wasn't still alive to appreciate it.

"Mum's accompaniment with everything living is still working," Jenny was starting to fill out and grow taller and more pink cheeked. Having Mum back was agreeing with her.

"Accommodation," I corrected.

I sneaked a look at the hole high up in the wall of the kitchen. I still sensed that something watched us. A something that was warm and somehow smug and approving.

In science we were learning about radiation. I brooded about leaking microwaves. Radiation was supposed to be dangerous. What effect could enough radiation have on spiders, vermin and other insects? Could it alter DNA, and genes or affect the intelligence of things?

"All right, accommodation," Jenny said again. "But it has always worked, hasn't it?"

I guess this was true. Mum had an accommodation with everything living—except Dad, I suppose.

"Yeah," I agreed again.

If it wasn't the universe on our side, something was.

Margaret took to writing (mostly fantasy) instead of drink when raising children. She has had children's and teenage novels published, three romances released with Robert Hale, and several more published as ebooks. She lives in Australia, and currently lurks in an underground flat in the Dandenongs — still writing.

CHARLIE'S WEEKEND

Ellen Barnes

Swamped with fear, I put my hands on the center of the man's chest, I began to count: one two, one two. Thirty compressions in eighteen seconds, two inches deep. Repeat compressions. At least that's what I thought I was supposed to do. I'd been trained in first aid, but not CPR.

The ambulance rounded the corner, siren whooping, lights flashing and squealed to a stop by the prone figure on the sidewalk. The EMT jumped from the front seat "Okay, miss. We'll take it from here." Seconds later, the police arrived on the scene.

I stepped back two paces next to my friend Carole and thought, "We're in deep shit." The cop began asking questions. "Do you know this guy? Name? Address?" Carole and I did, indeed, know him.

It had started out as such a lark… Oh Jeez. What possessed us? The idea had started simply enough and my thoughts drifted back to an evening a few weeks ago.

* * *

It was the same story every night at Restful Acres: "Move back, move back" barked one of the staff.

The waiting line of walkers, wheelchairs and canes snaked through the lobby blocking the entrance to the dining hall. Softened strains of Big Band era hits were piped in an endless loop over the lobby and elevators. When the doors finally opened the residents slowly shuffled to their assigned seats.

Charlie, one of the newer residents, had been the last to be seated. He'd just completed his ritual of bringing me coffee in a doubled up Styrofoam cup at the front desk where I worked as the receptionist. He stood there grinning and reeking of Old Spice as he handed me the cup. Charlie couldn't see well, so the second cup was insurance, like double bagging at the grocery store.

Carole had dropped by the front desk to chat for a minute or two. Management frowned on kitchen help coming into the lobby unless absolutely necessary, but Carole and I were friends. In fact, best friends. We had just graduated from high school together and were now roommates. Plans for Community College were put on hold for a semester while we tried to save money. Rules/schmules, I thought as we tried catch up without getting caught. While chatting, we spied an elderly woman, with her shirt on backwards, her skirt bunched up in the back and two different colored shoes. Clearly, her caregiver wasn't doing her job. It wasn't funny. The woman's dignity had been violated, but the absurdity of the vision was too much and Carole lost control. She started to snicker, and I helplessly joined in. We knew better, but sometimes the stress and rigidity of our jobs caused the safety valve to blow and the more we laughed, the more impossible it was to stop. The laughter and hysteria bordered on tears. For a brief moment, I pictured myself a resident, and the prospect was impossible to contemplate.

"I'll never get that old and that'll never happen" I told myself. After the manager shot a warning look, Carole quickly retreated to the kitchen.

The odor of evening meal wafted into the lobby. Smells of cabbage and boiled beef swirled through the miasma of orange scented disinfectant and a few leaky Depends. Most of the residents never thought to complain, their palates having been compromised long ago by age and medication. The closest thing to a revolt had been a group complaint over the loss of cranberry sauce that used to be served with roasted chicken. New management had initiated cost-cutting measures and cranberry sauce along with bottled water had been on the chopping block. Bottled water was replaced by a leaking urn with Dixie Cups.

Minutes later, I spied Carole waiting for the elevator with the food cart to deliver dinner to the "Memory Care Unit" on the second floor. With only one elevator, it was a losing proposition at mealtime. Only two wheelchairs and one walker could fit in the tiny elevator at one time. The housekeeping staff was also waiting to take the linen carts downstairs while Carole waited to go up. Neither was going anywhere soon since residents had priority, and this became a problem with a "no overtime" policy. Management monitored timecards mercilessly and expected staff to scan out and leave the premises within five minutes of shift change. Most of the staff were part-timers, a policy embraced by the owners to avoid paying health care and vacation benefits with the net result of an expanded staff that knew the residents less well and were not as invested in the community. It was hard for part-timers to form relationships with the residents, to learn their likes and dislikes, their families, and maintain a feeling of continuity for them.

After dinner, Charlie wanted to help Carole clean up. This was not allowed, but he usually managed to come in before meals and help lay down the place settings. At 95, Charlie was spry and fit and a shameless flirt. He'd done construction work most of his life and had a remarkable memory for man even 20 years younger. He'd told us he'd lost his wife ten years earlier and it was clear he was lonely. He'd lived with his daughter Margaret and her husband

Bill for years, but they decided it would be better for him (or, more likely, them) if he had a more structured environment. Charlie felt abandoned in a sea of old people. He didn't feel old himself. He had plenty of opportunity to spend time with the many available widows at the residence, but Charlie preferred the company of younger women. We thought this was a hoot! He had two great granddaughters in high school, not much younger than us.

Carole and I usually stopped in Starbucks after work to de-stress and gossip before heading home. We talked shop and I told her I would never end up in a place like Restful Acres. Both of us agreed we'd never go into residence, even if we could afford it, but what would happen if we started losing our own memories? Would we be able to make decisions about our care in advance? I hoped I'd have the courage to end it while I still had control of my life and I vowed I would never end up like grandma. Then again, the thought occurred to me that the closer to the edge I got, the more I might want to cling to the cliff. I didn't know. I decided to reserve judgment on others' choices until I walked in their shoes.

Sipping a latte, our talk turned to the residents, Charlie, in particular. We laughed and joked and were amused that he wanted to take us to dinner. He asked us out all of the time.

"He must have been hot stuff when he was young," Carole laughed.

I agreed. The charm still dripped off of his lean, 95-year-old frame. You could tell he'd had an active life and the sedentary atmosphere at Restful Acres did not agree with him. He was allowed to walk around the building at least an hour a couple of times a day. Sometimes he took a buddy with him. Even though he couldn't see well, he was designated the "responsible party" on these walks when he took a memory-challenged resident for company. Charlie had no interest in participating in elder activities. No bingo, sing-alongs, and crafts for him. Carole and I noticed he was losing some of his spunk lately and he deserved so much more. It really was a shame.

The weather was getting warm and Carole and I had planned a beach weekend at the end of the month. It had been a long time since we had a girls' weekend out. Ocean City was definitely on the menu. Then, a wicked idea occurred to me. "What if we take Charlie on this trip? He'd have the time of his life!" "Not possible." Carole stated the obvious. It was true.

It seemed as if he was a prisoner in effect, if not name. Adult children with POA always had the final say. The ultimate indignity: the parent being treated like a small child. There was also the unspoken, unwritten rule: No fraternization with the residents outside of work. Still, if Charlie maintained all of his faculties, why couldn't he check out briefly and "visit a friend"? Why not? The thought of this old guy flirting with young girls on the beach was irresistible. We, of course, were off limits but egging Charlie on seemed like great fun. Once the idea had sprouted, it would not go away.

"Can we do this?" Carole asked.

"Might spell trouble" I replied.

Carole started looking for hotel deals. "Whether he goes or not, we're still doing this, right?"

"Absolutely!" I replied. "I think you should drive. Your Subaru is good on gas."

The next day, Carole stopped by after the lunch shift. "I found the perfect place for us. The Ocean Plaza Hotel. It's on the Boardwalk."

"How much?" I asked.

"Oh, about $135 a night for two full size beds with a sofa. As long as it's before Memorial Day."

"Who gets the sofa?"

"Charlie, of course," I said with a mischievous grin. "They also have one of those old-fashioned beachfront wrap-around porches. The kind with all the rockers."

"Perfect! Book it."

"We'd better put in for time off." Weekends off were hard to come by. "Let's not ask Charlie yet. He might get so excited he spills the beans." Charlie knew a good time, and it wasn't happening at Restful Acres.

"Right," I agreed.

The next Monday rolled around, and Carole announced she'd made reservations. Two weeks to plan and request time off. Our leave was granted, since it was the weekend before Memorial Day and Restful Acres was assured full staff to work the holiday.

Two days before the trip, Carole asked Charlie if he'd like to sneak out for coffee after we finished our shifts. He would, indeed, and during his approved walk outside, we picked him up behind the kitchen dumpster for a quick visit to the nearby Starbucks. Since Charlie was allowed out unsupervised, though required to stay on the grounds, this was an easy escape since his usual walks lasted an hour or two.

Carole and I ordered caramel lattes and Charlie drank black coffee. Carole lit up a cigarette and inhaled deeply. No smoking on work property made for a long day. Charlie wagged his finger at her. He'd given up smoking years ago. We giggled over coffee and told him about our upcoming trip to the beach. Charlie begged to come along, as we'd predicted.

"Well, you won't be allowed to go," teased Carole.

"I won't tell 'em" replied Charlie.

"I don't know...," I said.

"Please, please. I won't be no trouble" pleaded Charlie.

"Well, you can't tell anyone," I insisted.

"I won't. I won't."

We silently crossed our fingers, hoping this was true. This trip was starting to feel like planning a keg party when your parents are out of town.

Friday rolled around and Carol and I packed for the beach — shorts (check), tee-shirts (check), sunglasses (check) and sun-block (check), cell phone chargers (check), plus a pack of cigarettes for Carol (check). We watered the plants and put out extra large bowls of kibble and water for our cat Frances.

Car loaded, Carol and I drove to the back of the Restful Acres parking lot. What a perfect day! The weather was warm and sunny. The scent of iris and peonies was in the air. Charlie was waiting behind the kitchen dumpster all dressed up in his best blue-checkered shirt and khaki pants – and the ever-present Old Spice — a fact that did not go unnoticed by the gaggle of widows watching TV in the lobby.

Jeez, talk about not "flying under the radar," I thought catching a whiff of Charlie's cologne. "Hurry up and get in the car if you're coming. It's all over if they see you."

Charlie climbed in and crouched down in the back seat with his best clandestine pose raising two fingers in the "Victory" sign. I looked over the head rest into the back seat. His excitement was palpable. Carole backed out of the parking lot and we were on our way.

"Did you bring anything with you?" I asked.

"No" Charlie replied.

I told Carole, we might have to shorten our stay. Charlie was unprepared. More importantly, we were unprepared. This probably wasn't such a good idea after all, I thought, silently cursing myself for failure to make adequate plans. I knew Charlie didn't have any serious health issues. Perhaps we could manage a quick overnight. We began to realize the weekend meant more to Charlie than to us. One last hurrah! We reminded Charlie to call in and say he met up with friends outside of Restful Acres and would be home in the morning. The old man sneaking out smacked of a teenager pulling a fast one on his parents. Hell, we were teenagers and could relate.

This could have more consequences, though. Nagging doubts began to flutter in my head. I could tell Carole was having second thoughts, too.

"Hey Charlie, what if we just do lunch today?" I ventured.

"No! I wanna go to the beach. You promised! I never get to go anywhere!" Charlie whined.

Cooler heads did not prevail, and we caved.

Though we'd gotten a jump on the weekend beach traffic, the drive took 3 ½ hours punctuated by numerous bathroom stops and coffee breaks along the way. Carole shifted smoothly in and out of traffic while Charlie chattered non-stop. He was so excited he could barely contain himself.

We learned about his late wife, Bernice. How they met and married in New York after World War II, that he'd fought in the Normandy invasion and sustained a wound to his leg but recovered quickly. Charlie said he'd worked construction his whole life, a testament to his good health, I thought. He told us he had two children, a son Richard and a daughter Margaret, but Richard had been killed in Vietnam. He had three grandchildren and two great granddaughters, whom he doted on. He was interested in Native American artifacts and played guitar. After his wife's death ten years ago, he had had a girlfriend or two. He seemed most fond of the "flower child" refugee from the sixties named Suzie, much to his daughter Margaret's dismay. He was an interesting guy. We let him do the talking and kept our own lives a relative mystery. After the Bay Bridge, we stopped in Easton for a quick lunch of crab cake sandwiches at a local produce stand with picnic tables. Charlie walked around the fruit stand, touching all of the fruit and vegetables until the exasperated proprietor told him to stop. We rolled our eyes and then bought local strawberries to take with us. Forty-five minutes later, Carole registered us at Ocean Plaza. We left Charlie's name off of the registration and walked down the corridor.

Charlie was ecstatic when he saw the room. "Ocean view!" he exclaimed. As we'd hoped, the room had two full-sized beds and a small sofa, a microwave, tiny refrigerator, table and chair and the all-important bathroom. The room was a little stale and the smell of a previous smoking occupant remained in the air, so Carole opened the window to let in the ocean breeze. Ahhh! This might turn out after all.

After a half hour rest and people-watching on the porch rockers, we strolled out onto the Boardwalk. The air was breezy and refreshing with a salty tang. The sunset frosted tangerine on the horizon. Life was beautiful.

At least where we were was beautiful. We didn't know it at the time, but back at Restful Acres a full alert was in progress. Charlie had called in with his "staying-with-a-friend" story. He was immediately designated missing and the staff was losing its collective mind. The state police had been notified and sped to the residence to take a report. Not exactly an "amber" alert but the word was out.

Charlie's family had been apprised of the situation. His daughter Margaret tore into the lobby screaming "How could you allow this to happen?" The director was making a full effort to soothe her. "I'm sure there has to be some explanation. He's never done this before. I'm sure he's all right." In addition to Charlie's phone call, he had been seen getting into Carole's car by one of the residents who neglected to mention it to staff until dinner. Things were not adding up.

***

On the boardwalk, we dodged the usual crowd of skateboarders, teenagers, and families with toddlers. Charlie was lagging a bit trying to dodge sticky chewing gum and cigarette butts on the boardwalk and I stopped to wait for him to catch up.

"What cha doin' Charlie? Don't you want to enjoy the beach before sundown?"

Charlie swayed as he held an oversized cell phone to his ear. He was taking too much time and I felt a frisson of fear chill the nape of my neck.

"I'm callin' muh muh mm daughter. Uhh I wanna t-t-t-tell her what a g-g-good time I'm havin'…" he stuttered. Charlie stumbled mid-conversation and collapsed face-down on the sidewalk.

"Oh My God! Carole!" I called out. "Carole! Help!"

Carole dialed 911 and I rolled him over. Charlie was clutching his chest. I moved his arms to his side and attempted CPR, but I had no idea what I was doing, and I was terrified. The arrival of the paramedics rescued me from my indecision.

Lights flashing and siren wailing, the ambulance transported Charlie to the hospital.

A quick check of his ID and a radio call in was all it took. The officer in charge told us there was an APB out for us. Carole and I sat handcuffed in shock in the back of a patrol wagon. At the precinct we were fingerprinted and photographed, then interviewed separately. We both were terrified. We'd never been arrested before.

The cops were incredulous at our story. We told it straight. No one believed we could be so stupid.

The lieutenant informed us we were being charged with kidnapping.

"Kidnapping? What? He's an adult! I want to make a phone call!" I shouted in panic.

Escorted to a pay phone, I dialed home, collect. "Please, Mom. Help me! I've been arrested. I need you to meet me in Ocean City."

"What have you done now?" she shrieked.

"I'll explain later. Can you help?" I wasn't sure she could, but I knew she'd try. Carole was making the same call to her family. There'd be some serious "splainin" to do. The situation was not funny, but the Ricky Ricardo accent from "I love Lucy" reruns kept popping into my head. "God, I'm losing it," I thought.

We were returned to the holding cell. Being the weekend, we knew we were in until Monday at the very least. The drunks were starting to filter in and the tank was filling up. It was noisy and stinking with a lot of yelling and screaming going on hours on end. One drunk peed all over herself and we tried to move to a new corner. The fluorescent lighting was giving me a migraine.

"Oh God! Now what? It's going to be a really long weekend," I thought as the minutes crawled by. We constantly asked how Charlie was, but no one was talking to us. The arraignment wouldn't take place until Monday, as I'd predicted. I kept rerunning the tape in my head. How could I be so stupid? I must have taken leave of my senses. All we had wanted was a short escape from the daily grind. Just a little fun. We never thought taking Charlie with us could be considered "kidnapping." The problem is, we didn't "think."

Neither Carole nor I could sleep. We started blaming

each other for the idea to include Charlie on the trip. The other women rotated in and out of the lockup all weekend. Some bailed out while new ones took their places. With a kidnapping charge, our bond wouldn't be set until Monday. We tried to sit unnoticed in the corner. Meals were stale baloney and cheese sandwiches and half-pint cartons of milk and an occasional mealy apple. Neither of us slept, and I had a pounding migraine that wouldn't end…and no medication.

On Monday morning, stinking and sweating, Carole and I were herded into a police van for the short trip to the courthouse. Shackled and handcuffed, we shuffled in along with the other assortment of drunks and miscreants and spied our mothers sitting grimly in the spectators' gallery glaring at each other. They'd never met, and this wasn't a great introduction.

My mother whispered loudly "It's your daughter Carole's fault! I warned my daughter about her!"

Carols mother shot back "If it weren't for your daughter's bad influence, we wouldn't be here today!"

The deputy "shushed" them and warned they would be evicted from the courtroom if there were any more outbursts. The two mothers silently glared at each other.

The judge appointed counsel for us and as he was setting bail, Charlie's daughter Margaret appeared in the courtroom. She had consulted with the district attorney and asked to approach the bench. She stated for the record that Charlie had an anxiety attack that mimicked a heart attack, but that he would be fine. She was feeling guilty that her father had felt so alone and neglected after he'd been put into residence and was torn by our stupidity but touched that we wanted to pay attention to him. She said Charlie claimed he'd pressured us to take him with us. (This was not entirely true, but he was the consummate gentleman.)

After hearing the description of Charlie's panic attack and subsequent treatment, I broke out in a chilled sweat and my stomach knotted. CPR would have been precisely the wrong procedure for a panic attack. My God, I could have killed him! My best intentions always seemed to cause more harm than good. How could I be such a screw up? What an ill-fated trip!

Margaret and her husband Bill were requesting that the case be dismissed. The district attorney did not object. Charlie's daughter and her husband had decided to remove him from Restful Acres immediately and also planned to retain an attorney to sue for negligence and inadequate staff training. After a few minutes of consultation with the prosecutor and counsel, the judge granted the request and the charges were dropped after giving Carol and me a stern lecture. The judge banned us permanently from Ocean City.

Carole and her mother walked out of the courthouse, arguing already, and retrieved her car from the impoundment lot. My Mom and I left in her car for the awkward drive home. I wasn't looking forward to it.

Restful Acres. We lost our jobs, of course. No legal action was taken against us, more likely because a local newspaper had gotten wind of the story. Restful Acres hired a PR firm to tamp down the fall out. Publicity would not be good and the less notoriety, the better. Orientation and training manuals were updated to specifically state staff was not allowed to have contact with residents outside of Restful Acres. A gag order was issued that applied to all staff.

The one silver lining from this misadventure, Charlie got his life back. He'd escaped, but the remaining residents were more restricted than ever — on lockdown.

Ellen Barnes has spent a lifetime stockpiling stories from rich and varied experiences, which now cascade out in writings filled with fact and fiction. She isn't on social media, preferring to be found between the covers of a good book in Baltimore, Maryland curled up with her cat Missy.

TO PROTECT AND SERVE

John Peel

Maybe this wasn't such a great idea after all. Bedwyr, eyed the thick forest entanglement ahead of him. He shifted his grip on his father's sword, wishing he'd thought to bring along the scabbard as well. He was starting to understand how badly he'd planned this little "quest" of his. Last night, his vow in the chapel to God not to come home until he'd had an adventure had seemed brilliant.

Of course, last night he'd been intoxicated in more than one way, and probably anything would have seemed brilliant to him. He'd just turned sixteen, and his father, Pedrawd, had thrown a big feast for him. Bedwyr had overindulged on the thick Grecian wine his father liked, and his head had swum. Then there had been that rather fetching maid, Mawr, who had shown him pleasures he'd heard joked about but never experienced. That had been as heady as the wine, and a lot more pleasurable. Having bedded his first wench and been drunk for the first time, he had believed that he was ready to take on the responsibilities of a knight. True, he hadn't yet been dubbed, but that was a minor point when you were drunk. It was the *thought* that counted, the intent, the desire. So he had stumbled to the family chapel, and made that vow. Then he'd collapsed and slept off the effects of the wine.

Well, most of them, at least. His head felt as if it was wrapped inside a woollen blanket and some blacksmith was pounding on the inside, trying to break out. Other than that, he was perfectly fine.

Except for the fear, of course.

If there was one lesson his father had drummed into his thick skull it was never to go into the deep forest. *Nobody* went into the forests—and came back again. His father and grandfather—the Bedwyr he had himself been named for—had explained that the Isle of Albion had once been home to creatures and monsters born at the dawn of time. When Christianity had come to the country and the light of the True Cross had shone upon the fairest isle, then the spawn of darkness had retreated into the depths of the forests. In the deep woods, deeper evil dwelled.

Hence the reason for Bedwyr's oath the previous night in the chapel. He had vowed to slay evil to repay God for the goodness he had been granted. When he was drunk, that had seemed like a very fair and honest payment. Now that he was sober—and a little hung-over—it was starting to look like youthful stupidity. But—another thing Bedwyr's father had driven home to him—a knight always keeps his word, no matter how inconvenient it later becomes. "A man who backs out on his given word," Pedrawd has growled, "will back out on anything."

Bedwyr would not back out. No matter how much he wished to.

But the forest looked evil. A normal forest would start as a small cluster of light bushes, a copse of trees, a smattering of ferns, before getting to the oaks and ashes or tall sycamores. There would be proud chestnuts, or bowed willows. Bedwyr, even though he was the son of a noble, was also a son of the fields, and he knew his trees.

He couldn't name a single one of the gnarled, warped growths he was looking at now, though. It didn't look like a forest as much as a defensive barrier set up about the hollow beyond—a living wall, all but marked *keep out*. He knew that if he was sensible, he would heed that warning. But, then, there was his vow...

Swallowing hard, he moved forward again, pushing his way past the first of the twisted branches, and so on into the forest. Here the shadows intensified, sucking the light and warmth from the air. He shuddered, and not only from the fear crawling, spider-like, up his spine.

"Who are you?"

He whirled around, bringing the sword up in a clumsy attempt at defense, before he realized it wasn't called for. The person who had spoken so jarringly was a woman—perhaps only a girl—who looked at him from around the bole of an ancient tree. All he could see of her was her pale hands, her paler face and her silky yellow hair. Her eyes were large and black, and boring into him.

"I'm Bedwyr," he told her. "Knight."

"Bedevere?" she asked, pronouncing his name in the Saxon fashion. They could never get the timbre of the old names correct, but he was used to it. "You look a bit young to be a knight."

He was on a holy quest, and knew that he was bound to tell the truth. "Well, I'm not, yet, quite," he said stumblingly. "But I hope to be one soon."

"Then you'd best turn around and go back to the open fields, *knight-to-be*," she said, and there was distinct mockery in her voice. "This is no place for a boy."

"I'm not a boy," he growled stubbornly. "I'm a man. I'm sixteen."

"Not by much, I'll wager," she said. But she seemed less timid now and came out from her hiding place. She was small, but well-shaped. Her clothing was poor and old, but she wore the dress as if it were of finest silk of the orient. Bedwyr had never seen silk, of course, but the traders sometimes spoke of it with awe in their voices.

"By a day," he admitted, being committed to being honest with her.

"Well, if you'd like to be sixteen and two days, the way is the way you came in."

"I'm on a quest," he informed her. "I've vowed to God not to return until I have slain something evil, an abomination in His sight."

"Have you indeed?" She was mocking him again. "And what makes you so certain that *it* won't kill *you*?"

"I'm on a *holy* quest. If I'm righteous, then God will protect me."

The girl-woman shook her head. "Somebody should protect you," she observed. "In this wood dwells a *thing*."

Bedwyr felt a prickle of fear and exhilaration. He'd been right to hunt here! "What sort of a thing?" he asked.

"I don't know. What sorts of things are there?"

"All sorts," he said. He knew about this from the traveling singers and harpists. "There are dragons and their kin. There are the wolves and their folk. There are the goblins and the fair folk. There are the banshees, and spirits and—"

"Things that go bump in the night," she said, tossing her head and laughing. "Oh, I've little doubt such creatures exist and roam about, but they're not what lives near here. This is a creature of pure evil. A man-eater."

"How come it didn't eat you?" he asked her, a little piqued by her belittling of him.

She pushed out her bosom a little more. "Do I look like a *man* to you?" she laughed. "Or are you still too young to know the difference between a man and a woman?"

Bedwyr recalled the delights he had touched and tasted the previous night and reddened. "I know the difference!"

"And so does this *thing*," the woman replied. "It takes only men." She looked him over again. "And, despite your youth, there are clearly the makings of a man about you, Bedevere. If I can see them, so then can it. Don't provoke it by going further into its range. It may be that it has eaten last night and isn't hungry enough to come after you yet. But if you tread its pathways and challenge it, it could hardly allow you to live, now could it?"

Bedwyr burned with her mockery. "I have taken an oath to slay evil," he repeated. "And a creature that kills men simply because they are men is clearly evil."

"Or more human than you are," she said lightly. "Nothing kills man as easily and frequently as another man."

There was some truth to that, of course, but she seemed to be speaking only to confuse him. "Do you seek to defend this monster?" he asked, puzzled.

"No, you idiot, I'm trying to defend *you*."

This didn't make a lot of sense to him. "I'm a knight," he tried again to explain. "Or shall be soon. It is my task to protect and defend you, not yours to protect me."

"Perhaps," she suggested, "you should seek first to find out what I wish to be defended *from*. This creature is of no threat to me."

Bedwyr blinked. He wished his head was a little clearer, because this strange girl was confusing him. "But you are a beautiful girl—woman," he said, quickly, lest he should offend her. "And someday you will want to take a husband. This *thing* will clearly seek to prevent it by slaying your would-be spouse. So by slaying it, I am serving you."

"Amazing," the girl muttered. "You men can find an excuse for killing *anything* if you really want to." She shook her head. "I can see that I'm not getting through to you. All right—if you *must* get yourself killed, on your own head be it. Just for the record, you're not doing this for me, you're doing it for yourself." She gestured behind her. "Follow this path, and you'll find it. Or, rather, *it* will most assuredly find you." She pointed back the way he had come. "Or go that way, save your life and I promise never to speak of this to anyone again, so you needn't be afraid you'll be labeled a coward."

She really knew how to hurt him, this girl! "I am *not* a coward!" he snapped, reddening again. "And I am a man who keeps his oaths."

"Well, I'm sure both will comfort you in your grave," she replied, shrugging. "I did my best. On your own head be the results of your foolish pride."

He shrugged and moved on. She moved aside to let him pass, and he thought he saw a momentary look of real concern in her eyes. Then she hardened her expression and half-turned away. "Idiot," she muttered. Then she lunged out and planted a kiss on his cheek. "You're worse than the others," she said. "At least they deserved their fate. You're simply too stupid to realize that nobility is an empty shell to hide within."

"If a man believes in nothing larger and better than himself," Bedwyr replied, "then he is truly hollow, for he has no support in times of crisis." He wasn't going to stand here debating with the woman, for he knew his courage would drain away if he did. While the after effects of his drunkenness and his oath still numbed him a little, he pressed onward, not looking back.

The woods, already dark and depressing, managed to draw even more gloom about them. He pushed aside branches that seemed to reach for him like wooden fingers, all the time listening and scanning the area carefully. In the deep shadows, it was hard to see anything, and he could hear nothing. No birds moving, let alone singing; no animals scurrying or burrowing, or hunting for food. Not even any insects. Perhaps within this forest, nothing but the trees were alive.

So, where was this *thing* of which the girl had spoken? He saw no signs of any life at all. Even the trees didn't seem to have fresh leaves on them. It was as if something had sucked the vitality out of this twisted mass of growths. He stepped carefully, though, looking and listening. He had an odd feeling, as though there was indeed something out there in the shadows, unseen and unheard, and yet moving closer to him. His senses could not confirm his fears, but that did not make them any less certain.

There was something here, something ancient, something evil.

He wanted to take the girl's advice, to turn and run, to leave this forest and never return. It wasn't yet too late. The thing out there was moving closer, but he still had time to escape. True, he had taken an oath, but would God hold him to such a naive vow? Wasn't it the equivalent of suicide, and wasn't suicide a sin? To avoid death here would not be dishonorable, but sensible. He could turn and flee.

No! Bedwyr caught his runaway thoughts, and tried to rein them in. That was his fears speaking! Justifying cowardice and breaking a vow were not the actions of a true knight. He had no option now but to press on and to confront this ageless evil. If it slew him, then it would prove that he was not fit to become a knight, and if he were not to be a knight, then he was better off dead. Tightening his grip on the sword and his nerves, he pressed on.

Besides, what would Mawr think of him if he turned and ran? Even if the girl he'd met had been telling the truth, and would never speak of his cowardice to anyone, *he* would still know. Last night, Mawr, laughing with pleasure, had shown him some of what it meant to be a man. He still hoped she would show him more. But how could he allow her to treat him like a man if he was nothing but a coward? Mawr! He couldn't help thinking of her again, picturing her in his mind. He hadn't known what to expect, not exactly, when she had slipped out of her clothing. He'd been delighted with what she had offered, and she had gently led him to pleasures he'd never known. He really wanted to return to those explorations. But he never would, if he didn't turn back now. The monster would stalk him and slay him. His flesh would be eaten, his bones cracked and the marrow drained. He would be dead, and would never again know such pleasures as Mawr had shown him...

The darkness of the forest was creeping into his soul. He jerked his attention back from within to without. If he didn't focus his thoughts, he would be simple prey for any creature that came along, even a hedgehog, let alone a monster. Fighting to retain control of his thoughts and not to give them over to his fears, he realized that he had stopped moving. He had to keep going. He managed to stumble forward a step.

His mind returned to a vision of Mawr's delicate skin and memory of her scents and tastes, and he licked his lips. When he returned, he prayed that she would be interested in sharing more of her secrets and pleasures with him. Of course, actually, she couldn't refuse. She worked for his father, didn't she? So she could simply be ordered to do as he wished. If she didn't, she would be punished.

Maybe, Bedwyr realized, stunned by the thought, maybe that was why she had come to him in the first place. Maybe she hadn't shared herself willingly, but out of fear of being punished if she refused the wishes of the lord's eldest son? As he thought about it, he began to see that this was indeed how it had been. She hadn't been giving of herself freely, but out of compulsion. She had been *forced* to serve his needs, and he had taken advantage of her weakness and powerlessness. There was nobody that she could complain to that he had raped her.

And there was nothing to stop him from doing it to her again.

Women had neither rights nor recourse if they disliked how they were treated. Men held the power, power of the sword and of wealth. Women were dependent upon men in all things. And, as a result, they could not deny him anything he wanted of them. It wasn't just Mawr who he could force to show him their secrets, and to share his bed: it was any woman he chose. He would soon be lord in his own right, and then their lives would be his to deal with as he desired. That was, of course, how it should be: the weak were helpless captives of the strong. Women were weak, and men strong. They had to do as they were told, when they were told. No. He could not run.

No! Again, Bedwyr rebelled against the thoughts that

were flooding his mind. He was ashamed and disgusted by these concepts. True, women were weak and reliant on men, but that didn't mean that they should be taken advantage of! They were to be protected by a true knight. After all, Christ, who was true God, had emptied himself of his power and majesty and deigned to be born on Earth, mortal son of a weak woman. If God himself had such an exalted view of women, how could a knight have less?

But Bedwyr knew in his heart that he wanted Mawr again, and that he would do anything to get between her legs once more. She would have to do as she was told, and to submit to his will. After all, she had done so once, hadn't she? Out of fear of punishment, she had shared her body's secrets with him. Even now, she was probably back home, sobbing and ashamed of what he had forced upon her. Bedwyr felt the strength draining from him as he realized what it was that he had inflicted upon the poor child he had so savagely abused. He fell to his knees, sobs jerked from his tight throat, his grip on the sword loosening. He could feel the darkness within his own soul reaching out to choke him. This forest was the rightful place for such a person as he was—the gloom and blackness of the trees echoed the darkness and despair of his own evil soul.

It felt as though the branches were closing in about him, making a cage of his body. He didn't care. He had looked into his own heart and seen nothing there but selfishness and hollow pride. A knight? He couldn't even make a decent serf! He had forced himself upon an innocent girl, ruined her life, perhaps left her with child, scandalizing her family and friends. She would be forced to bear a bastard child, or else to commit the sin of suicide to assuage her shame. And it was all his doing. He didn't deserve to live...

Mawr! How could he have done this to her? How he had enjoyed her laughter, and now he was about to still that bubbling merriment forever...

Laughter? Dimly, Bedwyr focused on that remembered sound. Mawr had laughed, tinkling sounds of pleasure as she had guided his clumsy, untrained fingers about her delightful body. Laughter... That had not been faked. Mawr had not been terrified, pleasing him out of fear. He concentrated harder, recalling how it had truly been. *She* had come to him, flirting, laughing, teasing. *She* had taken him from the feast, and led him to his room. *She* had slipped her hands into his clothing, touching, tantalizing and then delivering her whispered promises.

She had not been forced, or raped. She had acted willingly, delightedly. The sound of her laughter again filled his mind, and Bedwyr blinked and awoke.

Tendrils of woody growth were trailed about him, slipping and sliding in a black mockery of an embrace. With all of his strength, he raised his father's sword. Crying out wordlessly, he spun about, and slashed with the blade, cutting through the woody fingers, and deep into the trunk of the tree that was embracing him, and draining his life. The judder of the blow shocked his arms, but the scream of pain that ran through his brain pained him more. He dragged the sword free, and struck again and again. The mental howls grew softer and softer with each blow, as chips of wood flew under the force of his attack.

The tree-thing tried to escape, but it moved terribly slowly on its roots, dragging across the ground. Bedwyr would not allow it to retreat. He finally understood. *This* was the man-eater of which the girl had spoken. Somehow it sensed the fears and weaknesses of its prey, and projected them outward. Stunned by inner contemplation, the prey would stand still, allowing the slow-moving tree-thing to creep up on him and envelop him in its branches/arms. Then it somehow drained the life of its victims and awaited fresh prey.

But Bedwyr had awakened, seeing the illusion for what it was. True, like all men he was a sinner, but he was not the one that the tree-thing had tried to paint him. The truth had broken through the illusion and the truth had set him free.

He hacked and slashed at the monster, severing branches and limbs, gouging into the trunk. The waves of mental attack upon the darknesses in his soul slowly faded, and finally the tree shuddered a last time and collapsed. Bedwyr realized that it was finished, dead at last. He stood, panting, leaning on the hilt of the sword. It was dripping sap, and he couldn't restrain a bubble of laughter. He had expected to blood his father's sword, and instead had wielded it like a woodsman's ax! Well, either way, he had kept his vow: he had confronted and slain evil.

Staggering a little, but immensely lighter in his soul, he started back the way he had come. The monster had used his own doubts and fears to attack him, but there certainly had been some truth in the visions. Bedwyr resolved that he would be more careful in his dealings with women from now on. It was the task of a knight, he knew, to protect and serve a lady, and not to take advantage of her.

On the other hand, if she *offered*, freely and willingly....

Bedwyr grinned at the thought. He really hoped that Mawr would offer.

Or maybe that bewitching young lady he had met on the way into the woods...

―――

John Peel was born in Nottingham, England, but moved to New York to marry his penpal. They live on Long Island with their dog, Dickens. He has written over 100 novels, including the Diadem—Worlds Of Magic *and* Dragonhome *series, as well as tie-ins to TV shows such as* Doctor Who, Star Trek *and* The Outer Limits. *Find him at* Facebook.com/JohnPeelAuthor.

PASSAGE

Terry Korth Fischer

Too keyed up to sleep, I spent the night listening to the ocean breathe through my open window. My mind looped through an unending replay of yesterday's phone call. I counted the tropical night cries, and finally, when I could endure the wait no longer, rose.

Early morning left the room edges blended in shadow, while I fumbled with the door and limped onto the lanai. The birds stirred and a spider monkey screamed from the coconut palm. Taking the single lounge chair, I rested my cane against the stone wall. Forty years. The shore of Costa Rica had been my home for forty years. A beautiful land, yes, but I missed the city.

The long years had taught me prudence and a need for constant discretion. Soon Chita would come from Santa Cruz and bring the day-old newspaper. Tangible proof. Then, I, Elmo Paci, would see my exile's end. Until then, I would sit with the macaws and watch the pelicans and the Pacific. I closed my eyes, listening to the ocean lap, and drifted into the past.

***

I slipped back to Brooklyn, to a time when I was young and foolish; Angela, gay and carefree. We were enjoying, Indian summer, the warm autumn of 1971. I idled behind the hardware counter, my mind more on Angela than on nails and plumbing supplies.

Angela. I could see her: slight, with a mischievous secret in her eyes, and a glow radiating from her heart-shaped face, her shock of shimmering hair. I was impatient to be with her. The day was too full of overlapping hours, the minutes never moving forward until at last the short hand found its way to seven. I locked up the store at the same time the cold envelope of air moved in from Canada bringing rain. I rushed to the elevated train and was whisked back to the Old Italian neighborhood.

Angela waited, chaperoned by family: aunts, uncles, and Joseph, her overprotective brother. I wasn't deterred. We huddled together in the family pizzeria, filling the room with laughter and loud talk, while I slyly held her hand under the red and white checkered cloth. Angela's eyes shone; her hair glistened. Her touch seared me. Joseph, the notorious Joey the Knife, kept a watchful eye. It was well after midnight when the Uncles went off to smoke cigars and the women went upstairs to tuck the little ones into bed, that we were, finally, alone. Angela giggled and pushed me away. She said there would be time. A better time. The rest of our lives, she'd said. I was allowed to steal one kiss.

Later, in a steady rain, I made my way from the pizzeria to the elevated train. I flew up the stairs preoccupied with my dreams. Passing disembarking passengers, I ascended, two steps at a time, arriving on the platform lost in whimsical thoughts. I eagerly crossed, looking down the tracks; fog had swallowed the vista and the tracks led into muted dim. Looking into a middle distance, I saw familiar brick buildings morphed to faded outlines. No train in sight; the automobile noise from the street below was muffled in the haze. I was alone, just missing the Number-10 train, and twenty minutes until the next.

I backed up to lean against a cement pillar and focus on Angela's promise. The rain didn't dampen my spirits. I wanted to run up walls; call out to the sky; do handsprings.

I was so full of energy that my skin twitched. A life time, I thought, warmed from the inside out. A sudden gust sent me ducking around the pillar, out of the wind.

In the mist, a man scrambled through the station doorway and onto the platform. Peering from behind my shelter, I couldn't make out his face. He had substantial girth and a bold swagger. He, too, stopped to look down the tracks. Cursing, he walked further down the wooden boards. I thought he might be making his way home, when two figures appeared out of the fog. I didn't hear them come. Maybe, they had been on the platform when I arrived, silent in the shadows. They moved with ominous hostility. Disturbing menace radiated from their dark forms. Their faces were swallowed in the shadows, and a vapor rose from their shoulders, as if they were made of molten evil. There was something familiar, something threatening, but before I could put my finger on it, they overtook the large man.

He shuffled toward the platform edge; unnerved, he shouted, "Get away!"

"Where is it?" they demanded, pushing in on him.

"Get away! I don't... No... No!" His screams hung in midair. There was an unmistakable thud as his body dropped to the platform floor. I heard the vicious kicks as they landed on his fallen body. The man's moans echoed in the fog until he finally fell silent. Peering around the pillar, I watched one search his pockets; while the other, arrogantly looked around. *Mafioso enforcers!* I shivered and dipped behind the post just in time to stay out of sight.

I heard them drag the body. Their voices were husky and raw, and although their words were lost in the fog, their venomous intent didn't elude me. I feared discovery and stayed hidden. *Surely, someone would come?* But as I worried, no commuter noise broke the silence. Five minutes... ten... I waited. There was no change, except in me. My warmth and hope bolted. Steady drips fell from the station roof. Icy fingers of rain water found their way down my collar. My trembling legs began to cramp, and I wondered if they were gone.

Cautiously, I emerged from behind my shelter. The men were less than twenty feet away. I looked directly at their backs as they carried on a conversation. The man's crumpled body lay to their left against the wall. A growing pool spread around the body, outlining the dead man in his own blood. His mouth was open as if he'd just popped up in the middle of a pond for a gulp of air. Sickened, I froze. Then panic set in. I needed to make it from my hiding place to the stairway.

Without a Hail Mary, I sprinted toward the stair. Grabbed the side of the wooden rail, propelled myself around and down. When I reached the bottom rung, I stumbled and looked fleetingly up at the platform. Silhouetted in the night, the threatening ogre looked back.

No time to waste, I raced across the street and up the block, never looking behind. Hoping youth was on my side. Hoping the enforcer wasn't carrying a gun. I prayed that I could get out of sight before my luck and nerve ran out. I traveled several blocks headed toward the pizzeria before I slipped into a doorway to catch my breath. I couldn't go to the restaurant; maybe, I hadn't been recognized—but, that didn't seem likely. Home, the room above the hardware store, might be safe, but was miles away. Could I get there before the enforcer closed in?

I heard the footfalls on the damp street. I'd waited too long. Shuddering, I poked my head out to find a formidable shape barreling down the pavement in my direction. A low slung Pontiac screeched to the curb. The driver's window rolled down.

"Elmo, quick! In the back."

No hesitation. Sprinting over the concrete, I wrenched the rear door open and fell in. The car sped off, a hole in the muffler drowning out the enforcer's protests.

"Stay down," the driver said, and I was thrown against the door as we rounded the corner. "What were you doing at the station? Don't you understand the danger you're in?"

"You know!" I exclaimed. From behind the wheel, Joey the Knife, scowled into the rearview mirror and locked on my eyes. "How?" I stammered and lost purchase in a sharp right hand turn.

"Angela worries," he said. "Elmo shouldn't ride the train. Can't I give Elmo a lift? She is in love, and it is late." His voice mimicked hers in an infuriating whine.

"Joey, I saw a man murdered at the station!" Too late I remembered Joey was mob connected.

"Shut up!" he said, and I saw his pupils contract. "Get down."

I threw myself to the floor. The headlights of a car behind momentarily lit the interior. I curled into a ball. From the front seat, Joey talked into the steering wheel, I didn't miss a word. "You shouldn'ta been there," he said. "It's family business."

I waited for him to go on. He said no more. A cold sweat broke out on my forehead and my palms were moist. We flew through the empty night pinging loose gravel against the undercarriage. We squealed around corners and roared up streets; turning so many times I completely lost my bearings. Then one uphill spurt and we were still, idling, the engine purred. He turned it off. The engine ticked. The street noise echoed in my head, and I was unsettled by the darkness surrounding us.

Minutes passed. I couldn't see what Joey was doing. It made me all the more anxious, startling me when his head popped over the top of the seat. "I'm gonna go," he said. "I'll see if there's word. Make arrangements." When I didn't comment he continued, "I might be awhile. Stay here. Don't go near Angela. Got it?"

"Sure, Joey," I said.

"Sure what?"

"Sure, I'll stay here. Sure I'll wait." The whole time, thinking of putting distance between here and the entire family.

"Youse better," he said and he left me still crouched in the back. I could hear his footfalls. They echoed in the hollow night, and I waited until they were completely out of earshot. Then, I climbed out.

The car sat in a parking garage. It was cast in gloom, illuminated by a single exit sign high up on a far wall. Steel beams hung overhead, and grease stained the concrete floor. Joey's Pontiac was the only vehicle. Looking out toward the city, I gauged he'd parked on the second floor. I could see the rain coming down against the adjacent building and heard a steady trickle as rain made its way down the parking structure. I could smell the docks: diesel oil, garbage, and salt water. *This was crazy. I couldn't afford to wait.* I crossed to the waist high garage wall and looked down. I found Joey's figure almost a block away, moving down the street with a purposeful stride, his chest leading the way, strutting duck-footed with his arms swinging loose behind—a caricature of his uncle, Vito Castellitto. My mind jerked back to the sight of the dead man on the platform.

For some time after Joey left, I wandered around the garage, feeling helpless and confused. I could tell by looking out at the street that I was in a tough part of the city, rougher than the neighborhood I had escaped, with the help of Mr. Watt, the hardware store owner. This was not the old familiar Italian neighborhood, where I might be in danger, but at least knew the terrain. I hesitated, afraid to go too far from Joey's vehicle. Perhaps, he would bring help. But, I wasn't going to be stupid enough to wait patiently, seated on the floor in the backseat, hoping he wouldn't lead the Mafioso straight back.

I found a place where two cement columns ran parallel to each other, supporting the floor above. There was a space between the posts large enough to squeeze into. I tested it out. I could keep an eye on Joey's car, while I kept an eye out for anyone approaching. I confirmed escape was possible, both forward and back. Satisfied, I took a position on the floor next to my hidey-hole, with my back against the wall, poised to disappear.

An hour stretched by, and Joey didn't return. I thought about my vulnerability. I was defenseless, and when the concrete structure began to seep into dampness equal to my spirits, I went out in search of protection. The trunk of Joey's car produced a winter jacket and a grimy sweater. I grabbed both, tossing them blindly out behind me, and looked for more. In the process, I uncovered the bowling bag. Joey didn't bowl. Hoping for an extra pair of socks, I opened the zipper. Joey's knife tumbled out.

I couldn't believe my eyes. The bag held not bowling shoes, but thousands and thousands of dollars. Greenbacks still in ten-thousand-dollar bank straps. I didn't wait to count it out. I closed the zip and threw the bag, as best I could, toward the rear of the trunk. I grabbed the knife and a tire iron, slamming the lid down and collecting the sweater and jacket from the ground. I retreated to the wall.

It was too much money. I tried to reason it out. Joey hadn't conveniently driven past. Joey hadn't been on the elevated platform. He was the most brutal man I knew, but he was Angela's brother. He wouldn't hurt me, even if he was part of the Mafioso family. It took me a while, but finally I worked it out. And, when I did, I crept back to the car, and made a substantial withdrawal, stuffing the bundled bills in my shirt.

On the first floor of the parking garage I found a pay phone, dropped in a dime, and called Mr. Watt. He answered groggy with sleep. I told him I was somewhere near to the waterfront—in trouble. He didn't need more.

I worked my way toward the docks, giving Mr. Watt time, and searched for another bank of phones. I tried to calm myself, breathing slowly, and stayed tight against the buildings. I'd put on Joey's coat and sweater, shoved the tire iron down my pants and secured it with my belt. I held his knife tight in my fist. With each intersection crossed, I thought I saw dark silhouettes against a darker background. But the enforcer didn't materialize.

Finally, outside an all-night drug store, I found a phone booth. I inserted my coin and sunk down to an uncomfortable crouch on the floor, with the hope the street remained deserted.

"Elmo, it's not good," Mr. Watt said. I breathed deep, squinting at the closed door; the tire iron poked into my stomach, and I let my air out slowly. I listened as he said, "I can get you out of the country. That's the best I can do."

"But..."

"There's big trouble, Elmo. Paletti was murdered on Knickerbocker tonight. The streets are crawling with gumbas. They're searching for his bag money. I'm not going to ask if it was you, but Paletti's compadres are searching for someone of your description. I hear there was a hit on the train platform near the pizzeria. You gotta go. You gotta run. Now."

"Sure," I said.

"I set it up with a longshoreman I know. His ship is at the docks. You just need to find him. He'll get you out. You'll need money. I don't know how to manage that."

"I got it, Mr. Watt."

"He's mean, and he's big," he continued, "You'll have to grease his palm."

"I got it, Mr. Watt," I said again. The tight spot, the overhead light, and the night were closing in. "Give me a name and the slip number."

* * *

I left the phone booth, relieved to be moving. An early ferry left the dock, signaling with a blast of horn; like a ghost, its shape floated out into the fog. The closer I got, the stronger the stench of garbage and sewage. Chains rattled as anchors were hoisted, and the air sang with the monotonous drone of diesel motors. I was soon surrounded by the giant cranes that moved cargo. All around me, men shouted out under the glare of overhead lights. I went unnoticed as I futilely searched for slip 330, a ship with Panamanian registry, and a longshoreman called Culebra.

I was ready to give up when I found the ship where a dockside crane loaded modular containers. A crane operator picked up the containers, moving them into the ship amid the sounds of metal on metal and cargo shifting. Maybe as many as one-hundred-fifty steel boxes were stacked and waiting, brought from the warehouse full of cargo destined for foreign ports. I checked for laborers, and then slipped cautiously down an alley of triple stacked eight by eight-and-a-half foot containers, wondering where to find Culebra.

He found me. Dark hair, dark skin, stark eyes, he stepped out from between towering walls. He swung a fist, thumping it into an open, beefy palm. "Passage?" he asked. I heard it as a threat.

I'd prepared his payment. I thrust the C-notes in his direction and raised Joey's knife by way of greeting. My knees knocked, and the tire iron felt heavy in my belt. He opened his mouth in a gap-tooth sneer and grabbed the bribe, shoving the bills into the chest pocket of his coveralls. Distracted by the sight of a coiled, serpent tattoo on the back of his hand, I missed his left hook. I dropped to the ground ripping the knee of my pants, then staggered up. He had the dominant angle of attack and his roundhouse knocked the knife out of my hand with such force the blade slashed my exposed skin. I fell, crumpled, to the ground. The tire iron jabbed me sharply, forcing all the air from my lungs. I lay in the gravel at his feet. I heard running. He picked me up like a bag of grain and threw me into an open container. My head bounced off the floor, my legs folded awkwardly beneath me. He slammed the door. I could hear him outside, but before I could collected my wits and lodge a protest, the shouts came. My heart leaped into my throat.

"Hey! Hey! What are you doing down there?"

I felt the wall of the container give and was deafened by the hollow bang of someone hitting the outside wall.

"This container wasn't sealed," Culebra called. "I'm fastening it."

"Get out of this area. We're loading cargo." The voice was close.

"I'm moving. Just buttonin' up."

A parade of hollow thumps echoed through the steel box as Culebra hammered his way down the side. Double whacks on the far end.

I still had the money, and the tire iron, and my life. I was lucky he hadn't searched me. That was before the biting sting started in my knee. I was exploring the extent of the knife gash, when the crane grabbed my container and I was thrown from wall to wall, and swung aboard the ship.

***

A backfire echoed in the trees, bringing me back to Costa Rica. I opened my eyes. I heard the moped, its engine whining along the road, bringing Chita and the newspaper. There were young lovers walking along the beach, honeymooners. I watched their progress while absently rubbing the scar on my crippled leg. From the back of the bungalow, I followed Chita's progress through the house. She deposited bags on the kitchen table and opened the doors.

"Meester Smeeth, here is paper," said Chita, holding the folded bundle out. Her hair, crystal jet, floated around her shoulders, escaping from the fiesta-colored bandana tied around her head. Her round face flushed; cheeks like mangos, eyes shiny and moist. I took the paper and spread it out on the table. *There had to be proof.* She jabbered as I hunched over the New York Daily News combing for the substantiating article.

I ran a finger down the newsprint, noticing the back of my hand covered with liver spots. Protruding veins which twisted from wrist to bulging knuckles, told me just how many years had passed in isolation; a road map revealing the time I'd survived—in fear. I found the article in section D, page four:

> As a hit man for the mob, Vito "Fat Vinny" Castellitto was considered "the most dangerous killer on the East Coast," according to members of the New York Police Force Organized Crime Division. Castellitto, who spent twenty years in prison before being released to live with his nephew, Joseph "Joey the Knife" Castellitto in Brooklyn, died early last month. He was eighty-nine. The U.S. Justice Department linked him to more than two dozen contract killings. He was convicted of only one; the orchestrated murder of Frank "Three Toes" Paletti, a bagman for the Bondanni

family, in 1971. Even in his eighties and behind bars, "Fat Vinny" remained an intimidating man.

Yes! It was safe to return. I was going home. I stood, ignoring the pain in my leg, and grabbed Chita, whirling her around on the veranda. It would only take one phone call. Mr. Watt would make the necessary arrangements.

A dark, foreboding figure filled the back doorway. It was only when he opened his mouth to speak that I detected his presence. Even so, the coiled serpent tattoo on the back of his hand wasn't visible until I whirled Chita past. *Culebra!*

Like most pit vipers, he moved swiftly from his defensive stance, and delivered an effective strike. He spit out his mission with a gap-toothed sneer. "Joey sends his regards."

I shoved Chita into his menacing figure, hobbled to the brush, and retrieved the machete I'd stowed beneath its lower branches. Without Uncle Vito, Joey wasn't a threat—nor any of his men. I'd had forty years to prepare. No more hiding. No more fear. I raised the blade above my head and with a piercing scream, lunged at my deadly nightmare.

So determined was I in my plight, Culebra didn't stand a chance. Nothing would ever stand between me and home again.

And, by God, this time, I wouldn't leave until the fight was won.

Terry Korth Fischer lives in Houston, Texas. Retired from a career in IT, she uses her time to read, write, and relax. Her memoir, **Omaha to Ogallala** *was published by S & H Publishing, Inc. She has contributed to many anthologies. Terry is a member of Sisters in Crime International, Clear Lake Area Writers, and Pennwriters Inc.*

THE WERE FOUR

Alethea Kontis

"I told you he was going to freak out," said Quinn.

"Quick! Grab him!" said Peter.

"No way, man. I'm not going anywhere near those teeth," said Sam.

"You pissed him off, Peter," said Quinn. "You save him."

"*You* made the joke," said Peter.

"*You* renamed the band," said Sam.

"You are both pussies," said Peter, and he ran to get his mom's heavy-duty gloves from the kitchen.

"Who's talking, fuzzy ass?" Sam yelled up the stairs after him.

Peter dove into the cupboard under the sink. No gloves. What the hell? Didn't all moms keep gloves under the sink? Peter growled his frustration.

"What's up?" asked Natalie. Sam's little sister was perched on the counter eating Girl Scout cookies and reading a *Gothic Beauty* magazine.

"Get your giant stompin' boots off the counter, Natalie."

"Shut up your mother loves me." It was mostly annoying because it was true. "What's going on?"

"Romeo flipped."

"Aw, jeez." Natalie leapt off the counter. It was an impressive move, as the knee-high platform leather boots she had gotten for Christmas must have weighed a third of her body mass. She threw open the door to the basement, spread her arms to grab a railing with each hand, and slid down the stairs, which annoyed Peter even further. He still couldn't do that, even without shoes.

By the time Peter reached the bottom of the stairs, Natalie had taken off her hoodie and tossed it over Romeo's flipping, snapping body. She quickly scooped the bundle up in her arms.

"Where's the tank?" she asked.

"It busted a couple of months ago," said Sam.

"'Cause Sam tried to use it as an amp stand," said Quinn.

"We haven't gotten it fixed," said Peter. "Romeo's been fairly calm lately."

The bundle thrashed wildly in her arms. "Toilet then."

Quinn ran ahead and opened the door to the bathroom for her. Peter thought Romeo might have preferred the sink, but before he could even suggest it, Natalie flipped her hoodie inside out and Romeo splashed into the toilet. It took him a moment to recover, but he quickly started swimming angry circles around the bowl.

Natalie dropped the hoodie and put her hands on her skinny hips. "What did you say to him?"

Peter stared at Sam, but Quinn and Sam stared back at him harder. He sighed in defeat. "I signed us up for the Annapolis Battle of the Bands because we forgot to do it before 'cause we weren't sure we were even going to do it at all 'cause we only have like three songs, but I signed up just in case 'cause we can always change our minds whenever and the deadline was today, but when I did I changed the name of the band," he said in one breath.

"Good," said Natalie. "'Maelstrom' was kind of stupid." She preemptively crossed her eyes and stuck her tongue out at Quinn and Sam.

"I forgot how to spell it," said Peter.

"Sam kept calling us 'Male Storm' anyway," said Quinn.

"So now we're The Were Four," said Peter.

Natalie snorted. "Okay."

"And then nerd-ass here had to go and quote Shakespeare." Peter punched Sam on the shoulder for good measure.

Natalie groaned. She scrunched up her nose and said, "Were-four art thou, Romeo." Quinn did a spit take and laughed so hard he doubled over. Sam smiled that famous shit-eating grin of his. Okay, fine. Peter had to admit it was kind of funny. He remembered Romeo's reaction and snickered a little himself. The piranha in the toilet jumped and snapped at them.

"Dude," Natalie said to the fish. "They're *your* friends."

"He is going to be so pissed when he calms down," said Sam. Quinn was still laughing too hard to comment.

"Just remember not to flush him," said Natalie.

"Finding Romeo!" said Sam. "Quick! Call Pixar!"

"Oh, god," said Peter.

Quinn guffawed and wiped tears away. "Holy crap," he said, gasping for breath, "I'm gonna pee my pants."

"Just as long as you don't use the toilet," said Natalie. "I'm going to get his clothes. Here"—she threw her hoodie at Peter—"I'd rather not smell like fish."

"Romeo wouldn't mind if you did," said Quinn.

Sam punched Quinn, who gave up at that point and fell over. "Don't talk about my sister."

"Just talk about his mama," said Peter. Sam slapped him in the back of the head. Peter tripped over Quinn, still laughing in a fetal position, and they all went sprawling on the floor.

"Excuse me." Natalie gave Sam a courtesy kick in the ass with a giant boot as she stepped over them. She folded the clothes neatly and set them beside the sink. Peter managed to get Sam in a headlock. Quinn yanked the hoodie out of

Peter's hands and whipped it around his head. The room went dark and smelled like Dad's tackle box right before Quinn and Sam sat on him.

"I ha-ave to pe-ee!" laughed Quinn.

"Get the hell off me, douche!" yelled Peter.

He heard Natalie shut the bathroom door, and then the clomp of her boots before the basement lights blinded them again. "Give me this. Morons."

Once Quinn ran upstairs to pee, it was easy enough for Peter to shove Sam's puny ass onto the floor. He hopped onto the dryer and watched Natalie shake the Tide bottle. "You got any more of this?" Peter shrugged. "Fine. I'll just try to rinse out what's in here." She pulled the knob on the machine and filled the empty bottle with water, then dumped out the suds.

"I suppose I could have put Romeo in the washing machine," said Peter.

"I'm sure it wouldn't be the first time," she said.

"So what do you think of our new name?" he asked.

She shrugged. "It's fine." She threw her hoodie in the washer and closed the lid. "When's this Battle of the Bands thing?"

"This weekend."

She raised an eyebrow. "Aren't you grounded this weekend?"

"Technically."

"*Technically*?"

"Well, I sort of have a way around that."

"Really."

"And I sort of need your help."

Natalie raised both eyebrows this time.

"*We* need your help."

"So what's the prize for this Battle of the Bands?"

Thinking about the prize energized Peter all over again.

"The winner gets to open for Stephen Kellogg and the Sixers when they play Annapolis."

"Stephen Who? Never heard of them."

"It's four guys—they're influenced by Tom Petty and Pearl Jam and their lyrics are a-ma-zing."

"You guys don't sound like Tom Petty *or* Pearl Jam," said Natalie. "And if I had a dollar for every time you rhymed 'death' with 'breath,' these Sixers would be opening up for *me*."

"Stephen Kellogg's motto is 'Dare to Suck,'" said Sam.

"He should have dared you to practice more," said Natalie.

"We're gonna go and we're gonna be *awesome*," said Peter, because it was true.

"The second thing's a matter of opinion," said Natalie. "As for the first...good luck with that."

"That's where we need your help," said Peter.

"She's going to say no," said Sam.

"As much as I hate to agree with my brother, he's right," said Natalie.

"Come on, Natalie. You don't even know what I'm going to ask you yet."

"I know that I've never once been invited to join your little boys-only club, unless it's to make brownies or rescue Romeo," she said.

"You do make good brownies," said Sam.

"You've never let me practice with you," said Natalie. "And I play drums better than Sam."

"My dog plays drums better than Sam," said Quinn. He skipped down the last two steps and vaulted the back of the ratty green couch.

"Hear me out," said Peter. "I have a plan."

Natalie sat down next to Quinn. The ten rows of buckles on her ginormous boots scraped by each other as she crossed her legs. "This not only better be good, but it also better include some serious financial gain on my part."

"We could let you play with us sometime?" Peter said hesitantly.

"Or NOT," Quinn and Sam said in unison.

At a splash, thump, and growl, everyone turned to the bathroom door. After a few minutes Romeo emerged, redressed in ripped jeans and vintage TRON t-shirt. His dark skin still glistened with damp, and what short black hair he had stuck up in crazy spikes. "The toilet? Really?" The words echoed in his barrel chest. Not for the first time, Peter wished he had filled out a little more in his junior year. Romeo was built like a Polynesian linebacker and could easily eat the rest of his band mates for breakfast. Natalie, whose lanky height combined with her boots made her the only one who could see eye to eye with Romeo, attacked him in a flying leap. Romeo caught the hug and swung her around. "Hey, little sista."

"Romeo! I'm so sorry I put you in the toilet. Those idiots gave me no choice. I was afraid you were going to die."

"We were afraid you were going to bite us," said Quinn.

"I still might," said Romeo. He pointed at Sam. "Except for him. Him I'm gonna kill."

"Can I watch?" asked Natalie.

"You know you love me," said Sam, with less confidence than he probably meant.

"I'd love to put my hands around your scrawny neck," said Romeo. "But I will restrain myself out of respect for your sister."

"Aw," said Natalie.

Romeo shot Quinn a look and he quickly vacated the couch so Romeo could sit. Natalie cuddled up to him. Platonic brotherliness aside, Peter suspected the reason Natalie really loved Romeo so much was because he was the only one of them who had the ability to make Natalie look small. "So," he said. "Where were we before stupid got the better of me?"

"Natalie was just agreeing to drive us to the Battle of the Bands on Friday," said Peter.

"I did what?" asked Natalie.

"She did what?" asked Sam.

"Sweet," said Quinn.

"You know I only have a learner's permit." Natalie narrowed her eyes at Peter. "And Friday is the full moon."

"That's what makes this perfect!" His plan really was perfect. "Nobody's ever out on the roads during a full moon." It was true. In 2012, the world hadn't ended, but life as they'd known it did. Without warning, some crazy celestial event timed with that damned Mayan calendar turned ninety-nine percent of the population into their totem animal. The city now ground to a halt during the full moon. Sure, some weres still did the Jekyll and Hyde thing, like Romeo, or the physical exhaustion thing, like Sam, but that one inevitable night every month, every human in Northern Virginia was considerably indisposed. Every human, that is, except the less-than-one percentage of the population who were Unwere. Like Natalie.

"Jerk," said Natalie. For some reason, she still didn't like anyone bringing her normalcy to attention. Peter didn't understand why. It's not like he looked forward to sitting around for an entire night watching *Phineas and Ferb* and scratching his stupid furry butt with his stupidly long beak. It wasn't like he'd matured enough to have venomous spurs on his hind feet, and even if he had, it's not like he planned on doing anything with them. While he was a platypus, he was only ever concerned with where his next worm or shrimp was coming from or if the webbing between his toes was drying out.

The way Peter figured, it was better to be *no* were than a *lame* were. All the athletic guys at school were wolves and bears and elephants. All the hot chicks were ponies and swans and cats. He looked at his friends: sloth, mosquito, piranha. Sure, Romeo was dangerous, but how dangerous was a single piranha, really? Romeo had ditched his buff sham friends after the third time he came within an inch of death at a frat party. It was like the Celestial Event cemented them all in their current status and doomed them to never be cool. Ever.

Natalie could do *whatever she wanted*. It was like being the only person in the world on a regular, temporary basis. Oh, the things he would do... For some reason, all Natalie did was break up with all her very old and very popular friends, dress in black, and dye her hair rainbow colors. She always had her nose stuck in some book or another; she didn't really talk to anybody anymore. In fact, Peter realized, he'd spoken to Natalie more in the last ten minutes than he had in the last five months.

"Just hear me out," he told her. "Wait until everybody's in were form, then just shove us all in Romeo's van and drive to Annapolis. It's only like an hour and a half away, and there will be *no traffic*. Who gets no traffic in D.C.? Like, ever?"

"I'll have to spend the night somewhere. I am not sleeping in the van with you and Sam's drum kit."

"We'll get you a hotel room," said Romeo. When the others balked, Romeo repeated, *"We'll get you a hotel room,"* just in case he hadn't gotten his point across.

"I'll leave Mom a note that I'm staying over at your place," said Peter.

"But you're grounded," said Natalie. "Am I the only one who remembers this? You and Quinn tried to walk to Walmart that one night, and the cop picked you up with four cans of spray paint?"

"Yeeeeah," said Peter. "Well, she hasn't said anything. I don't plan on bringing it up. And if she does remember, it'll be too late. I'm gonna have to play forgiveness versus permission on this one."

"This is really worth that much to you?" she asked.

"Yes," said Peter. More than chocolate and Cheetos and peanut butter sandwiches. He made his most pitiful, depressed kicked-puppy face.

Natalie rolled her eyes. "Fine."

Sam, Quinn, and Peter attempted a three-way high-five and failed miserably. Romeo shook his head and rummaged in his pocket for keys. "Come on," he said to Natalie. "Let's take the van around the block a couple of times so you can get a feel for it. These yahoos need to practice."

"Perfect," said Natalie. "Outside the house is the best place to be for that anyway."

* * *

Peter woke naked and shivering in the back of Romeo's van. He stretched his limbs and splayed his no-longer-webbed fingers wide apart. He shifted to pull the drumstick out from under his lower back and took a few deep breaths as his eyes slowly adjusted back to human. Romeo had already de-wered and left the van. Peter didn't blame him. Sam still laid there, a blanket bunched beneath his still body with its long limbs, flat face, and tiny ears. Peter didn't have a blanket. He shivered again. Doubtless that was part of Natalie's subtle revenge. He ruffled Sam's backward fur and decided that sloth-Sam didn't look all that different from human-Sam.

He couldn't tell if Quinn had changed back or not; he certainly didn't see a mosquito or hear one buzzing about, but who ever did until it was too late? Peter pushed himself into a sitting position and felt a bundle of clothes under his hand. His clothes. Maybe Natalie wasn't so mad after all. There was another bundle by Sam, but no other. Quinn was up and about then. Good.

As he pulled his jeans on, his phone fell out of his pocket. "Ten o'clock? Already?? Shit!" They had to be set up and ready to perform their first song at noon. "Sam." Peter shook the sloth's body. "Sam!"

The back door of the van opened to reveal Romeo and Natalie, standing in a parking lot Peter had never seen before. Annapolis. He smiled—part of him had been worried that Natalie would kidnap them all and then just leave the van parked in the driveway. But his relief was short lived.

"Good morning, Sunshine," said Romeo.

Natalie's greeting was less amiable. "Which of you morons gave Sam energy drinks last night?"

Peter winced. "Quinn brought a six-pack of them. We had to practice as late as we could. I didn't know Sam had any."

"What do you think?" Natalie pointed to the sloth. Sam was kind of hyper ADHD anyway, but when he got worked up, he crashed hard. Too much caffeine or too little sleep, and Sam could be a sloth for days afterward.

Quinn squeezed in beside Natalie and pulled out a blue milk crate of supplies. "He'll wake up. He's just being an asshole and making us unload everything."

"Yeah. Probably," said Peter, passing Natalie a snare drum.

"You better hope so," said Natalie.

"I'll go download a drum machine app on my phone," said Romeo.

"We'll get this all set up and ready, and Sam will wake up just in time to walk on stage," Quinn predicted. "Bastard."

But Sam did not wake up. He didn't wake up when Natalie, acting as the band manager—with some choice words to say about improving her taste in bands—signed them onto the BotB roster. Sam didn't wake up when the guy from the radio station warmed up the smallish crowd in the freezing warehouse. Sam didn't wake up when the first band played their song, nor did he wake up when Peter, Quinn, and Romeo changed into their costumes.

"You look like you've got a job interview," Natalie said of their suits and ties. "Did you find an app?" she asked Romeo.

"I found EZ Beats and a couple of others, but they take off points for using them," he told her.

"Every point counts," Quinn reminded her.

"We need all the points we can get," said Romeo.

"Hey, Natalie. You know our songs, right?" Peter asked. He held Sam's bundle of clothes in his arms.

"I hate you." Natalie snatched the bundle of clothes from him. "My giant ass is probably not going to fit in Sam's pants, you know."

"So don't wear the pants," said Peter. "It'll be fine."

"Bathroom's over there," said Romeo.

"We go on in three songs," said Quinn.

Natalie was already walking away. "I'll be there," she said, "but I'll still hate you."

"I'm gonna kill Sam," Peter said to his bandmates.

"I was already planning on killing him," said Romeo.

"Let's just tune up the guitars and stuff, okay?" Quinn asked, hurrying over to their gear.

"I left Sam in the parking lot," Romeo said, "with blankets and clothes and a note saying where we are. It's cold, but I figured it would be better than him waking up in a strange hotel room somewhere."

"You're probably right. Good thinking," said Peter.

"Man, if he misses all this, he'll be pissed."

"If he misses this, I'll be pissed," said Quinn.

"Natalie might be able to pull it off," said Romeo. Peter and Quinn paused long enough to give him a what-the-hell-is-wrong-with-you-and-the-planet-you-fell-from look. Romeo shrugged it off. "I'm just sayin'."

"The only thing Natalie's good at is stomping around in those boots," said Peter.

"And she's not even great at that," said Quinn.

"I'm not great at what?" asked Natalie.

Peter was on his knees plugging in a pedal when the boots in question stomp onto the stage. He looked up at Natalie, and up, and up. She was wearing Sam's collared shirt and tie, and those damned boots. And nothing else.

"Woah, girl," said Romeo.

Peter cursed. "Sam's gonna kill me," he said.

Quinn turned red and looked away.

"I told you those pants wouldn't fit," she said innocently.

Peter snapped. "I said don't wear *his* pants. Not don't wear *any* pants!"

Natalie bent her long arms and put her hands on her hips the way she always did. Not that Peter could be sure those were her hips, since he was fairly certain her legs just went all the way up to her armpits.

At the first catcall, he realized they were drawing a crowd. *All* the crowd. He peered around Natalie to where the assembly could probably see her underwear. If she was wearing underwear. Oh, god, they were all going to go to jail.

"Let the girl play!" screamed an audience member.

"Let her do whatever she wants," shouted another.

Romeo caught Natalie up in a bear hug and physically moved her to the seat behind Sam's drum set. Had Peter thought Sam's bass drum was huge before? It clearly wasn't big enough. He could still see Natalie's white knees peeking out from behind it above those damn boots.

"Play!" yelled an audience member.

"We're not up yet," Peter yelled back. He pulled his guitar strap up over his shoulder.

"You are now," said the guy from the radio station. He leapt on to the stage with them. "We'll shuffle people if we have to. All I know is that this poor crowd is freezing their asses off, and they need something to be excited about. Are you guys ready to rock?" He said the last part into his microphone.

Peter strummed a chord in answer.

"Ladies and Gentlemen, I give you The Were Four!"

The crowd went wild.

It was the only time the whole night the crowd went wild. Unfortunately, all that enthusiasm didn't make The Were Four suck any less. The pace was too fast, the monitors stank, and the guys constantly yelling at Natalie to take her clothes off distracted Quinn and Peter, who suddenly couldn't seem to remember which verses came before the chorus. To make matter worse, every time he sang the words 'death' and breath' he tried not to cringe.

It was horrible. By the time they got voted out of the third round, it didn't exactly hurt anyone's feelings. They only had three original songs anyway.

Romeo and Quinn gave Peter a consoling pat on the back, but it didn't matter. Peter was still elated. He remembered the way the crowd had gone crazy in anticipation. He wouldn't be opening for the Sixers now — or any time soon — but he had that feeling. One day, he'd feel it again. He bent down to unplug his guitar and saw boots. He tried not to look at anything else as he stood up.

"You must be freezing," he said.

As always, she ignored him. "I'm sorry we didn't win."

Peter shrugged, still smiling. "It's okay. We sucked."

"At least we dared to," said Natalie.

"Yeah," said Peter. "We did."

Natalie flipped the drumsticks around in her fingers. "Do you think I can play with you guys again sometime?"

"Maybe."

"You'll have to change the name of the band, though," she said.

"Oh, right. What about 'The Not-Entirely-Were Four?"

"How about 'Natalie and the Were Four?'"

Peter laughed. "I'm gonna have to think about that one."

"You do that," she said, and then she kissed him. On the lips. Not a box-office sizzler, but not a sisterly kiss either. "Thanks," she said.

Peter didn't say anything. He didn't know what to say. He just watched those very tall boots and those very long legs walk away. He felt a tap on his shoulder and turned around long enough to get punched in the face.

Sam was awake.

Alethea Kontis is a princess, bestselling author, stormchaser, and geek. She is the host of "Princess Alethea's Fairy Tale Rants" and Princess Alethea's Traveling Sideshow every year at Dragon Con. Alethea contributes regular YA book reviews to NPR. She currently resides on the Space Coast of Florida with her teddy bear, Charlie. Find Princess Alethea and the magic, wonderful world in which she lives at patreon.com/princessalethea

FAR HORIZON

C. M Stucker

Thick gray dust hung in the still, parched August air. Josiah Stubbs watched the lean gunman pace toward Lucky Dan's Saloon with a twinge of envy. Josiah was a short, thin, towheaded lad with, save for a receding chin, no distinguishing features. He wore simple homespun and his hand-me-down boots had low heels for walking. The stranger, dark eyes glinting beneath his lowered sugarloaf hat, radiated menace. Miss Braun, the schoolteacher, crossed the street to avoid his path while Brad Whittaker, Johansen's hired man, flinched and looked down rather than face that fierce regard.

Josiah stood beside his uncle's fine buckboard, waiting in the hot sun for his aunt to have the store clerk load her purchase. Despite the wealth his uncle enjoyed, in no small part because Josiah's father died intestate at Shiloh when Josiah was but a toddler and Uncle Manfred gained all the property, Josiah himself was given only the oldest castoff's and begrudged every morsel he ate. Yet every time he tried to get a job at another farm, his uncle talked to the owner and kept him tied at home, a slave in all but name.

Aunt Irene stumped out, the clerk beside her with a basket laden with packets. The clerk had just placed the basket behind the seat when staccato shots rang out from the saloon. Josiah, recalling his youthful experience of getting shot while watching a shootout, grabbed his aunt and pulled her to the ground, shielding her with his body.

The shots stopped and Josiah waited to see if they would continue before he looked up. He saw a man from the back, running toward a roan tied to the hitch before the post office. Irene shoved Josiah. "Get off me, boy. What did you think you were doing?"

Josiah rose and absently reached a hand to help his aunt off the ground, all the while watching the rider disappear over the far horizon as the roan galloped north. Men swarmed out of Lucky Dan's like hornets from a poked nest. Several shook their fists in the direction of the fleeing man. Irene slapped Josiah to get his attention. "Lazy boy. Get to work loading the buckboard. You go no call to gad about while there's work as needs doing."

"I reckon the sheriff's gonna have some questions. I better head over to answer them."

"You'll have a long walk home if you're not back here by the time I'm ready to leave."

Josiah nodded his acceptance and headed toward his date with destiny.

* * *

Inside the saloon, men and the women who served drinks clustered around a table where the sheriff waited, his shirt open while the doctor looked at his wound. Josiah waited while several men came forward to tell what they had seen. All agreed it had been a Mexican bandit, who came to rob the bank and only left because too many folks had seen him shoot the sheriff. Eventually, the crowd thinned enough for Josiah to approach. The saloon keeper, his normally pristine apron stained red from the sheriff's blood, glared at Josiah, who never had money to spend. The sheriff noted the glare and glanced over to see Josiah waiting. He motioned Josiah over.

"Joe, you see what transpired?" Sheriff Beck asked through teeth gritted against pain as the doctor bandaged his wounded right shoulder. The doctor told him to hold still and pulled the bandage tighter.

Josiah took a moment to compose himself before replying, "I saw a stranger, wearing a dark suit and a butternut-colored sugarloaf hat, head into the saloon a couple of minutes afore the shooting begun. I pulled Aunt Irene down at the first sound of shots, so I cannot say for certain sure that he was the one who ever-body else saw running out after."

"Could you identify him?" Beck leaned close, dropping his voice. "I could surely use a deputy right about now. You up to chasin' after him?"

"I don't got a horse or a gun." Josiah felt his heart sink like lead in his chest. He wanted to be a man, to ride in a posse, but he lacked the minimum essentials.

"I got both to spare." Beck nodded toward the crowd. "You're about the only one I trust to try and see the fella back for trial. Those as would chase him would shoot him, and that's God's own truth."

Josiah felt his heart leap into his throat. Being entrusted with one of the sheriff's horses was like a dream from Ivanhoe. He could be that gallant knight, riding out to save the kingdom, or in this case, to get the bad man. "I can try sir. I can try."

* * *

Josiah crossed the Red River into Oklahoma as the last rays of the setting sun limned the cottonwood and mesquite trees on its banks along with lowing cattle on the horizon. He had no jurisdiction, but the six day chase left him determined to catch up with the man who had shot Sheriff Beck. A whiff of smoke tickled his nose, and he spun to face the wind. He had no doubt, it was a pipe. Perhaps the owner had spotted the man he wanted. He followed the scent to a small clearing and stopped short when he noted the man in the hat. The man he wanted to bring in. The man pointing a pistol at him.

"I ain't got jurisdiction here." Josiah eased his hands away from the holster at his side. "I just aim to have a peaceable palaver and decide if why you shot Sheriff Beck was good enough for me to tell him he got it wrong."

"You're just a boy sent to do a man's job," the stranger said.

"Maybe, but when Ted Dillon got to be my age, he done shot a passel of folks." Josiah eased forward, not too close, but near enough that the other man would not think he was trying to run. "I got sent seein' as how I been shot before and ain't too scared about it happening agin'. Sheriff Beck thought as how I'd talk and try to bring ya back, not just shoot and haul in a corpse."

"You have never shot a man." Josiah caught a trace of Hispanic accent. "That is what makes him so certain."

"So why for did you shoot him?" Josiah looked closely, but the man appeared as white as most.

"He tried to stop me." The man cocked his pistol and pointed it at Josiah's belly. "Just as you are trying to stop me."

"No sir." Josiah took off his hat, fumbling with it as he would when addressing a prosperous businessman. "I aim to try and find a way for you to get what you want and still go back to tell our judge as how you're powerful sorry about the shooting. I cannot, in good faith, argue your case if I know nothin' about it."

"You speak as one who wishes more education." The man leaned back and holstered his pistol. "I am Diego Castillo. I once belonged to a good family, but after the war, gringos stole it all. A particular one debauched my sister and I seek his blood. Your sheriff stood against me. I had no choice."

"Diego, it sounds to me like you and I could ride back all peaceable like and explain, and then the sheriff would arrest whoever it is. We can pack him off for trial. At least tell me the fella's name and I can go tell the sheriff and that'll be the end of the matter. You could a shot me, but didn't. Makes it pretty clear you ain't as bad as you think."

Diego nodded and the pair spent eight days returning, resting their mounts as they chased the southern horizon. Along the way, Diego and Josiah shared tales of their lives and each gained a measure of respect for the other.

"Bob, the sheriff asked me to fetch you down to town." Josiah nodded to the dusty cowhand as he spoke, keeping his expression bland. He never liked the older man, but it was important to get him to the jail without commotion.

"I gah work t' finish." Bob spoke around the wad of tobacco in his cheek. He spat on the ground. "Now git on with ya."

"I done spoke with mister Jorgensen." Josiah nodded toward the main house. "He allows as to how you can go on into town with his blessing. I never shot a man and your name was the last words I heard from the stranger the sheriff sent me out to fetch. I'd expect as you could tell me if you knowed the man."

Bob scowled, but joined Josiah and rode back into town. Nothing of note occurred until they reached the door to the sheriff's office. As Bob opened the door, Josiah calmly reached out and took Bob's gun from its holster. Bob spun to grapple with Josiah, but the sheriff's voice stopped him. "Bob, you let go of my deputy before I put a bullet in your back."

"Ya ain't got no call t' do this," Bob got out as Josiah overpowered him, his youthful energy and muscles hardened by long years of hard work overpowering the dissipated strength of the cowhand. Bob struggled briefly then slumped on the ground. "I done nothin' wrong."

"I disagree," Diego spoke in a flat emotionless voice. "I told them of the warrant for you in California. They have agreed to let me take you back."

"Lyin' dog." Bob spat, literally spraying Josiah with tobacco juice. "He gonna take me to his beaner town and hang me fer bein white."

"Don't you worry about that," Sheriff Beck replied. "I'm sending Josiah to make sure as you get a fair trail. He can even testify to your character. My reckoning is you'll get ten years in a state penitentiary."

Josiah noted that Bob easily identified Diego as Mexican despite his white appearance and clothes. Any latter attempt to deny all knowledge of Diego would be fruitless. Josiah exchanged a look with the sheriff and decided to not bring it up. "Sheriff, you aim to let me keep usin' your horse all the way to California and back?"

"I'll have someone go with you to the railhead. Then you can take a train to California."

At that moment, Manfred Stubbs, wearing a black suit he had ordered from a tailor in New Orleans, stormed in, with Mister Quinn, the town's only lawyer, trailing him. "God damn you Beck. What do you mean, sending my nephew out to chase bandits then treating him like an errand boy when he gets back?"

Josiah, still holding Bob to the ground, stayed still, hoping Sheriff Beck could weather the storm of his uncle. Bob sensed the wind shifting and made his play. "Mister Stubbs, Sheriff Beck is in cahoots with this here beaner. I ain't never seed him afore, but your nephew, he want to—" Bob ended with a shriek of pain as Beck stepped back, over balanced and barely caught himself as his boot-heel came down clumsily and heavily on Bob's elbow.

"Manfred, I know you cheated Josiah out of his father's farm. Want I should set the law on you for it?" Sheriff Beck bristled, taking a step forward, away from Bob, and into the doorway, managing to retain his footing and avoid Josiah.

Josiah's eyes widened. He felt rage flood through him at the notion of owning his own farm and being the prosperous one, rather than the poor relation begging charity.

"The time has passed to contest any speculative irregularities which occurred during the tenure of a different nation regarding the disposition of a man's worldly goods when his mortal coil shuffled off. Do I need to cite statutes and case law?" Quinn pressed back. "I can make a case of slander against you for those accusations."

"That farm's worth a damn site more than shown on county tax lists. I can tell you got at least three hundred acres."

Bob, realizing he had a chance to turn the tables, kneed Josiah savagely in the groin and grabbed for the hand holding his pistol. Josiah, momentarily stunned, fought to keep from having the pistol turned on him. He gritted his teeth against the pain in his privates and put both hands to the task of moving his pistol to the side, away from his head. Above them, with tempers short, the debate raged without heed for the struggle at their feet.

"I had a state fellah survey it for my taxes," Manfred said. He punched a finger forward at Sheriff Beck. "You got no call to waste county money to do 'er over."

"My client expects a written apology expressing your contriteness over this issue as well as an official recognition of the validity of that survey," Quinn added when Manfred took a breath.

Pain sapping his strength, Josiah nearly wept as he watched the barrel of his borrowed Colt swing mercilessly toward his face. Sweat slicked his hands and he tasted blood where he had somehow managed to bite clean through his lip. Above the two protagonists, Sheriff Beck prodded Manfred Stubbs with a shove to the shoulder. "Back up, I got a deputy wrasslin' with a felon and I need to get it under control."

"You back up," Manfred stood still as a statue. "That's my kin. You got no call to make him a deputy. He ain't even full-growed yet."

"So I should let a thief keep a slave?" Beck shoved hard enough to overbalance Manfred, but it was too late.

With a look of glee, Bob managed to shove the gun right into Josiah's face, its barrel touching his cheek. A boom and blood splattered the floor as Diego, forgotten in the dispute, had waited until he had a clear shot. Josiah barely managed to push the barrel to the side before Bob's fingers spasmed in death and fired the Colt. The bullet creased Sheriff Beck's holster before it lodged in the ceiling.

Beck pulled Josiah to his feet, looked at the lip and said, "None the worse for wear. I'll have doc stitch up that lip and it'll be good as new in a week or so."

"I been to thinking Sheriff Beck," Josiah began. He stared at his feet, mumbling around his swollen lip. "I know we got the best part of three sections, call it nigh on to four-hundred and eighty acres. What if my pa left me most of the farm and Uncle Manfred a small part. He showed the will to that state fellah who measured his part off and give him a tax receipt. Would that hold up? I know sure as certain that Mister Quinn is wrong as can be about the law. All I heard back when I was about eight or nine, was how White agin' Texas was a robbin' folks by saying we never actual seceded. But if that's the right of it, then I'm due my farm."

"That boy don't know what'all he's talkin' about," Manfred bellowed. He tried to slip past Sheriff Beck to clout the boy, but Beck quelled his rush with a hard look.

"Funny how that about matches what Mike Carson wrote. I had a letter a couple of days before I got shot and sure enough, Mike was with Josiah's pa at Shiloh. Promised to look in on Joe when things got settled. What with the Carson family gettin' killed and their mule farm stole before he got back, well... That was a sad story all around."

"My client denies any knowledge of a speculative will. Without written evidence, there is nothing to back these claims."

"Now that is where you erred, Yankee." Sheriff Beck grinned broadly. "I got a message back from Austin earlier today. The surveyor clearly noted that the land was divided with forty acres going to Manfred as payment for holding the remaining land in trust for Josiah and seeing to his raising proper. Way I reckon it, Manfred failed at his duties and is forfeit his claim on any of the land."

"I don't aim to make my uncle a pauper," Josiah said.

"Then I propose we settle this now. I want a deed to all the land what ain't shown on the state roster as belongin' to Manfred Stubbs. It goes to Joe, who I would recommend sell to a speculator from back east who is offerin' the fine price of six dollars an acre. Then go west to where Mike lives and set up a small ranch there. He wants you in the newly reconstituted Ranging Battalions."

"I ain't sure," Josiah said. "My family lived here since the Austins brought folks in."

"Your uncle, perhaps, is not above hiring your murder and taking your land," Diego Castillo said. "You would be safer away from him. Go and chase your dreams. Make your horizons broad."

C. M. Stucker is literally a rocket scientist who lives in Houston with his wife and two cats. He hopes to soon have novels published as he has multiple manuscripts ready for editors. His short story "The Odd Case of the Widow Merovigian" appeared in Saints & Heathens *published by S & H Publishing.*

FOREVER GONE

Azure Avians

Riding the wind above the ocean, her strong wings stroking with power, Sierra raced to make it to the Gathering on time. The elders would greet her with either derision or affectionate dismissiveness if she arrived last. Worse, with disdain or contempt if discussion had already begun.

Even Aevigshon would attend this time. Sierra refused to look bad before the most ancient of all of them.

Sierra plummeted straight downward through the crystalline cerulean sky. She delighted in plunging through the stray cloud or two, so ephemeral as to appear more azure than white. The moisture, however sparse, still caressed her sapphire-blue scales as she dove. Tranquil turquoise waters rushed to meet her. At the last moment, Sierra pointed her snout and stretched her long, graceful neck, pressed her massive wings and four legs tight against her side and belly, and extended her tail out behind her.

Barely had the scent of salt reached her nostrils when Sierra dove beneath the surface. Her momentum carried her deeper than the prismatic flickering of sunbeams reached, yet even in the depths, the tropical waters remained warm.

She rolled, thousands of bubbles rising with her as she stroked with her webbed feet, quickly swimming back to the sun-lit shallows and heading away from the rocky coast.

Sierra took her duties *very* seriously—far more so than those two nestmates who had hatched with her almost a thousand years ago took theirs. In the next few decades, a new batch of eggs in the nursery would hatch and they could no longer call themselves babies. Sierra thought the others would cope badly with the realization. They cared only about games and dancing and stories.

Not Sierra. Sierra wanted the respect and admiration of the rest of her clan, and even of the other clans! But that would come in time. She needed to keep proving herself.

Even this simple mission would help her do that.

Especially this one.

Simple.

Easy.

Vital.

Absolutely, incredibly vital.

Sierra filled with pride that the elders had entrusted *her* with the mission.

The water warmed even more as she neared her destination. Illumination ahead came not from the golden rays from above but from a deep red glow emanating from a fissure in the sea bed below.

The Fire Clan reached even deep beneath the oceans, just as water from the Ocean Clan touched the highest heavens before falling back to earth. All interconnected. Everything intertwined.

Soon the fissure would erupt. Lava would spew forth, shooting up and turning the water around it to steam. The magma would rain back down, and would continue gushing from the volcano as well, spreading over the ocean floor for the next decades, eventually resulting in the birth of new islands from the desolate submerged desert.

The elders of the Ocean Clan had ordered Sierra to take one last quick look to ensure no life had swum or wandered into the area and then to report back.

Powerful strokes of her feet and a corresponding swish

of her tail propelled her swiftly forward. The red glow suffused the area. In the motion of the water, Sierra could see the heat rising toward the surface.

Fish disliked the hot water and swam well clear of the area. Not even the occasional kelp or anemone or crustacean broke the monotony.

Then Sierra drew up short, recoiling in horror at the sight.

No!

It couldn't be.

A colony of thirteen-legged shtaernshen clung to the rocky ground few dozen feet from the volcanic crevice. Suction cups on the bottom of their legs gave them purchase. They held tight or walked with three or four of their narrow legs while the remaining nine or ten legs swayed gracefully in the current. They shouldn't have been there at all.

How? Why?

Why now?

Ocean currents, and certain other sea creatures, transported the shtaernshen all over Teerrock yet they returned to one single place to reproduce.

Why had they abandoned their usual—no, their *only*—spawning ground hundreds of miles away?

As Sierra looked more closely, her horror and despair increased a hundredfold. The delicate jewel-toned creatures, every glittering shade of blue, had already deposited their eggs on the rocks. Hundreds of them, the entire population in the world, stood sentry over tens of thousands of eggs—the indigo foam jelly more precious to them than anything else in existence. Moving the eggs risked destroying them and wiping out the shtaernshen entirely. The fathers died shortly after fertilizing the eggs. The mothers would guard them literally with their lives, and die as the thousands of babies hatched.

Sierra had to stop the volcano. If it erupted, it would obliterate the shtaernshen forever. They would vanish for all eternity, lost forever.

Sierra surged to the surface and exploded into the air. As she soared eastward she emitted a roar the likes of which she had never mustered before. She had no idea who might be close enough to hear, but she needed to sound the alarm as early as she could.

The ocean gave way to sprawling dunes of sand which transitioned to magnificent canyons, revealing glorious strata of rock in reds, golds, yellows, oranges and pinks. Gradually, the hardiest cacti and scrub took hold. The desert tones gave way to browns then greens, then to verdant lushness as forest took over the foothills to the mountains in the distance.

Spotting four dark flecks in the sky near the horizon, Sierra roared again. Four answering roars echoed over the countryside as she and her clansmates converged on the Valley of the Eternal Gales, the designated meeting place for the current Gathering.

As Sierra flew nearer, the snow-capped mountain turned to look at her.

Not the mountain!

Aevigshon!

The largest, the oldest, the mightiest of them all, if Aevigshon spread her alabaster wings, they would span the entire valley. Her origins lost to all but the oldest among them, Aevigshon had led the clans for a few hundred millennia.

"Little One, why are you distressed?"

Wind from the words buffeted Sierra. She imagined she could see the earth tremble with the power behind the statement. Never had Sierra felt so tiny, not even when she had just emerged from her egg and stretched only a foot from the tip of her tail to the end of her snout.

Aevigshon waited patiently, head tilted quizzically to one side and one brow ridge arched high over one fierce golden eye as she regarded Sierra.

Sierra's voice caught in her throat as all eyes turned to her. Although Sierra had arrived ahead of time, if not by much, everyone else was already there.

The twelve elders, three from each clan, the greatest among them measured only half the size of Aevigshon. Now they all fixed their gazes on her. Some conveyed curiosity or concern; others, impatience, annoyance, even anger.

The leaders of the Ocean Clan, their glistening scales either sapphire or turquoise, betrayed their embarrassment. Sanvell's face wore its usual smirk, pained at the moment. Shenlon yawned and flexed his turquoise wings, tail twitching restlessly even as he feigned disinterest. Senrae's silver eyes narrowed as she glared at Sierra and gave small snorts of flame.

The remaining nine elders radiated every bit as much disapproval. Either jade or emerald in color, the three other members of the Earth Clan dwarfed Sierra with their immense size, yet Aevigshon still made them look small. The gleaming alabaster or opal of the Wind Clan stood out most glaringly against the greens and browns of the mountains and valley. Even the garnet and ruby of the Fire Clan blended better with the surroundings.

Sierra gathered her courage and found her voice. "It's the shtaernshen. They moved...I mean, they changed...I can't explain it. They didn't go to the right, to their usual spawning place. They're next to the fissure. They've already laid all their eggs."

"Ah." Aevigshon closed her eyes in contemplation and

leaned her head back.

No one else among them said a word. Senrae even stopped snorting fire.

The silence grew heavier and heavier, all of it pressing down on Sierra. Not even the wind stirred. In the Valley of Eternal Gales, not a breeze!

"That is sad," Aevigshon said, deep voice shaking the ground with tragedy as if the whole world were about to weep with sorrow. "It is to your credit that you want to help them. Yet inaction is not an option. We tend to all of Teerrock. The pressure must be released or it will burst forth elsewhere. The waters need the heat. The plants need the nutrients. More than the shtaernshen are at stake. Life will spread to the islands that will be born."

"But…but…the shtaernshen."

"All things die, Little One. Nothing goes on forever."

"I know that!" Sierra huffed, suddenly angry. Did Aevigshon think she was stupid? "But we don't have to let them. We don't have to *help* it happen." Sierra's fury grew. "We don't have to kill them. It's wrong to do nothing!"

Sanvell roared in rebuke. Senrae blew a plume of fire high into the air. A glance from Aevigshon quelled their outbursts.

"Would you sacrifice the forestland instead? Or have the great schools of bluefish die of cold as their waters chill? Or delay the rains that will awaken the desert?"

Sierra's confidence wavered. "There has to be some way. The eggs will hatch in a month. Just a delay…"

"The delay will destroy the bluefish," Aevigshon explained gently, her tone full of pain. "Which means the bigger fish, and the eels, and many birds will have nothing to eat. And the bluefish will not spread the kelpin seeds, or the mogs that attach to them and then drop off. And with no kelpin, the whales die. With none of the larger fish, the sharks and other types of whales die. " She paused, and it seemed the entire assemblage held its breath. "Are the shtaernshen more important than all these?"

"No," Sierra admitted, then found renewed conviction in another flash of fury. "They aren't less important either! They deserve to survive. We have to help them!"

Aevigshon curved her neck around and swiveled her head to look directly at Sierra. "Then it is up to you to find the solution. We can only wait two days without risking further catastrophe. Find an alternative by then, or we will have no choice."

"Two days!" Sierra could scarcely believe it. Yes, the task was daunting, but at least Aevigshon had given her a glimmer of hope. What could she possibly do in two days? She had to try. Doom and failure loomed inexorably, yet she refused to give up.

Two days. She had to find a way. Anything less would not stave off extinction.

Terror gripped her, and panic.

What should she do? Where to start?

Before Sierra lost her composure in front of all the elders, especially Aevigshon, Sierra shouted, "Thank you!" and flew blindly away, heading in the general direction of the volcanic fissure.

Whoooosh. Womp. Whoooosh. Womp. Whooosh. Womp. Whoooosh.

As her mind cleared and settled into a greater level of coherence, Sierra became aware that someone flew beside her. Sierra recognized her. Among all the clans combined, only fifty or so eggs hatched every millennium. Everyone the same age knew each other.

Nixel's garnet red scales glistened like flames in the bright sunshine as befitted a member of the Fire Clan. Not as long and sinewy as most, instead Nixel intimidated others her age with her greater size and bulk. Some others, but not Sierra.

"Where are we going?" Nixel asked. "What are we going to do?" The pauses between the words showed Nixel was expending effort to keep up with Sierra's brisk pace.

"We?" Sierra hoped she sounded more startled than hostile. Especially since she was stalling and had no better answer than that.

"I can help. Maybe," Nixel said. "You were so brave, speaking up like that!"

"For all the good it did," Sierra snarled. Then, contrite that Nixel might think the emotion was directed at her, Sierra confessed, "I don't know what to do." She slowed ever so slightly, making it easier for Nixel to keep up. "What's your idea?"

"I'm the one who found the chasm," Nixel said. "Before the shtaernshen were there. I'm the one who picked it. When it was clear. But there was a second choice."

Sierra stopped short and hovered in mid-air, wing-strokes swirling the desert sands beneath them. "What? Tell me."

Nixel wheeled around to face her. "The next best choice—the best choice, really; the eruption will be more powerful and build an island chain faster, warm the water more—was a few hundred miles south. There was only one problem. The eruption there would cause a massive wave that would sweep inland and cause great death for miles. Well, and the whales don't want to leave. But only because they like it there. Nothing is really holding them to the place. They haven't grazed all the kelp yet."

Sierra nearly screamed at her in frustration. She barely stopped herself. What kind of solution was a mass drowning? There had to be a better option. "Can you get the whales to leave?"

"What?"

"Can. You. Get. The. Whales. To. Leave?" Sierra felt the fire burning in her chest and throat. She swallowed it down and fought back her rising temper.

Nixel regarded her with a deep frown as if she thought Sierra had lost all reason. "Yes, mayb—"

"Good. Do it. I need to talk to my clansmates."

With the Gathering at hand, many had congregated in the Sea of Great Waves, one of the common meeting places. If she could convince those she found there, they could help her convince the three elders—and Aevigshon.

The Ocean Clan held sway over the water. They should be able to handle a wave, no matter how gargantuan. And if her clan needed assistance—especially from the Wind Clan—well, Aevigshon had emphasized that everything was connected.

She could reach the Sea of Great Waves in a few hours. The true question: how quickly could she convince the rest of her clan?

She skimmed low over the water, the tips of her wings barely touching the surface at regular intervals. Ahead, a circle of towering rocks rose from the sea, perpetually beset by dangerous currents, mountainous waves, and fierce winds. No clan except the Ocean Clan sought out the perilous location. Perilous only to others. The Ocean Clan gloried in it.

Some perched on the rocks, the diameter of the formation over a mile across. Others floated on the calmer waters outside the perimeter and basked in the hot sun. Still others swam and played in the thunderous foamy white waves. A few circled lazily in the sky overhead, or danced or played games of chase.

Sierra roared, and over three dozen of her clansmates rose as one to join those already in flight. They all soared to meet her.

"I need your help!" Sierra called out. "There is word from the Gathering that we need to change the location for the birth of an undersea volcano. Lives depend on it. The new location will likely cause a massive wave. It's up to the Ocean Clan to prevent it from reaching shore and causing death there instead."

"What foolishness is this?" Snitfen scoffed. Of course, she would protest. She hated anything not her idea, and considered herself an expert in all things. Quite an accomplishment for one of any age, let alone someone not yet ten millennia old.

"Quiet," one of the older clan members admonished her, before pivoting in air to regard Sierra. "Explain," he told her.

"The Fire Clan picked a location where they were going to cause an eruption. When they picked it, it was deserted. But Sanvell ordered me to check one final time. All the shtaernshen had gone there to spawn. We haven't found out why yet, what disturbed their usual location, but it doesn't matter. They've already laid all their eggs. There's no way to move them without killing them all. But the eruption will also kill them all.

"There is a second choice the Fire Clan can use for the volcano, they've already told me. It's an even better location for new islands, and will warm and revitalize the waters just as well.

"But it will also create a huge wave. We need to counteract the wave and stop it from causing terrible destruction on land."

Snitfen opened her jaws wide to continue her ridicule, but again the senior clansmate Sonelle forestalled her. "That is no easy thing, to manage such vast power," he said.

"Yes, you're right," Sierra talked fast. "But the entire clan is here. We can do it! And the others, the other clans, they can help."

Sonelle contemplated, going perfectly still except for the rhythmic flapping of his turquoise wings keeping him aloft. The rest began talking amongst themselves, some praising the idea, others questioning or outright mocking it as they swooped or glided or hovered.

Finally Sierra could no longer hold her tongue, or contain her desperation. "It's been done! History tells, it's been done!" They all knew the accounts, passed down to every generation. "We can do it again."

"We have to!"

"What you ask will not be easy. When must we do this?" Sonelle asked.

"Within a day and a half. The Fire Clan can't wait any longer."

Again Sonelle retreated into his own thoughts, apparently oblivious to the chaos swirling around as the rest of his clan argued and exclaimed over the dire situation. He fixed Sierra with a stern look, before giving a sly wink and letting out a roar of his own.

Sierra could feel its power course through her as it echoed off the rocks and the ocean.

"Come!" he commanded. "We go to the Valley of the Eternal Gales."

Sierra easily matched his speed despite Sonelle's far greater size. Some of the others lagged behind, but not her. Joy welled up in her despite the urgency. She'd done it. She'd convinced them. Surely the rest of the clans would agree.

Back in the Valley of the Eternal Gales Sierra noticed that Aevigshon had moved to the other side of the valley. And many, *many* more members of all the clans had arrived.

They lined the valley walls, high and low, and some had landed on the valley floor as well. The vista sparkled as the sun shone off scales of sapphire and turquoise, emerald and jade, ruby and garnet, and alabaster and opal.

Interspersed, she also spied flashes of gold, silver, copper and iron. Even some of the loners had come! Far fewer in number than the clan members, Golds, Silvers, Coppers, and Irons most often kept to themselves.

Sierra marveled at the sight; it looked as if a magnificent rainbow had settled from the heavens to enshroud the ground.

She held back so Sonelle could surge ahead by himself. Better that someone far older and more respected than her speak. Sierra settled atop one of the ridges as Sonelle circled the valley, greeting Aevigshon and the rest of the elders.

Sierra watched so closely as Sonelle and Aevigshon fell into intense conversation, that she almost didn't realize when Nixel landed beside her.

"Have the whales moved?" Sierra asked.

Nixel's mouth twisted and her golden eyes narrowed. "They were *not* pleased about it, but yes, they moved."

"Thank you!"

Nixel curved her neck and swiveled her head toward the elders. "Did you convince them?"

"Yes. My clan, at least. Now the elder is convincing Aevigshon." Sierra dipped her head toward Sonelle. An elder—Sierra didn't know which one—from the Fire Clan had joined them.

The stiff breeze turned to a steady wind as deep purple clouds gathered on the distant horizon.

Not a portent of failure to come, Sierra hoped.

Leaving the trio, Sonelle flew over to her. "Well done, Sierra. Well done. Stay with the rest and help. I'm going to protect the shtaernshen from the rough waters we're about to cause." He flew off before she could reply.

Aevigshon got to her four feet and spread her wings wide, demanding everyone's attention. The ground shook and the very air vibrated when she spoke.

"The Fire Clan will go to the fissure further north, not the one taken over by the shtaernshen. The rest of us, led by the Ocean Clan, will go to the coast east of the eruption. We must stop the wave from wreaking havoc. It is imperative. Otherwise we will have caused far more damage than we prevented."

She raised her alabaster wings, and with a powerful downstroke took to flight, trailing a rainbow of color behind her as everyone else followed.

Sierra leapt skyward, weaving among all those others to avoid clipping anyone else with her wings. She soon found herself at the front with only a few elders and Aevigshon herself maintaining the same swift speed.

Aevigshon glanced over at her and smiled. "You are as fast as they say, Little One."

Unsure how to respond, Sierra smiled back and dipped her head in acknowledgment. She'd always known that. It had never occurred to her that she had gained a reputation for it.

They flew toward the storm, although it remained a ways off when they reached the coast. A narrow beach of shimmering white sand separated the waters from the flourishing tropical forest. The clansmembers organized themselves, each clan finding its own.

A band of glistening sapphire and turquois blue formed the first line as the Ocean Clan arrayed itself along the coast, spacing out to stretch several miles. The opal and alabaster Wind Clan fell in behind them, followed by the emerald and jade Earth Clan.

A flash of flame shot into the sky far out at sea. Several moments later, the combined roar of the Fire Clan reached them.

They had done it.

The volcano was born. Lava would be shooting up into the water and rushing outward on the ocean floor.

The Fire Clan raced toward them. They would take up a position behind the Earth Clan and lend what strength they could.

Sanvell, and Senrae had taken up position at either end of the line, with Shenlon in the middle where Sierra had made her spot. The three roared in unison, and Shenlon bellowed, "Ahead!"

The further out to sea they met the wave, the more they could disrupt it. So they streaked away from the land and, as the Fire Clan soared over them in the opposite direction, the Ocean Clan dove.

They charged forward, drawing the water with them. Sierra roared as the wave front smashed into her, nearly washing her aside. She pressed forward, battling for every inch of headway as the water bashed against her face and wings with blow after blow. She persevered, roaring again in defiance of the wave and pushing forward.

When she suddenly shot forward with almost no resistance, she knew she'd gotten through the entire breadth of the wave. From her talons to her tail to her snout, her whole body trembled with exhaustion. She could barely find the energy to point herself to the surface.

Her wings felt like they had to be the size of Aevigshon's, they were so heavy. She could hardly move them. Her tail seemed likewise huge and threatened to pull her to the depths of the sea.

She refused to sink down there and rest. They hadn't yet won the fight.

The longer she forced her wings to work, the less leaden they felt. Breaking the surface, she looked anxiously around. She could see Shenlon, Sanvell, and Senrae already making their way back toward shore. One after the other, her clansmates emerged from the sea with the water streaming off of them, rose up into the air, and followed suit.

They reformed the line to make a second run. This time, the Earth Clan and Fire Clan accompanied them.

The Wind Clan remained behind, marshalling their own powers. Hovering in place, the motion of their wings, and their roars, called on the full majesty of the wind. Wisp became breeze became wind became gale that swept out to sea, meeting the onrushing waters.

This time when Sierra slammed into the submerged wave, it had lost a great deal of its force. The impact wasn't anywhere near as severe as the initial one. And the size of the wave had shrunk. She broke free far more easily and more quickly.

Still exhaustion assailed her as she struggled to reach the air.

When she did, its hurricane force sent her tumbling snout over tail until she regained her equilibrium. The gales did not relent.

Sierra soared high, high above them to make it back to land.

The surf had retreated, leaving only packed wet sand scattered with boulders and driftwood.

Then a wall of water loomed up, surging in toward land with an entire body of water behind it. The fierce winds slowed it immensely but weren't stopping it.

Not yet.

She looked to her elders, trying to gauge if they should make one last assault in the water rushing in. They appeared reluctant to do just that.

No! Not after they'd done so much and worked so hard. Sierra refused to quit now.

She roared and attacked the wave one last time, heartened to see that the others followed. Yet after their third run, far too much of the deadly wave still remained, and it had nearly reached the shore.

They'd decreased it greatly, perhaps even decimated it. Yet its impact remained inevitable.

Sierra wanted to fly away and hide from their failure. From *her* failure, as she'd convinced everyone of this action. Her heart broke in her chest, and an epic wail of frustration and fury welled up in her. Her wings barely held her aloft as she glided shoreward.

But then, sparing the briefest of nods to Sierra, Aevigshon reared up and broke from her place in line, circling up and over all the rest of the Wind Clan. She swung around and passed under Sierra and the others to attack the wave.

With a roar the likes of which Sierra had never ever heard before, and never expected to hear again even if she lived to a greater age than Aevigshon herself, Aevigshon sounded as if all of Teerrock roared with her. The gusts, already hurricane intensity, doubled their force.

The thunderous wave slowed and shrunk as Aevigshon bore down on it. The rest of the Wind Clan followed.

And the wave grew smaller. And smaller. And slower. And slower.

And bubbled and gurgled its way up the beach, not even reaching the tree line as the last of the wind faded away.

Sierra dropped to the ground with a *thud*, landing sprawled on the wet sand and spitting out some grains that had ended up in her mouth.

She wanted to dance and sing with delight and joy.

She wanted to sleep. For a decade. Or two.

Her body ached and throbbed from the beating she'd just endured and, now that the crisis had past, the pains seemed to be getting worse, not better.

But . . . the Gathering!

Sierra hated to miss the gathering.

As she debated with herself, Aevigshon's tail slid tenderly under her and raised her level with her huge golden eyes.

"You did well, Sierra. The ocean has a most worthy steward in you." Gingerly, Aevigshon returned her to her spot in the sand, then took wing, calling the elders to follow. "The Gathering awaits!"

After a few minutes, Sierra flexed her wings and decided she'd rested enough. Her spirit soared with triumph. Sleep could always wait.

The Gathering wouldn't.

Azure Avians writes in several fantasy worlds full of magic, mayhem – and cats. In "A Tiger's Tale of Two Sisters" and "Vanishing Angel" two very different sisters must team up to deal with two very different felines, only one of which is a tabby. Amazons, Pirates, and Assassins take center stage in other tales. Plus magic runs amok in the series Sorcery & Steel, now up to book three. For more, please visit http://www.BluetrixBooks.com/.

WONDER WOMAN

John Jeffire

I dress alone. Alone, always alone. Yes, my wife is in the bedroom with me, like every morning, but she is still sleeping, like every morning, her breathing heavy, labored. After showering, I open the drawers of my dresser slowly, deliberately, closing them the same way, quietly, very quietly, so I don't disturb her. After throwing on my underwear and setting pants and shirt on the edge of the bed, I sit in the bedside chair to pull on my socks. Her sleep is deep. Scary deep. I am always listening for breaths. The bones of her face are delicate scrimshaw, the story of her life etched lightly into the moons of her cheeks, the olive of her skin humming softly. I love this woman.

Like air.

Like water.

Like the fragrant body that rises from fresh April earth after a heavy rain.

In minutes, I must leave for work. Lately, it seems I am always behind, glancing over at the clock, wondering where the minutes have gone, knowing the white-knuckle traffic will set my temples throbbing if I don't get onto the road soon. Our schedules have become the ends of like magnets, repelling each other—when I am awake at home, she sleeps, and when she is awake, I am asleep or at school teaching. I perform the same ritual every time I must leave her. I bend over her body curled beneath the covers, lower my lips to her face, and place a light ring of kisses over her cheeks and forehead. I make sure she is breathing.

She is asleep, but a faint grin forms in the corners of her

mouth, and her smile makes me smile. I am her husband, but also her guardian, her nurse, her friend, her protector. In her sleep, she loves me, and for that I am grateful and thankful. From her eye, though, a tear forms and slips down her cheek before melting into her pillow. A gentle, content smile still lights on her face, yet, somehow, this single tear.

I touch the bare roundness of her shoulder under the comforter, her skin soft, smooth, warm.

"Baby...."

I stop short of shaking her—when she sleeps, she is free of pain, or is at least not conscious of her pain. I don't want to break the spell of serenity, but the tear, I can't ignore it, she might be in some sort of trouble. Living with someone with an incurable brain disease has taught me that nothing, even one tear, is insignificant.

"Honey...."

Her eyelids flutter. Her lashes are thick and long, forming rich dark rainbows around her eyes. She awakens, and it takes her a moment to recognize me.

"Honey, are you okay?"

She takes another moment to gain her senses. Where does she go during these split-seconds it takes to set foot in our shared world? Past lives, childhood, former husbands, to a mystical future without chronic pain, some fantastical world made so by its benign, quotidian normality? Cerebrospinal fluid—CSF—has been building up in her skull, causing unbearable pressure and headaches. Most nights she lays awake, all her pain meds taken but none helping, surfing the internet, researching and firing off messages to members of chatrooms dedicated to the illnesses they share, seeking reasons to be hopeful but mainly searching to keep occupied, to keep the mind away from what each day appears inevitable.

"I'm...I'm fine. What's wrong?"

I brush away another tear.

"You're crying."

Puzzlement takes her face.

"Crying? I'm not crying." Her voice is low, caked with sleep, slightly confused.

"Look," I say, pointing to another tear. She reaches up, touches the tear, lowers her hand and surveys as she rubs the tear into nothingness between thumb and forefinger. She has the presence of mind to reach for the glucose meter she keeps on her bedside table. She inserts a test strip and when another tear forms, she tests it. Tear drops—and sinus mucous (good old-fashioned snot)—do not contain glucose, but CSF does; lately she had been draining fluid from her nose without suffering a cold or allergy symptoms, so a nurse friend from one of her chatrooms suggested we purchase the glucose meter to confirm exactly what type of fluid it is. She tested the drainage from her nose later that night—glucose. She was leaking CSF. When the pressure of backed up fluid has nowhere to go, it seeks the path of least resistance to escape, in this case her nose.

She tests the tear.

Glucose. She is leaking brain fluid from her eye socket.

Her face is a stir of dread, fear, and resignation. What emotions my face conveys I cannot know. I try to reassure her. *It'll be okay. We'll find a doctor to figure this out. We can do this.* But do I even believe my own words? We have been married less than a year. Her sick days far outnumber her healthy ones. The illnesses she faces are degenerative, but the pace has quickened more rapidly than either of us could have predicted. It takes a toll on us, both of us. Pain has gripped her and will not release; she now sleeps sometimes twenty hours a day, and when she is awake she is prone in bed, the only position that does not spike the immense pressure in her skull. It's not much of a life for a one-time model and advertising exec, someone used to traveling about the country, zipping off to meetings, relishing another successful ad campaign. Me? I grow more powerless by the day, becoming little more than a water-bringer, meal cooker, laundry washer, medicine bringer, kiss giver. I have no power to ease her physical pain, and instead offer trite phrases of encouragement. I am useless.

And I am late again. I must rush out to the car and begin the grind to work.

The night before, we had the talk, confronting, even if only with a glance, the elephant that had shouldered over the living room lamps and crushed the couch and chairs. We acknowledged the interloper who had derailed all our plans before we married to sunbathe on a Spanish beach and drink into a wine-fueled fit of laughter in France. We did not take a honeymoon and our dream of owning a home fell aside as bills mounted for her treatments. Her disease was winning.

"You didn't sign up for this," she told me, dry-eyed, even voiced, but I knew her too well, even after only a few months of marriage: she was afraid. She told me I was free to leave her, that she would move back in with her parents, who could take care of her as they did after her first brain surgery years before we met. What she said was both true and untrue. From our first meeting, I knew she had some type of brain condition; she explained to me in basic terms what Chiari Malformation is, and I then researched more about it on my own. Chiarians have a defect in the formation of their skulls, most likely genetic, that allows the cerebellum to begin sliding into the spinal column and, if unchecked, eventually leads to death. Konnie had undergone a surgery already in which the back of her skull was removed and a titanium plate—a sort of net or pouch—was inserted to keep the cerebellum in place. She had one hell of a sexy scar that ran from the top of her head to the base of her skull, which she hid with a few deft waves of a blow dryer. Her previous husband left her when it became apparent her illness was not going away. Yes, she is afraid—of being abandoned again, of being alone with her pain, of dying unloved.

The talk expanded in other directions. Death, for Chiarians, is always lurking. Always sitting down at the dinner table. Always slipping in under the sheets. Every week on Facebook one of Konnie's comrades in suffering passes; most are far younger than she is, and some are even little children. When a Chiarian dies, Konnie always posts a personal message on Facebook with a picture of her fallen friend: "Another Chiarian has earned her wings. Fly high, my sister." She feels these losses deeply, and I feel them because she feels them. We already discussed a living will at one of her previous hospital stays. She didn't want to be kept alive if she became incapacitated. No machines, no life support, no breathing or feeding tubes, no extending the suffering—if she fell into a coma with little to no chance of recovery, I would know her fighting was done and act accordingly.

I look at her and think of the Konnie I had courted and married. I'd fallen in love with one amazing woman. When she is healthy and her pain driven to a standstill, she is vibrant and lively and feisty and fun. That is my Konnie. Yes, she needed lots of rest when we first met, but when she was awake we were out at the local bar on a Saturday afternoon watching her beloved Wolverines play football, dancing to local bands at a familiar club, cooking out, caring for our beloved dogs, philosophizing about politics and religion until well after my teacher bedtime. She could talk relief pitching, toss a shot of Patron, offer the sweetest kiss I had ever tasted. I was swept away. Within a month of meeting, we booked a trip to St. Louis to visit Scott, an old college roommate of mine, one of my dearest friends in the world, a mammoth step for a small-town divorcee living in

Frankenmuth, Michigan. We flew to the city of blues, we ate barbeque, we sang to the Funky Butt Blues Band, and we told stories with Scott and laughed long into the night. I knew then I would marry her. I had found my road dog. My mate. My travel and drinking buddy and my let's grow old in each others' arms companion. She was my forever, and in less than a year we were man and wife.

Tonight, I consider her offer. Freedom. Unconditional, no strings attached. I would be free. Free, as she told me, to have "a healthy woman." One who would not sleep for twenty hours a day for days on end, need to be fed like a child, walked to the bathroom, cooked for and cleaned up after. I could find someone who was not a slave to a brutal physical curse. Free, but how free? From what? To do what? Free to be alone. Free to abandon someone who truly needed someone like me in her life. To begin the solitary hunt again. To step back out into the darkness. To be unneeded, without purpose, alone.

I don't need more than a second to answer her. I take her hand and look straight past the wall of her doubts.

"Konnie, enough. Believe me, I'm not going anywhere."

* * *

I am writing in Konnie's hospital room at the University of Virginia. About an hour before she was taken on a gurney for an angiogram of her brain. Like a heart angiogram, a catheter is inserted in the groin and run through the body, but in the cerebral version the tube doesn't stop until it reaches the brain. In Konnie's case, the final destination is the transverse sinus vein, which allows blood to drain out of the skull. A previous angiogram done before her last surgery discovered her vein to be severely blocked, accounting for her massive headaches; the vein was backed up, the blood unable to flow normally, and the ensuing pressure resulted in agony. Typical movement of blood through the transverse sinus measures in the 0-1 range, meaning flow is unimpeded. At a measurement of 3-4, doctors know that a major blockage exists—Konnie's flow was 7. Now, less than a month after two stents were inserted in her brain, she is back, her symptoms returned, her pain still unrelieved and dominating her life.

The gurney rattles outside the doorway and I am up, pushing pen and paper aside. When I reach her, I first see the tear welling in the corner of her eye.

"Baby, you okay?" Of course, it is an idiotic question, one ignoring the obvious.

"I hurt." Her voice is quick, labored, gripping anything to hold onto. I run a hand through her damp hair. Konnie's connective tissue disease, Ehlers-Danlos Syndrome, causes thin, fragile tissue and for some reason leaves its victims notoriously immune to opioids and other pain-killing substances. Whatever she was given to manage her pain has not worked.

"I felt...everything. I could feel it moving...around in my brain."

Here is the bane of the caregiver. What do you do? Where do you place your hands? What words do you offer? What emotion do you quickly sketch onto your face, no matter how far removed it is from the emotion you are actually feeling? You better do *something*. How do you tear through the outside to be of some damn use on the inside of this scene?

Figure it out. For Christ's sake, don't just stand there. *Do something*.

"We're going to slide her off the gurney," the lead nurse says. She grabs two handsful of the sheet beneath Konnie. She will not be strong enough to do it herself, and her assistant is trapped on the other side of the gurney in the cramped room. I am likely violating all accepted rules of protocol, but I grip the sheet with two hands, so the nurse moves her grip down toward Konnie's lower body, I make eye contact with her and wait for her nod, and we then pull gently but purposefully until my wife is back in her bed. The tear breaks free and slides down her cheek and I brush it away — I am wearing her wedding ring as all jewelry had to be removed before the procedure, and the diamond catches a spark of dim fluorescent light.

Another tear forms. She is a rabbit caught in a coyote trap. The nurses turn their attention to the incision where the catheter was inserted. Konnie has bled through her sheets and hospital gown, and when they peel back the layers of cloth blood is streaming unchecked from her inner thigh. The nurse removes the bandage and saturated gauze over the incision and the wound gushes; she applies a wad of fresh dressing.

"This might hurt."

She presses down on the wound to create pressure to staunch the flow of blood. Konnie convulses, her body lurching slightly upward — it hurts. It hurts bad. Whenever she is forced to strain, her pain is magnified and the pressure inside her skull spikes. The tear lets go and streams down her pale face and I catch its path with the back of my hand, absorbing its wet warmth. I brush her hair and with my other hand I grasp hers. Her grip is strong. I let her squeeze, welcoming her strength. The nurses work away. The lead nurse stands on tip-toe, her arms extended as she presses down, finding the right amount of pressure to exert. After ten minutes, the river of blood has been driven back into her. In moments, though, another wave of bleeding surges, and her dressing becomes a sopped, bloody mess. The process is repeated, ten more minutes of continuous exertion. I give a small squeeze to Konnie's hand — how much more can she bleed? How much more pain can she endure? She grips my hand — it must be all the strength she possesses. The blood floods into the crevice of her thigh, drenching her bedding, and her face becomes a crease of pain. The lead nurse labors like an athletic short order cook, pressing, pushing, keeping pressure.

Finally, the flow of blood is beaten back. The nurse has won. Konnie has won. Her forehead glistens with a light mist of perspiration, her damp hair falling limply to the side of her pale face. I thank the nurse and turn to my wife.

"You did it, girl."

Konnie nods, another tear filling the corner of her eye.

***

Her favorite sleeping mask is adorned in leopard print. Jungle huntress. Sleek, powerful, unconquerable. Independent. Morning sunlight causes her head pain to spike but, medical bills still mounting, we can't afford blackout shades. While restful sleep is near impossible, she enjoys the stylish touch of leopard print. I am sitting across from her gurney we have set up in our bedroom next to the bed we used to share. She asks me if I've seen the eye mask. I find it on the floor between the beds.

"Here you go."

Her pain meds begin to kick in. Fentanyl, dilaudid, diazepam, whatever Hospice can provide. Her eyelids grow drunk heavy. Her speech slurs, exacerbated by the neckbrace she must wear, which restricts movement of her jaw. The fifth—and we know final—brain surgery has shown no positive results. I try to stretch the eye mask over her head but she reaches up, takes it from me. She struggles the eye mask on.

"Need my mask. Gonna be flying around."

"Oh yeah?"

"Yeah. Wonder Woman needs a mask."

"So where you flying to?"

"Everywhere. Gonna get the bad guys. Fly up over top them, swoop down. Kick ass and take names."

I take her hand. Thin. Pale. A papery sliver of light. She is a wonder. My wonder woman. My leopard queen. No primetime family friendly network time slot. No magic bracelets. No shield. No invisible plane, but she is taking flight, soaring off somewhere, eyes set on the infinite beyond. I am here on Earth, sitting on the bed we shared next to the gurney we brought in to give her some comfort, and I watch her drift off to sleep.

What can I say about her?

I want her here.

What would I say *to* her, if she were awake, not taking to the clouds, soaring over everything, prowling through the high grass, fighting monsters and the malignant powers that forced her onto this gurney?

I cover her hand in both of mine.

I listen to her breathe.

Woman, I want you here.

I want you here.

I want you here.

———

John Jeffire was born in Detroit. His novel Motown Burning won the 2005 Mount Arrowsmith Novel Competition and the 2007 Independent Publishing Awards Gold Medal for Regional Fiction. Detroiter and former U.S. Poet Laureate Philip Levine called his first poetry collection, Stone + Fist + Brick + Bone, "a terrific one for our city." For more on the author and his work, visit writeondetroit.com.

THE WHOLE KITTEN CABOODLE

Patricia Powell

The Powell home and family always included pets: birds, fish, rabbits, hamsters, turtles, horses, and dogs—always dogs. We were a dog-loving family, and I can hardly remember a time without residents of our home and cherished members of the family of canine persuasion. Boots, Cinnamon, Dukey, Foots, Ginger (I-II), Mummy, Penny (I—III) Rags, and the list goes on... Cats? An altogether different matter. It wasn't that we didn't like cats; we just never presumed to have any legitimate claims of ownership or binding family ties to the footloose and fancy-free feline vagabonds that occasionally dropped by, unannounced and uninvited, for a few days' meals, and then were on their way again, continuing their lives and journeys, their comings and goings, as they pleased.

Things changed the summer of 1981, when my parents and I flew to California for a visit with my former sister-in-law and two of the four children who comprised my brother's family with her. Upon our arrival, Bea apologized for having taken in another visitor, unexpectedly, a few days before we were due. She hoped we wouldn't find the townhouse too crowded or our privacy violated by the additional presence. When my sister-in-law reluctantly succumbed to the frantic urging of the children and agreed to a 'one night only' stay for the stray they had in tow, little did she know that the accommodations provided would prove so comfortably inviting that their visitor would deliver five offspring, while her hosts slept, oblivious to the momentous event occurring under their roof. Finding mother and children snug and safe in their ad hoc home the next morning, Bea's firm demand that the kids go out immediately after breakfast to find a real, permanent home for their foundling underwent quick revision. The just-born kittens and their mother could not be moved for a while; others in the household would simply need to deal with the situation, and so we did, quite happily.

The mother cat, dubbed "Duchess," for her self-assured, aristocratic bearing and demeanor, was a beautiful, flat-faced, tortoise-shell Persian. And her royalty notwithstanding, the sophisticated stunner proved herself an admirably capable and competent parent.

Determined to find the ideal environment in which to nurture her babies, Mama Duchess searched the townhouse over for the best spots, transporting her quintet, one-by-one, from closet to closet, bedroom to bedroom, undaunted by other occupants. The meticulous mom finally settled on the living room as an ideal site for development of the children's aesthetic sensibilities and on the family room for its opportunities to refine their social skills. She made no effort to hide her maternal pride and relished all the attention a house full of doting adults lavished on her and the babies. New to full-time, up-close and personal cat care, we human novices would soon come to appreciate the truism long understood by veterans in the field: "Dogs have masters; *cats* have staff." We probably handled the kittens before we should, but Duchess took "staff" fascination with her little brood in stride and was never out-of-sorts with us as we played with the nearly newborns.

For more than a week, the townhouse family room and

living room became oversized playpens, in which human fascination with feline antics developed right along with the kittens themselves. Duchess had a collection worthy of her beauty and dignity: four handsome boys, one cream-colored, one black-n-tan, one tiger-striped, and one a soft amber tone, joined by a lone, lovely gray/white lady. Proud Persians all, they were all delightful, and their human admirers spent hours caressing and cuddling kittens while catching-up on lots of family conversations, as well. For folks who had arrived in California generally indifferent to cats, my parents and I were now utterly captivated by these charming creatures; we were completely, hopelessly, kitten smitten.

As leisurely days wore on toward our scheduled return to Texas, the thought of leaving such precious wonders behind began to gnaw at me. I asked if I might have my litter favorite, the striking, lover-of-a-gent, who seemed to select me, even before I named him "Jasper," for his milky quartz coloring. The answer was, "Of course you can," followed immediately by "but how will you get him home?" Then Bea offered to ship Jasper to Houston when he was older, but I couldn't bear the thought of one single day's separation, let alone weeks. I called the airline to arrange passage inside the cabin for my child of choice, but was told that the quota for such pet passengers was already full for our flight. Spurred by the urgency of an impending departure and the absence of any other feasible solution to the problem, I introduced the notion of smuggling Jasper home, since we could not pay to take him with us legally, and since he was far too young and delicate to travel alone as cargo.

Nothing demonstrates quite so forcefully or dramatically the extent to which my parents and I were infatuated with these feline infants as the fact that there was no immediate, unequivocal outcry from two very sensible, traditional, rule-respecting adults, when their usually level-headed, risk-averse daughter suggested the smuggling idea. There were the obligatory but understated reminders that I/we could be denied entry to the airplane or required to deplane, if the stowaway was discovered, and that meant financial loss that would be painful for us, while still not solving the issue of how to get Jasper—or us—home, together. Absent adamant parental rejection of the blossoming smuggling scheme, my reckless resolve was emboldened and encouraged.

In a textbook example of "Give 'em an inch, and they'll take a mile" (or in this case, "give 'er one smuggled kitten, and she'll take four) I began pitiful musings about how heartbreaking it would be to leave sweet, delicate little gray female behind, it we took brother Jasper away from her. Then, one lazy afternoon, sitting on the sofa with lap full of kittens, as usual, I watched a local Los Angeles TV interview with Richard Chamberlain. To the question of what quality he found most attractive and appealing in a woman, or what adjective would describe his ideal woman, the actor replied, "Winsome...winsomeness." Then followed discussion about just what distinguishes or best characterizes a winsome person. Qualities of quaint and elusive charm, among other traits mentioned over the next few minutes, supplied the only possible name appropriately befitting the dainty but fiercely independent little gray girl, who was, from that moment, "Winsome," immediately shortened in daily, familial usage, to "Winnie." And once named, like brother Jasper, Winnie was mine—all mine!

What had begun gradually now continued as a rapid,

relentless unraveling of anything even slightly resembling rationality or caution. Jasper and Winnie must travel home with us; that seemed obvious to me, at least. Then I began to talk about what a wonderfully unexpected surprise it would be for friends back home in Houston to receive one of the kittens on my return. Within a few short months of my moving to Clear Lake City to join the faculty of a still-under-construction Clear Lake High School, I found a circle of friends who invited me to accompany them to the annual Houston Cat Show. These new acquaintances had aroused my curiosity by their devotion to cats, and as a way to know and understand the ladies better, joining them for the cat convention seemed a good idea. It might provide insight about people who gave all indication of feeling for cats what I thought only dog-lovers experienced. Wouldn't they get a kick out of seeing me a cat conquest, after all my low-to-no enthusiasm for their pet of choice! And wouldn't they be absolutely blown away by my generosity (and daring) in transporting kittens from California to Texas, on the sly, just to please them! That meant two more of the fabulous five must be included in my expanding clandestine scheme.

Looking back these many years since the plot was devised and executed, I find it even more amazing and inexplicable that my very principled and proper parents never just said, straight out, "NO! You're talking crazy! Forget the whole thing—DROP IT, RIGHT NOW!" I vaguely recall practical observations about the dangers involved and the high probability of detection, with all the embarrassment, inconvenience, and expense that would entail. But, with no overriding word or act of sensible seniority raised to trump my madcap determination to take home all of Duchess' jewels, save one, it was time to decide which two additional kittens went, and which one stayed behind.

It was a decision I regretted and resented. Had my nephew not already promised "one of the kittens" to an employee at the supermarket where he was working part time during the summer, we could have latched on to the entire litter, which was what I really wanted. The Duchess had managed to win the favor of my sister-in-law, who wasn't about to part with her. Of the three kitty candidates for two remaining travel slots, the tiger stripe was a hands-down, sure-thing, no-brainer-of-a-pick. Self-appointed king of the litter, he was an out-going, fun-loving, self-confident tease. Those very qualities that made him such a natural choice for the traveling troupe proved, in the end, precisely the reasons that it was decided he should stay with Duchess, until claimed by the supermarket lady-in-waiting. His independence earned him a consensus vote as the kitten best able to make it on his own, without the companionship of brothers and sister to bolster his spirits and share his bed and adventures as they matured together. By process of elimination, by dropping the natural selectee from consideration, the final twosome was chosen by default. With all travelers selected, the hard part was over. Now, we had only to figure out how the heck to get the bunch of them from Orange County California to Harris County Texas. No sweat! No sweat?

Our* first concern (*Note: what had begun as individual insanity had, of necessity, devolved into conspiracy, since transporters—plural—would be required to pull off the crazy caper) focused on the harm we might cause tiny, nursing infants by earlier than advisable separation from their mother. Next worry was any potential for damaging radiation from security equipment. In light of today's drastically altered air travel, fueled by fears of terrorist attack, our devious smuggling plans of 30+ years ago now seem inconceivable. Who would be crazy enough to dream-up such a scheme? Who, even crazier, would actually try it? Fortunately, (Fortunate on oh, so many levels) that was then...a kinder, gentler, more trusting era, when even friends and family seeing travelers off were permitted to accompany passengers all the way through a terminal and out on the tarmac, without requirement that either travelers or their companions must undergo any kind of personal security check. At the Orange County/John Wayne Airport there was a security scanning process for carry-on luggage, only. When an attendant questioned us about the near-empty square basket (with attached lid) on the conveyor, we truthfully described the contents: a few newspapers to read in route, plus a towel and wash cloth, should air sickness cleanup become necessary. Upon completion of their carry-on inspection, airline personnel turned their attentions to my mother, whose measured steps and use of a cane (evidence of an earlier hip replacement) caused them to suggest and supply a wheelchair, to make her trek out to the waiting airplane less physically taxing (and time-consuming?) Mother had found mercy in her disability, since the physical limitations had ruled her out as a viable candidate for smuggler, leaving Dad and me responsible for concealing and carrying two kittens each.

   The era was also marked by much greater attention to attire than is evidenced in what most current travelers wear (or don't wear) on their journeys. Air travel, especially, seemed to call for Sunday-best garments. For our trip home to Texas, my father wore a suit, its long-sleeve shirt accessorized with a traditional necktie. It was a fortuitous wardrobe choice, as he explained later, since one of his kittens made several energetic escape attempts, thwarted only by Dad's tightly-secured collar and tie. The most significant component of my flying ensemble was an open-front jacket with large patch pockets on each side. The kittens were so small and, generally, so still, that I could put two in one pocket, to soothe and control with one hand, while leaving the other hand free to handle purse and boarding pass.

Remembering the nervous milling-about and excited chatter that occupied our party of fliers and family just before we all headed out of the terminal toward the waiting plane makes me understand why, even if there were no worries over potential terrorism, it makes all kinds of sense to stop non-traveler companions at a point well before the actual departure area. But for us, at that time, in that place, and under those circumstances, a little chaos provided useful cover. And, for reasons I can explain only in terms of extremely good luck, or as a merciful act of the God who is reputed to accord special protection to fools and babies (for which we qualified on both counts) our flying threesome, including one partially disabled member, was not PRE-boarded, as is operational routine these many years later; instead, my parents and I were the final passengers to head out of the terminal, at direction of the airline staffer in charge.

Amid all the hubbub of hugs and promises about a next visit, and wheeling Mother out, my father mistakenly picked up my sister-in-law's purse, thinking it was Mom's; so as we crossed the tarmac and reached the foot of stairs leading up to the door of the craft, the purse mix-up created still more confusion and delay. It was apparent that the stewardess greeting passengers and directing them into the airplane was beginning to feel serious schedule stress and was eager to get our bunch off the ground and on board the plane as expeditiously as possible. The tedious process of Dad's helping Mother up the stairs was accomplished, and I was relieved when the two of them disappeared into the airplane, leaving me as the final passenger at the top of the stairway, ready to enter the craft. Just as I reached out to hand the smartly-uniformed stewardess my boarding pass, one of the kittens in my pocket emitted a soft, but audible, easily distinguishable, and utterly unmistakable, "Meow!"

Never before, or since, has the phrase "pregnant pause" seemed quite so apropos to describe a moment in my life, as it did for that "eternity in a minute," while we two faced each other and the dilemma I had created. The stewardess knew that the flight was slightly late, already, and had been doing her best to hurry passengers along and into the airplane, while maintaining an air of helpful cordiality. She had exercised professional patience in dealing with last-minute delay caused by the purse exchange at the foot of the stairs and Mother's slow ascent. Now, with departure already overdue, this professional whose job it was to complete the boarding process and give an all clear signal to pilot and flight crew, so that the plane might take to the skies only a little on the late side, this very businesslike staff member faced a final passenger who was clearly NOT traveling in compliance with well-understood and strictly-enforced airline rules and regulations.

With my boarding pass thrust forward, I stood on the platform, linked, gaze-to-gaze, with the airline employee whose job it was to enforce airline policy, and who stood squarely between me and a seat on the plane where my parents (and two kittens) were now comfortably, thankfully, settled and waiting for me to join them. The stewardess knew that I had cat contraband; I knew she knew; she knew I knew she knew. And there we stood. Almost as audible as the kitten's cry was the "whirring" of wheels inside our respective heads and the thoughts that activity produced: "I have her red-handed, red-faced, and guilty as sin," she must have reasoned, "in a brazen violation of airline policy for which penalties are plain and simple." The burning question in my mind was not what the mistress of my fate could or should do, under the circumstances; it was merely *Will* she? Will she pursue the matter and further delay the flight, or make a spontaneous executive decision that some violations of the rules are just not worth all the bother – and the time – enforcement entails. Hoping to influence her decision-making and tip the scales in my favor, I forced the extended boarding pass into the young woman's hand and turned quickly into the aircraft entryway, fully expecting a raised voice or firm grasp of my shoulder to indicate that the escapade was over.

Instead, moving down the aisle without pause or a backward glance, I reached the row where Mother occupied the aisle seat, and stepped past her into the middle space, left vacant for me. The next words I heard from the stewardess came over the speaker system, as she instructed passengers to adjust seat belts and prepare for imminent takeoff. Never have I heard pre-flight instructions delivered with such lyrical, calming, poetic beauty as those words, at that moment. My family's collective, conspiratorial sigh was drowned out by the roar of engines, and as we taxied toward the runway, Dad removed two kittens from inside his shirt front, and I lifted my two from their sheltering pocket. The four babes, a cozy pile in their spacious, under-seat basket, slept blissfully for the entirety of what proved to be a blessedly uneventful journey home. There was one brief, scheduled stop in Phoenix, for a change of flight crews. Thus the beneficent flight attendant and I were spared the awkwardness of another encounter when the Powell party of three deplaned in Houston—all SEVEN of us.

———

Pat Powell lives in Clear Lake City (Houston), Texas, where she served as Audio Visual Librarian and then Coordinator of the CCISD Teacher Center. Retired now, Pat finds more time for writing and other similarly enjoyable and rewarding pursuits. Pat's memoir, The Quilt House, *was published in 2015.*

SYMBIOSIS

S. M. Kraftchak

Sleep had escaped me, yet again, so I lay in the loft bedroom, looking out the floor-to-ceiling window of my cabin. This was my refuge; a place with deep enough peace to keep my symbiote asleep.

The gray half-light of early morning lay like a blanket across the blue spruce-covered mountains snuggling my cabin. On the next ridge, I could just make out the sun-bleached granite jutting from the trees where the rock held a curve that fit my backside like hands around a teacup. From there, the view of the gurgling river wending its way along the valley floor eased my mind and cooled the fire inside me.

The crash of splintering wood sat me bolt upright and startled my symbiote. I watched, almost in slow motion, as two grenades shattered my window and heard them clatter to the floor downstairs among the tinkling of broken glass. Two more sailed through unimpeded, landed near the foot of my bed, and began hissing out a pale-blue gas. Instantly, I recognized the unusual color as the specially created CO_2-sleep grenades that TORTSS (Tactical Outcomes Reduced To Simple Solutions) used to subdue me.

I held my breath and scrambled from bed as my symbiote awoke. My safe place was downstairs, but I could hear the familiar scramble of boots; a tactical team systematically searching the main room below, before beginning to ascend the stairs. I'd have to jump from the balcony to make it in time. Lines of red light crisscrossed the air above my head. I placed one hand on the smooth, debarked pine tree that was my balcony rail and saw a small wisp of smoke rise from around my fingers before I hurdled the rail. I landed square on my bare feet and ignored the broken glass underfoot. I took two steps and doubled over when a fist in my gut exploded the air from my lungs. When I straightened and inhaled, the faint smell of burning wood wafted upward before I saw those green eyes behind a gas mask. I felt my symbiote panic and diminish and my body crumple to the floor.

"Got him," an amplified communicator voice said as I drifted into oblivion.

* * *

As consciousness returned, I heard a man's unmodified voice nearby. "He's coming around."

A woman's voice from across the room said, "Keep the enhanced breather on him." A moment later the woman was nearby. "How are you doing, Carl?"

"I was fine before you barged into my home," I mumbled into the oxygen mask over my nose and mouth, an obvious attempt to keep me docile or subdue me again if I didn't cooperate. Tugging gently on the metal restraints securing my wrists to my ankles, I pulled up to a sitting position on the floor. She was getting sloppy; escape was possible, but not without burning down my home and half the surrounding forests. Or was that what she wanted? I'd wait and see.

"Welcome back. That was a close one," the woman said.

"I could have taken you all out, but chose not to," I said as I looked up at Mela, the woman who had uncovered my symbiote I called Chōwa, over ten years ago and had used us for her own gain. "You know, most people simply knock. Oh, I see you've finally made Major. Was it on your own merits or did you find someone else to exploit?"

Mela squatted down in front of me.

Her straight, brown hair barely covered the top of her ears, and her green eyes were still stunning against her pale, freckled complexion. I loved and hated this woman.

"You never seemed to mind when it benefitted you as well. I just took my advantages in a different direction. Now I get to say what I want and don't want to do, and you…" she shook her finger at me. "Have been a bad boy."

I felt the tiniest bit of fresh air enter my mask as my brow creased in confusion; Chōwa breathed deeply. "What are you talking about?"

Mela chuckled as she shifted to sit cross-legged on the floor across from me. She snapped her fingers in the air and immediately a fluted glass of amber liquid with tiny bubbles was placed in her hand by a guard completely attired in camouflaged assault gear. She sipped her drink before continuing. "You see, I've noticed a number of incendiary *incidents* over the past few months that have your perfect signature."

I was unsure what she was talking about since I'd pretty much kept to myself, living peacefully and simply off the grid in the mountains; I saw no tactical advantage to letting her know I was clueless. I rarely lost at poker, even when the cards were stacked against me. I bluffed. "I don't have a signature."

"Carl, please, false modesty doesn't become you. No obvious source of incendiary, strategic target eliminated, minimal collateral damage? You have a bleeding heart, even when it's on fire. Who else are you working for?"

Shaking my head, I said, "Anyone with decent tools and a little skill could produce the same results, furthermore, I don't work for anyone. Remember, I quit after our last assignment together."

"Interesting..." she took another sip, "but I'm not looking for decent tools and a *little* skill, I need a master. One who has something to gain...and something to lose."

"I don't need anything and have nothing to lose."

"Oh, well then maybe," she reached inside her uniform shirt pocket, pulled out a surveillance photo, and tilted her head as she stared at the picture, "you don't care...she has your nose, and definitely your chin, but I think she's got my eyes. Wouldn't you say?" she asked as she turned the photo toward me.

As I stared at the picture of my daughter walking along a secluded path, I felt Chōwa struggle to flare with my emotions, but the higher level of CO_2 they were feeding us and my practiced control quickly subdued it; I covered with, "I don't have a child and neither do you." This was a blatant lie.

"I didn't think so either, but at my last physical, my doctor asked if I was planning to have any more children."

I just stared at Mela. I wasn't going to play her game. Some snippet or hunch had led her to uncover my most precious secret and she was taunting me to see what she could learn.

"That one mission that backfired on us...you saved me...I was unconscious for nearly ten months...a lot could have—"

"The mind often feeds our wildest fantasies. Maybe you should talk to someone about that."

Mela leaned forward and spoke in a low voice. "Maybe I should talk to you about the night before that mission. My wildest fantasy was no fantasy. It was...heat and passion; it was real," she took her cold glass, wiped the condensation on the side of my neck, and dragged it halfway down my chest.

I could feel goosebumps rising on my skin. "I don't

know what you're talking about."

With a smile, she gazed at me through her eyebrows, then leaned only inches from my ear and whispered, "It was the best night of my life. I'd love to refresh your memory." She turned the glass so fresh condensation ran down the other side of my neck and chest.

I locked my jaw to control the memory of that night. It was the only time I'd ever allowed Chōwa to have free will and the thought of doing it again tantalized me, but in the same moment, terrified me. There was no way I ever wanted that to happen again, at least not with her. "It was okay. I've had better," I said off-handedly knowing it would provoke her. I needed her angry, or at least wounded so she'd hopefully forget about my, our, daughter.

Mela threw her champagne flute aside and slapped me on the cheek, setting my mask askew.

Another surge of fresh air pumped vital life into Chōwa.

A guard stepped forward, readjusted my mask, and said, "Major Stanwitz, may I remind you—"

"You may not!" Her eyes narrowed when she looked up at the guard. "I'll deal with this in my own way, in my own time."

The guard nodded and stepped back.

Mela waggled the photo in front of me. "You may have control of your...talent, but your eyes betray you. We found her living with your mother's former housekeeper. It would be truly sad to have to deliver the news of her father's death. I'm *sure* it would trigger an 'enlightening' response." She made air quotes with her fingers.

I couldn't help myself. I leaned forward until my face was only inches from hers. I ignored the guard's grip on my shoulder and shouted into my mask. "You leave her alone. What do you want from me?"

"Ah, so the truth comes out." She sat back and smirked as she motioned to the guard to let go. "Does she have your same talent?"

"No. She has none."

"Are you sure of that?"

I held her gaze without flinching, but my mind raced through all the tests I'd put Harper through; it couldn't have been her.

Mela held out her hand to a second guard, who handed her an electronic tablet.

"Aww, now that's a pity. I was rather looking forward to a reunion." She tapped the screen several times and turned the display toward me. "I need whoever has been doing this. They need to work for us."

Slowly I lifted my cuffed hands and took the tablet. I scanned the display; data on each incident, each high value target was as she had said. No one except me, or someone who might have a symbiote like me, could have done this. "I can see where you'd think this was me. It appears, at first glance, to be well executed but there are some definitive amateur flaws. You don't really want this person."

"So, you are saying you'll come back to work—"

"Not even if Hell freezes over," I tossed the e-pad onto the floor and stared her in the eyes.

"Not even to help me find your…replacement?" Mela flipped the photo in her fingers.

"There is no one else like me. You'll have to learn to do your own dirty work, because I'm done working for you. I've made peace with my past and the atrocities you made me commit in the name of peace. I swore I'd never again use my talent"—she still didn't know Chōwa was more than a talent—"to further yours, or anyone else's agenda."

Mela tossed her head back and laughed, "Funny you should say that." She easily rose and stood with her hands behind her, looking down at me with amusement. "I have designed a process to remove your…talent…and transfer it to another person."

My heart and Chōwa seized in unison at the thought of being separated and that this woman knew our truth. I clenched my jaw to control our emotions as she continued.

"I thought someone young and strong, with so much to lose might be a good, compliant choice." She tucked the photo back in her pocket. "But I think I like your suggestion even better." She walked to the impatient guard and paused. "Put him in his safe box and get him to my lab. I'll send word to secure him some proper motivation."

"No!" I shouted behind my mask as two guards lifted me to my feet. With a quick twist of my head, I knocked my mask askew against one guard's arm and took a deep breath of fresh air. Instantly Chōwa flared to life. The heat, like a cup of hot chocolate on a cold day, blossomed in my chest and raced out my extremities. My clothes began to char and the guards began to scream as they watched their gloves suddenly ignite and flames surge up their sleeves. I saw Mela stop at the front door.

"Get him! Use the gas!" she shouted before she shoved her gas mask back over her face and took up a stance to block the doorway.

I didn't have time, or the stomach, to watch the guards as they screamed and tried to extinguish the fire that was quickly covering them like a second skin. A third guard came at me with a CO_2 fire extinguisher. Chōwa recognized it as death, and flared until flame encrusted all of my body but my head; I felt my shackles crumble away. We grabbed the nozzle and watched it melt. The guard quickly dropped the tank and turned to run but not before fire leaped onto his back and almost instantly engulfed him.

The wooden floor was now smoking where my bare feet stood, small pools of molten glass were beginning to sear into the wood, and fire reached out for the furniture with an insatiable appetite. I felt Chōwa's desire grow and feed on my own fear and rage at Mela threatening my daughter. I stared at the woman's frustrated and angry expression for no more than ten seconds before I called in my mind for Chōwa to return to me from the men and the furniture. As it did, I leaped out the broken window and sprinted along the gravel driveway through the woods, leaving the shouts of panic and commands behind me. Bits of Chōwa dropped along the path, trying to feed and grow, but only smoldered and went out in the heavy dew of morning.

I heard Mela's truck engine rev. She'd outrun me in no time, but not through the woods. I chose a path across round granite rocks scattered on the forest floor like lichen speckled mushrooms to avoid starting any fires. I knew where I was headed. I took my time, choosing each jump carefully as I battled to calm Chōwa. I was giddy with Its glee at being released; even the slightest spark set free could grow and swiftly consume the surrounding forest of pines. I couldn't let that happen.

Finally, I spotted the 'swimming hole' in the wide wandering river and managed to stifle a flare of outrage from Chōwa. It wasn't much, but the water would temporarily quench the fire of my symbiote and give me back control. I fell into the waist deep water and silently apologized to It as the water boiled and steamed around us. Once I was certain of control, I waded across the river and down the far side before getting out and heading up a game trail I sometimes used. Half-way up the opposite mountain that had been my bedroom view, I ducked behind a fallen tree when Mela's voice drifted up to me. I peered down at the swimming hole where she stood at the edge, scanning the river.

"You might as well come back. I can get to her much faster than you, and then talent or no talent she'll be all I need to get your cooperation. Make it easy on yourself and her."

Clenching my teeth, I let Chōwa seethe a little deep inside my chest as an apology for quenching It. Threating to use a child to gain my cooperation, much less one she suspected to be her own...was intolerable. My daughter was a means to an end for her and nothing more, as I had been for many years, but I refused to let that happen anymore.

* * *

Planning ahead with a cache of clothing and necessities hidden in my old jeep had paid off. After many times of being forced to beg for clothing with nothing more than my hands for modesty...you get the picture. The hardest part to explain had been the lack of hair all over my body, but still sporting a full head of hair. The worst part was several days later when the itch of hair growing in began.

Within half an hour, I arrived in the nearest town, Harmony, if you could call a diner, a gas station/grocery, and a barber shop a town. This was my only point of contact with the outside world and where I could activate the safety network I'd put in place for my daughter. I was exasperated and distressed that Mela had found Harper but knew with one call my daughter would disappear. I was banking on Mela's need to be 'tidy' about covering her trail. It would take a little while to take care of the three unfortunate guards.

The bell on the door of Danny's Diner clanged as I walked in. The smell of bacon, coffee, and toast filled the air of this lost-in-time luncheonette, with its round counter-side stools, black and white checkerboard floor, and green

Naugahyde booth seats; it was as unhurried and laid back as its owner who glanced over the top of his paper and took a sip of his coffee before calling, "Hey Carl. What brings you down so early?"

"I need to make a call." I tried to sound casual.

"At this hour? Never known a woman who liked being woken from her beauty sleep."

"Can't be helped," I said and slid onto a stool close to him.

Danny carefully folded his paper and moved to grab some dishes as he whistled some tune only he could identify.

I didn't turn to look at Sarge who had fallen asleep with his arms on the table surrounding his cup of coffee and was snoring softly, as usual. I'd already checked out the young couple who were making eyes at each other across one plate of half-eaten scrambled eggs, hash browns, and bacon; they were no threat. As I sat and assayed everything else, I realized my heart was pounding and Chōwa was cajoling me into release. So, I folded my hands, took a deep breath, and leaned my elbows on the counter to wait. Within two minutes, Danny slid a cup of steaming coffee and a strawberry Danish with a small flip phone on the side in front me.

"My coffee will tar and paper your insides. Sure you don't want no creamer with that?" Danny steadied himself with his one hand on the counter and waited with raised eyebrows.

"Yeah, give me seven creamers. No, I'm cutting back, give me just four."

"Jeezus, Carl, you sure do make for some interesting times around here."

"Yeah, so much for peace and quiet in Harmony. I gotta hit the head, I'll be right back," I said, slipped the flip phone from the plate into my pocket, and headed to the men's room.

As I sat on the closed lid of the toilet, I found my hands shaking. It had been nearly six years since I'd last seen my baby girl and this wasn't the way I'd imagined our reunion. I flipped the phone open and dialed the number I'd engraved on my heart. I checked my watch and felt Chōwa rise with my anxiety, eager for release again.

"Hola?" I recognized Sara's slight Spanish accent, even though there was a strange lilt to it.

"It's me."

"Oh, you telemarketers are so rude…"

"Is she safe?"

"Yes, of course I do my own baking and I have everything I need, which means I don't need any of your new-fangled appliances. Oh, Dios Mío, now I must go find out who is banging on my door. Good luck and Adiós." The connection ended.

My hands fumbled through disassembling the phone; I dropped the mechanical parts in the trash and flushed the sim card. Mela must have sent men to get Harper at the same time she came for me. "Thank you, Sara," I whispered at the sink as my hands steamed under the cold water; a trick I used to politely control Chōwa.

When I finally left the bathroom, steam tumbled out into the diner. Two more locals sat at the bar talking over their coffee. My white china coffee cup and plate had been replaced with a medium sized brown paper bag. I offered an apologetic smile and reached into my pocket.

Danny waved his hand at me. "It's on the house. You best get a move on. Mama's at the riverbend and Ernest says she don't look happy."

"Thanks, Danny. I owe you one," I said, grabbed the bag, and headed out the front door.

"You owe me plenty and maybe one of these days I'll collect," he called as he grabbed the coffee pot and began making his rounds to fill everyone's cups.

It had been four very long hours of worry and constant vigilance to keep Chōwa under control. Three was my fastest time when Harper had fallen and broken her collar bone at school, but the extra time on several switchbacks and a fire road or two ensured I hadn't been followed by Mela and her personal crew. Sara had let me know that Harper had already been sent ahead and that Mela's men had already been there, so I didn't even try to go past the house. She'd forgive me for not checking in on her. I took the back road into town and parked behind Pop's Hardware, two doors down from the bakery. I wasn't taking any chances.

As I wandered around front, I assayed the street. There were seven cars on their way through town and six more parked in front of the eight stores; only one in front of the bakery. I had no way of knowing for sure who was who, so I popped into Pop's to shop a little and watch. An electronic bing-bong sounded as I broke the laser eye inside the front door.

"Morning." Pop called from behind the counter to the right where he was busy unrolling small brown paper bags of hardware and dumping them into drawers with yellowed labels. The pipe he held in the side of his mouth had gone out but still left a sweet lingering smell of smoke to mix with the smell of metal and oil.

"Morning," I said.

"Anything in particular I can help you find?" He continued to talk around the pipe.

"Nah, I've got to see some things and think it through before I know exactly what I want." I peered out the multipaned window as I casually examined some calf-skin gloves.

"Know exactly what you mean. Sometimes jury-rigging things just takes the right inspiration. Let me know if I can help."

"Thank you." I forced my sense of urgency, and Chōwa, to be still as I pretended to look at things while going back to the window several times. Finally satisfied with the situations outside, I decided to leave. "I'm going to have to think some more on it. Thank you for your time."

"Not a problem. We'll be here," Pop called as I headed out the door.

I walked with a purpose toward the bakery, keeping an eye out for Mela's goons; either they were better than I thought or they were already with my daughter. A small wind chime ting-a-linged as I opened the door and instinctively inhaled the tantalizing yeasty smell of baked bread mingled with a hint of sweet icing. I sighed with relief. Just a few more minutes and Harper and I could vanish somewhere where Mela could never find us again.

My heart soared when my little girl, now a young lady of thirteen, walked out of the curtained off backroom. The expression on her face was composed, but the fear in her eyes seized my heart; Mela's men were here.

"How may I help you, Sir?" Harper asked as though I was any other customer coming into the store.

I smiled. She was playing our game. "Do you have two whole wheat bagels?"

"I'm sorry, we're out of whole wheat. Can we offer you three sourdough instead?"

She played so well, just like we had when she was little; she informed me there were three uninvited guests in back; even her voice didn't betray her fear.

"That's fine. What can I get with them?" I was asking for

more information.

When Harper laid the bagels on the cutting board, I suddenly felt like someone sucked all the air from my lungs. There, on the crusts of my bagels where her fingers had been, were toasted lines. Chōwa had spawned. All I could do was stare at Harper as I felt Chōwa surge and dance inside me like never before.

"Sir?" Her voice wavered slightly.

"Oh, I'm sorry, I'm not quite awake yet. What did you say?"

"We only have small tubs of regular cream cheese. Can you handle those?"

"That's perfect." They had small handguns, nothing more. I smiled to reassure her but was struggling to control my tumult of emotions: pride and fear that my girl shared my symbiote; apprehension that she might lose control, even though she seemed to be as calm as could be expected; and anger that Mela had threatened her to get to me, and that I had somehow let her.

When Harper pulled the small tubs of cream cheese from the counter top refrigerator, they melted in her fingers and splatted on the floor. She smothered a squeak of dismay.

"Here, let me help you with that." I rushed around the counter, grabbed the roll of paper towels from the sink at the end of the counter, and squatted next to her. There was only a moment to bridge six long years of separation. I kissed her hard on her forehead and felt a unique warmth under my lips as Chōwa and its progeny met for the first time.

Harper whispered. "Daddy, you came!"

"Of course, I came. You are my life. Where are they?"

"One is keeping lookout by the back door and the other two are sitting on stools next to the kneading table watching Mrs. Takuri. I gave them some pastries to try to distract them."

"Good, thinking. Now stay behind me." I pushed Harper behind me as I stood and walked toward the kitchen.

I peered through the slit between the curtain and the doorway. One man at the table had his back to me and the other sat to his left; both extolling the deliciousness of their pastries. In one swift movement, I was behind them with my hands on their shoulders. In my mind, I called Chōwa, inviting it to find the metal in the men's hands, but felt It flare with what felt like anger and surge toward their hearts. They didn't even have time to swallow the last bites of their pastries before both men slumped to the floor clutching their chests.

Mrs. Takuri glanced at the men on the floor and then up at me as she continued kneading her dough. "You *are* going to clean that up, right?"

"Hey! What—?" the guard by the backdoor said around a mouthful of Danish, drew his 9mm pistol, and pointed it at my chest.

"You don't want to do this," I said slowly walking around Mrs. Takuri, who kept working as though nothing untoward was going on. With my hands raised, and Harper's hand on the small of my back, I slowly advanced on the last guard.

"What did you do to them?" he asked glancing down at the two men on the floor then re-aimed his weapon at me. "Stay where you are! Major Stanwitz warned us about you."

"I'm sorry about them. I'm... kind of angry at having my daughter threatened. I lost control." One step at a time, I walked toward the man, who matched each of my steps, backing toward the door. "So, if you just let us go...I promise I won't hurt you."

A suppressed gunshot snapped like a mousetrap going off.

I flinched and grabbed behind me for Harper's hand; she was still there and her hand was as hot as mine.

I watched the guard's weapon clatter to the floor as the man pitched forward, revealing a single hole in the screen door. Mela stood outside with her weapon pointed where the man's head had been.

"I hate people who get in the way of reunions. Why don't you come out here so I can be properly introduced to my daughter?"

I held Harper's hand tightly. "I won't let you hurt her." Only years of experience allowed me to suppress it.

"Oh, I'm not going to hurt her, but I might hurt *you* if you don't bring her out here. I'm just going to give her what she's always wanted, a mama."

I squeezed Harper's hand and turned to look in her eyes. "You okay? Just stay with me. She won't hurt you. She's after me."

"I know who she is Daddy. I'm okay." I watched Harper swallow hard and swipe at a few tears before she smiled weakly and nodded.

"Aww, how sweet." Mela taunted from outside. "Get out here, you're wasting my time."

I carefully guided Harper around the body in the doorway and when she began to whimper, I tugged her hand. "Hey, don't look at him, look at me." Slowly I opened the door, stepped out first and pulled my daughter out behind me. "Now what?" I said staring into Mela's green eyes behind her still pointed weapon.

"Send her over here. I'd like to meet her."

"No. You don't care about her. You just want me to do another job for you. I'll do it. Just leave her out of it."

"You make me sound so cold and unfeeling…"

I raised one eyebrow. "Truth hurt?"

"Not in the slightest. When a job needs to be done right, sometimes you have to do it yourself."

A suppressed gunshot snapped again. Faster than I could flinch and encircle Harper in my arms, I felt Chōwa and its progeny burst from our entwined hands and instead of covering us like a second skin, they created an orb of fire around us, leaving us unscathed. Through the thin orb of fire, I watched Mela topple to the side with a wide-eyed expression.

"Like you said, sometimes you need to do it yourself. Ansendesu."

Still clutching Harper to my chest, I turned to see Mrs. Takuri lowering a pistol. She had shot Mela in the head.

She turned and bowed to us. "Ansendesu. Heiwa."

I felt Harper push away from me and un-entwine her fingers. She held out her palm and repeated Mrs. Takuri's words. "Ansendesu. Heiwa," and then added, "Come, Chōwa."

The orb of fire surrounding us suddenly evaporated. I felt Chōwa settle back inside me like embers of a campfire, instead of the raging flame I often sought to control, and watched as a small ball of fire appeared on Harper's hand.

"Daddy, meet, Chōwa. Its name means harmony."

I couldn't help that my mouth gaped like a baby bird at feeding time as I marveled at the ball of fire in Harper's hand. Finally, I collected my wits and asked, "How do you do that?"

Mrs. Takuri approached. "Talking to It is much better than commanding it. This, your daughter has learned in the years you were apart. You, too, can learn. But, you two have much time for this later. You are now under the protection of SAP, the Symbiote Alliance for Peace."

"There's more?" I closed my mouth so it wasn't wider than my eyes.

"Yes, Daddy, there's a whole network of us."

"Yes, and your first job is to clean up the mess in my kitchen," Mrs. Takuri said as she walked back inside.

S. M. Kraftchak spends most of her time with dragons, elves, and aliens, yet still enjoys sunrise on the beach, sunset in the mountains and portraying Elizabeth Tudor. She has three awesome daughters, two dogs, and one cat. Her husband is her best friend, harshest critic and most fervent supporter. See her website: smkraftchak.com.

MACHINATIONS IN THE MUSEUM

Madeleine McDonald

Charlotte scowled at the brightly lit display cabinets. Why had she agreed to this? Replacing his pottery with something made of torn-up T-shirts was a betrayal of Gramps and all he stood for. Gramps had put his soul into crafting the stumpy little figures, and soul was something a vulgarian like Mavis Chirk would never understand.

The previous night, the trustees and volunteers of the Congar Museum of Local Life had met to prepare the annual summer opening. The museum shut in winter, when few visitors braved the rain-lashed Welsh coast. It struggled on, from one government grant to the next, its collection of objects increasing as elderly miners and farmers died off, and their heirs donated tools rusty with disuse.

The old farmhouse which housed the museum had never been modernised. To American visitors "doing Wales" on a coach tour, that was its charm. They enthused over the uneven brick floors, low ceilings, tiny windows, dark corners and steep, narrow staircases. They cooed over the black-leaded range, the washtubs, dollies and mangles, the cast-iron fireplaces, the tables draped in yellowing, hand-embroidered cloths, and the mannequins in period costume.

The meeting was held in the activities room. In contrast to the mock-up of a forbidding 19th century classroom with scratched desks and wooden-framed slates, the activities room was brightly painted, with communal tables offering plentiful supplies of worksheets and felt tip pens. The volunteer guides always breathed a sigh of relief once parties of bouncy schoolchildren were corralled in a room devoid of exhibits, for the old tools could be dangerous in reckless hands.

The overhead lighting in the activities room was unflattering to the mainly elderly volunteers. They were barely a dozen in number now, despite regular appeals to the town for new blood. Charlotte's youthful face marked her out.

"Item 3 on the agenda, the gift shop," the chairman announced.

Mavis, self-styled manageress of the gift shop, marshalled her papers. Around the table, people stared at their hands.

"As noted in the treasurer's report, in our first year of operation, the gift shop exceeded expectations," Mavis announced. "If we double our floor space this summer, I expect to quadruple our turnover."

"Hold on a minute, Mavis. We're a museum, not an emporium. Why do you need extra floor space?" Derek Jones asked.

"A failing museum," Mavis snapped back. "A dismal collection of moth-eaten clothes and antiquated tools. It was my retail skills that kept us going last year."

"Why don't you open a high street shop then?" Derek countered.

Charlotte hid a smile. With his untidy hair and well-worn anorak, Derek reminded her of Gramps.

"A shop lowers the tone of the museum," Derek continued. "Before you came and turned us upside down, we offered a selection of books reflecting our ethos and purpose." As the author of two self-published books on the lost railways of Snowdonia, he had particular reason to dislike Mavis, who had moved books to the back of the gift shop.

"I agree with Derek." That was Ann Poole. The oldest trustee, she walked with difficulty after two hip replacements, yet insisted on taking responsibility for dusting fragile exhibits. "You're not interested in our work, Mavis. You're using us to get your name and photo in the paper as often as possible. We all know your husband wants to be the next town mayor. And you want to be lady mayoress."

"Ladies, please." The chairman took a handkerchief from his pocket and began to polish his glasses, acknowledging that he had temporarily lost control of the proceedings.

Ann and Mavis took no notice. Miss Roberts, in charge of the minutes, laid down her pen for the duration of hostilities.

"I will not resign, Mrs Poole, I will not give you that pleasure." Puce with fury, Mavis delivered her parting shot. "And, in case any of you have forgotten, it was my Arthur who secured us grant money from Europe." She glared round the table. "You don't get money just for being a worthy cause. You need to know the right people as well. You should all be grateful to my Arthur."

The mention of money silenced the dissenters. It was true the European Union had awarded the museum a substantial sum under some coastal regeneration programme, although the extra money had been diverted to repairing the slate roof. The chairman suggested placing on record the trustees' appreciation of Mrs. Chirk's diligence. Reluctantly, Charlotte raised her hand along with the others. Miss Roberts made a note on her shorthand pad.

Mavis gave a gracious nod and steamrollered on. "Now that we are agreed on the extra floor space, I can show you two new lines we will be introducing this summer." Mavis bent to extricate items from her shopping bag. Coming up, she breathed heavily and Charlotte had the irreverent thought that chains of office were designed for ample bosoms. Mavis would carry hers well but, standing beside her, Arthur would be weighed down by Congar's municipal regalia.

Born into a family of self-employed farmers, Charlotte had been out of sync with the clamorous left-wing views of her fellow students. At the same time, she nourished a visceral hatred for the Arthurs and Mavises of this world, festooned with chains of office and frothy Tory hats. Soft-living incomers like the Chirks had never known the precarious life of the hill farmers or the slate miners. She, Charlotte Davies, might be a shining example of social progress, having attended art college in Liverpool, but solidarity with her ancestors' existential struggle was bred into her bones.

After handing round an example of the new line of love spoons featuring the fire-breathing Welsh dragon, Mavis unrolled a bundle. She smoothed the bright colours flat. "And these are the rag rugs."

"No way, Mavis," Derek Jones said "My grandma's rugs never looked like that. She didn't waste money cutting up clothes until they were worn to threads."

"Aye, Derek's right." A couple of ladies with tightly permed grey hair voiced agreement.

Charlotte's only knowledge of rag rugs was seeing grimy rectangles set in front of the fireplaces in the various rooms. She rarely had occasion to step over the ropes that cordoned off the tableaux of village life, and could not recall having handled one.

Mavis bridled. "These are a modern version. Designed and made in Wales by Felicity Williams. Well, the originals are. I ordered one hundred."

"Without consulting us?" The normally emollient chairman bristled with indignation.

"I used my discretion. Made in China, they cost £5 each, and we can sell them for £25 each in the shop."

Around the table, heads jerked up. Even Charlotte did the mental calculation of £20 profit on a hundred rugs.

"Of course, if we want to encourage people to buy them, we'll have to find a place for Felicity's originals. I suggest we move the Duckfeathers Pottery pieces into one display case, instead of two."

"But Duckfeathers was Gramps' business," Charlotte wailed. Heads turned to look. "His pottery is part of Congar's history. He employed lots of local people."

"Quite, dear. And since you inherited his artistic talent I nominate you as the best person to make a selection of his pottery pieces." Mavis smiled at the table, not at Charlotte.

"Agreed," the chairman said, and Miss Roberts made a note. "And Charlotte, can you write something on Facebook? Those bright colours will make a good picture."

Charlotte could not refuse. Her degree in fine art had not led to a job, even at dogsbody level, and voluntary work at the museum was something to list on her CV. She had also taken responsibility for the museum's Facebook page, allowing her to claim *excellent social media skills* in her numerous job applications.

Derek Jones left the museum alongside Charlotte, chuntering discontent. "That woman is a vandal. I'll kill her if she pulls another trick like that. Plastic love spoons made in China! Time was a young man carved a spoon for his sweetheart with his own knife and only the two of them knew what the carvings said. Know what I mean?" His throaty cackle embarrassed Charlotte.

* * *

The next morning, Charlotte still seethed. Instead of kicking something, she scuffed the soles of her trainers across the wooden floorboards, producing an unpleasant sound in the small room. She did it again.

You'd hate it, wouldn't you, Gramps, fake Welsh culture. Another part of her brain snorted in contradiction, for Gramps had never turned up his nose at making money. Charlotte turned her back on the display cabinet and stared out of the window.

The anger she felt since last night's meeting intensified when Mavis arrived and suggested that she remove the sheep and ducks. "Leave the cups and saucers, dear, the colours are quite pleasant. But you must agree those 1950s ornaments are beyond kitsch. I'm not saying anything against your ancestor, he did well for a self-taught man, but I'm sure your art degree has given you a sense of perspective."

Shrouding the despised ducks in layers of bubble wrap, Charlotte dreamed of being in a position of power in the art world and refusing to renew the museum's grant. As a revenge fantasy, that was as puerile as the various Facebook posts she had composed in her head following last night's meeting.

She'll pay for this, Gramps.

Objectively, she conceded that Gramps' sheep and ducks lacked taste. She held one of the pottery figures to the light, examining its unnatural blue plumage. The duck stood upright, in a defiant pose. As an object it was so hideous you had to smile. Yet Charlotte recalled Gramps explaining the nineteen forties and fifties to her, when she was a child and Gramps was unimaginably old, for Gramps was Grandpa Tom's dad. "It was a grim time. We'd won the war, but conditions were hardly better than before. Our houses were always cold, and food was rationed." He'd ruffled Charlotte's hair. "You and your little friends wouldn't recognise it for the same country. So when the good times came back and people got a bit of money in their hands, they wanted things that were bright, and shiny and new. Think on it. If you lived in a cold, damp home, with a fireplace that smoked, you'd want something new to put on the mantelpiece and cheer the place up. That's what I gave them, little ornaments that put a smile on people's faces."

Throughout art school, Charlotte had defended Gramps' homely philosophy of giving people what they wanted. Now she was complicit in sweeping him aside. Rage seethed and roiled as she packed the ornaments.

There was nothing she could do. The discussion of the previous night swilled through her brain, underlining her spineless complicity.

She'll pay for this.

The museum was almost empty. Out in the courtyard, a portable radio was set to a local station as Andy Perkins sawed and hammered, working on a new bench for the garden. A jingle cut across the radio chit chat to announce the traffic news. Somewhere Ann Poole was progressing from room to room, feather duster in hand, removing every speck of winter's dust from the jumble of display items before opening day. Mavis was in the small office on the top floor.

Charlotte made a quick foray upstairs to find one of the genuine rag rugs, noting with satisfaction that it was almost invisible against the black-painted floorboards at the top of the precipitous back stairs. Downstairs again, she headed for the alcove where the electric kettle was kept. "Ready for a cup of tea, Andy?" she called on the way.

* * *

The trustees and volunteers agreed that the grand summer opening should go ahead, in tribute to Mavis's sterling work, with Councillor Arthur Chirk invited to perform the opening ceremony. "It's what she would have wanted," they told each other. The plastic love spoons and mass-produced rag rugs arrived from China, and were stored in the gift shop cupboard, thus offering the volunteers further opportunity to dissect Mavis's conduct.

Mavis had fallen down the unlit back stairs when Charlotte had called her to come and share the morning tea break. The tragic accident was blamed on her high heels. "Quite unsuitable for a woman of her age," was Ann Poole's verdict, and her cronies agreed.

The Duckfeathers Pottery display had been reinstated. The rag rug was also back in its place, for Charlotte was tidy by nature.

Madeleine McDonald lives on the east coast of England, where the cliffs crumble into the sea, and finds inspiration walking on the beach before the world wakes up. Her latest romance novel, A Shackled Inheritance, is based on the true story of a Scottish will.

THREE WISHES

Robert Kibble

I don't remember life without Joe. He was there in the background of my first memories of the park, and he was probably there on the day I got married, and on the day my mother died. He wasn't called Joe, but I didn't know that then.

That wasn't the first name we gave him. His first name, to us, had been "old boot-lace." He was called that because he had long straggly hair and had a boot-lace tied 'round his head to keep it back. I suppose in those days he was the local weirdo, back when you could be weird and not be beaten up. He'd ditched the boot-lace eventually, and gotten a short haircut, but that was after I knew him better. The first time I ever saw him was just after we moved up here. I was playing in the park, some distance from my mother, who'd met a friend of the family. They were having some dull chat about something completely uninteresting to a ten-year-old, and I was looking around for a good tree to climb. I eventually found one, with a couple of sturdy-looking branches slightly higher than I'd managed before but low enough to be possible if my hands were feeling strong. I walked underneath it and looked up, preparing for my jump. Joe was sitting on the third branch up, directly above me, and looking terrifying with his hair falling around his face in all directions. I was paralysed with my knees bent and my arms slightly back, just ready to jump up.

He smiled, and shiny white teeth shone out at me.

That's the image I kept for a good many years: of him, with the messy hair but clean teeth. I still feel he ought to have had awful teeth.

My mother heard my scream and came running over faster than I'd ever seen anyone run before, and I was in her arms before I'd realised I was screaming. I think my knees were still slightly bent, and she must have thought I was constipated or something. She yelled at the man in the tree, and if I recall correctly the police were called. They came round and asked me what he'd done, as there'd been a flasher reported in the area some time before and people were on their guard, and I said that he'd scared me by smiling at me. It sounded really stupid when I said it to them, and I remember wanting the policemen to go away, even though one of them did let me try on his helmet. It was so heavy.

As far as I remember he was never actually in a tree again, although he was always around one. He sat at the bottom of a tree, whittling away, or on a tree-stump occasionally, with his legs crossed. He was always whittling or carving something. When I got close enough to see what he was doing, I could tell that he was carving a statue of something vaguely person-shaped, but couldn't tell any more than that. I didn't get very close, because my mother kept an eye on me to make sure the gap didn't get too small.

* * *

I was twelve or thirteen when I exchanged my first words with the man. He'd become a legend at school, and various of my friends had stories about him that I was certain were made up. He varied in their tales from a terrifying monster who carried corpses back and buried them at night, to a benevolent misfit who was kind to the children he liked. Neither was really true.

It was a cold day, the wind was blowing strongly, and I had gone up to the park by myself to fly my kite. My mother hadn't minded, because she believed that I was going with a couple of friends, it being a half-term holiday. In fact my friends had said they couldn't make it, but I'd been so keen to go that I'd lied to my mother and gone anyway.

The kite flew high and well, although my hands got cold very quickly and I had to put my gloves on, which always made flying the kite more difficult. It got a little out of control and landed in a tree, one of the tall oaks between the park and the road, with bushes around the bottom. I'd sometimes cut through under them as a short-cut into the park. I walked over and saw Joe sitting at the bottom of the tree, staring up into it.

"Your kite?"

I nodded, but didn't move any closer. I was scared of him, but I was also scared of having to tell my mother the truth if I didn't have the kite when I got back. That was the only thing that stopped me turning and running the whole way home.

He stood, leapt up, and grabbed one of the branches. He climbed effortlessly, as if he were walking rather than climbing. He had the kite down in a matter of seconds, and leapt down after it, although he did stumble slightly as he landed. I knew that it was rude not to thank someone for doing something kind, so I said "Thank you" to him.

"My pleasure. It relieves the boredom, anyway."

It was probably at that moment that Joe made the transition from childhood fear to a real person. It had never occurred to me that he could actually have feelings as normal people do. "Are you bored, then?" I asked, forgetting my fear and walking forwards a little to hear better, as the wind was quite strong. He handed me my kite.

"Yes, very. No one talks to me anymore."

"They used to?"

"Well, not since the war, but they used to before that."

I was not a very bright child, it must be said, but it still amazes me that I didn't grasp the full meaning of that statement. Joe looked about thirty, if that. "How long have you been here, then?"

"Forever by your standards. About ten years. But I've been in this area for a hundred."

"You're a hundred years old?" I was a trusting child, and believed most things people said. I'd even believed it when a friend told me that the word gullible wasn't in the dictionary.

"No, I'm nearly three thousand years old. I've just been here, off and on, for a hundred."

"How come you're that old?"

"I did a favour for a god once, and she gave me three wishes in exchange. I used the first one to get immortality." There wasn't the slightest hint of a smile on his face, but I started feeling that he was having me on. I pulled my kite closer to me, turned around, and ran off. I heard him shouting "Good-bye" after me, but I didn't look back.

* * *

I never told anyone about our conversation, at least not until Andrea came along. In the week following my first words with Joe I alternated between believing that he'd been having me on and hoping that he was telling the truth, because then I'd be the only person who knew about him. Eventually I came down on the side of disbelief.

We didn't share another word for two months, during which time I grew increasingly annoyed with him, simply for existing. For some reason I got it into my head that his very life was an affront to me personally, and I went through a phase of sneering in his general direction whenever I was at the park and he was there too, which was most of the time. He seemed to spend a good two-thirds of his days there, including week-ends.

It was actually because a small part of me did believe him that I plucked up the courage to go over and call him a liar. I stood about fifty feet from him and shouted. He looked up from his carving, placed the knife and wood very carefully down in front of him, and asked me to repeat myself.

"You're a liar!" I shouted again.

"Why do you say that?" he asked, without anger or resentment.

"Because you are!"

"Well, that's certainly a concise argument. Not perhaps very informative, but nevertheless consistent in its logic. Perhaps you would care to elaborate as to which particular facet of my speech you consider false?"

I paused, waiting for the words to file slowly into my head, and then waited a moment longer to understand what he meant. I assume that was his intent, as he leant back, clasped his hands behind his head, and smiled.

"You didn't do a favour for a god at all. You're just a loony."

"As you wish. I know the truth, and you won't believe anyway, so there seems little point in attempting to converse on the subject."

The fact that he didn't mind me calling him a liar irritated me even more. "But I don't believe you."

"I know. I heard you the first time."

"So you're supposed to argue."

"Why?"

I stopped and tried to think of something to say. In the end I ran away again, leaving Joe laughing behind me. My memory of the event includes crying, but it's possible that was for another reason, as I think I had a slight accident while climbing a tree later on.

Two days later I ran across him again, and we spoke again.

"Good morning," he said to me. I was slightly startled, as I hadn't noticed him.

"What do you want?"

"Nothing. I was just saying good morning to you. That's all."

"Good. Okay then. Good morning."

He looked down again, and ran his finger along the piece of wood in his hands, turning it slightly to feel the other sides. It was a very light wood, almost white; I briefly thought it ivory, but he produced wood-shavings by running a knife along it so I assumed it was just pale wood.

"I still think you're lying." It still surprises me that I was so rude then.

"As you wish."

"Why would a god give you immortality, anyway?"

"Well, I did her a favour at the time, although I'd rather not go into details. But she didn't give me eternal life, she just gave me the chance to wish for it. She didn't think it a problem, because so many people had wished for immortality before and failed to get what they really wanted. When I came up with a wish that was impossible to misinterpret the gods were furious, but none of them could lift a finger against me. I tell you, I shook uncontrollably for a year after facing them down." He looked past me and off into the distance, obviously remembering something.

"But what did you do?"

He looked back at me, and his voice changed, became deeper and more serious. "I said I'd rather not say. It was a personal matter then, and should remain so, even now."

"So what did you do with the other two, then?" I was only asking to be flippant, to draw him out and get him to admit that he was lying.

"I waited a long time to use the next one, in the hope that the gods would forget how much they hated me, because I was afraid of them managing to misinterpret my next wish."

"And did they?"

"Oh yes. Very much indeed. But I thought you wouldn't be interested. Don't you believe that all of this is made-up, and that I'm lying?"

"Yes," I said, quickly. "You're still a liar."

"Well, I'm glad we're clear on that point. I would hate to waste your time telling you stories that weren't true."

I turned and left, annoyed that he'd noticed that I was interested, and also annoyed that I was so determined to stick to my guns and say that he was lying, even though I no longer really believed it. That's not to say that I believed him, either, because I didn't, at least not fully, but I was interested enough to want to hear more, and I no longer regarded belief as the important matter.

Anyway, the next day was a school day, and I didn't get to the park again for a week, during which time I lost my determination, so when I next met him I was quite willing to talk to him.

"All right," he said, settling back to talk to me more comfortably. "You want to know about my next wish, do you?" I nodded. "Good. Well, it's still quite fresh in my mind, because it was only ten years ago. I'd almost forgotten that I had two wishes left and had become quite contented wandering around watching people. The problem came one day when I was watching some people shooting arrows at some targets, slightly sad that not as many people do that sort of thing anymore. I remember winning a couple of small tournaments, a very long time ago, you see, and I've always been quite fond of the sport. Now these people weren't bad, so I walked closer and sat on a little grass verge watching them.

"My eyes happened to fall upon the prettiest of them, a young girl with reddish-orange curls, just touching her shoulders, and a pure white dress, just a couple of thin straps over the shoulders and a plain front and back, but perfect for her. The leather arm-guard on her arm, which looked like three leather bracelets from my side, made her arm look even paler. She lifted her bow, with her arm just off-straight, just the way I'd been taught, and pulled the arrow back. There was no movement anywhere else as I watched her two fingers open and the arrow disappear.

"The string moved, but there was hardly a twitch from her until the arrow was long gone, when she lowered the bow again, her arm still just off straight. I looked over to the target and saw it in the outermost ring and felt terribly sorry for her. To shoot so beautifully and not to hit the centre seemed so unjust. She looked down, her eyebrows raised, looking sad, and then looked around. She looked straight at me for a moment, and then looked away again. Whether she really saw me or not I don't know. But in that moment I fell in love. I used my second wish to wish that she would be my loving wife."

"Was she so awful, then?"

"I don't know. I haven't seen her since."

"But I thought your wishes came true?"

"It will. But I didn't say when she would fall in love with me, or indeed when we would be married. She is out there somewhere, and some day she'll come to me. That's why I wait here, you see. Someday, the most beautiful woman I've ever seen in my entire life will walk up to me, already in love with me, and we shall be married."

Back then I knew precious little about women or girls, and thought he was speaking a load of rubbish, but thought better than to tell him so. I couldn't have been talking to him for more than five minutes, but I worried that my mother would somehow realise that I wasn't home, so I decided to go back, to hide the fact that Joe and I had spoken.

* * *

That was the only one of our early conversations I can remember fully, word for word, and it isn't saying much, really, as it was only a few minutes long. It was also the only one of our conversations in which I got to do all the asking of questions. From then on Joe became interested in me, and as an annoying young brat I was more than keen to talk about myself given the chance. That's actually the reason I didn't know his real name for so long. Our conversation had moved onto the subject of his love again, and my interest was flagging.

"No, you don't understand," he said, slowly, and very much unlike the teachers at school. I didn't mind nearly so much when Joe told me I didn't understand. "Throughout my life I've wandered aimlessly around, never doing anything worthwhile. I've been depressed and I've been happy. But I've never done anything. Not anything real, or lasting. Somehow because I know I'll be around for so long I can't really plan for the future. That's the biggest problem with this life. It's not that I'm upset about being as I am, it's just that I need more, and she is... well, more."

He was about to carry on, but I wanted to change the subject, so I interrupted him. "Excuse me, sir?" I said, in much the same manner as I would have used to one of my teachers, who insisted on being called 'sir', even if you met them outside school.

"No, no, Jason. You can't call me 'sir', it sounds so formal."

Had I asked then what to call him, I would have found out, and a lot of the mystery and, I suppose, fear, would have disappeared from him. As it was, my own interest had been aroused by him calling me by my name. "How did you know my name was Jason?"

"You said."

"No. I didn't." I'd been very careful, in fact, to avoid using my name. I was afraid that he'd go to my school and tell someone that I was talking to him, and I wanted to make it difficult for him. There weren't any other Jasons in my school, at least not to my knowledge.

"Well maybe I heard your mother call you it."

"She didn't use my name either." In fact I wasn't as certain as all that about her not using my name, but I was convinced that he was lying.

"Okay, so I just know your name. Is that so terrible?"

The chances are that he read the back of my jacket or something, as every one of my coats still had my name on one of those little fabric name tags that my mother bought six-million of when I was three and never finished. But at the time, that didn't occur to me, and I thought he was using some strange power to find out. I was a little scared and was just about to ask him about it when he asked me a question instead. "Jason, what do you want to do with your life?" He placed the emphasis on the word 'your'.

"I don't know. Get rich, get a fast car, you know, that sort of stuff."

"That's easy, though. You'll have those before you're thirty." He was right, for what it's worth, but I think that was guesswork on his part. "But what would you do then?"

"Have fun."

"How?"

"I don't know. Get a video game of my own, or a full-size snooker table, or something like that, I suppose."

"Things, Jason. Things. What about people?"

There was silence after that, as I tried to work out a reply, but in the end the conversation just died, and I think I left at that point. On my way home I felt annoyed that I hadn't got his name, and from that day on I started thinking of him as Joe. Why I chose 'Joe' is beyond me, but I probably had a reason then.

"Good morning, Joe," I said, the next time we met. The other thing I don't understand now is why I didn't just ask him his name, but I didn't.

"Good morning, Jason," he replied, slightly coldly. "How are you today?"

And that was it. He never questioned the name once, and even used it to refer to himself. Occasionally I imagined he was trying to develop a wild-west accent, but that went away again after a couple of months.

Over the weeks and, subsequently, the months, that we were talking to each other I started telling him about my life and what I was doing. As I have already said that was a perfect subject for me then, and he seemed unwilling to say very much about his life. He would occasionally reveal the odd bit here and there. None of the conversations during that period were memorable enough for me to have any hope of repeating, but they were the most important of our times together. During my adolescence I had someone to turn to, to talk to, and someone I trusted outside of the family.

Why I trusted him I don't know, but it never occurred to me not to. When I got my first crush on a girl at the youth group, a girl called Wendy who had long straight brown hair and wore unbelievably tight jeans, and I started fantasising about her, he was there to hear. The simple act of telling someone made it seem so much more normal, and he just nodded and said something about remembering how it felt. Going down to the park every weekend became a regular part of my life, and I continued doing it until I went to University. I can remember our last conversation before I went.

As usual, I had arrived at ten a.m., and he was sitting waiting for me. I waved, and he put down his carving, which I had realised by this time was a statuette of the woman he loved. He waited for me to sit.

"Good morning," he said once I was settled.

"Good morning."

He normally waited for me to start, but I didn't know what to say, so I waited, too. "Is something wrong?" he asked.

"Not really. It's just I'm leaving tomorrow. For University."

"I know. I remembered. Enjoy it."

"I just felt..."

"Oh, don't worry about me. I'll still be here when you get back, and I've grown used to the long waits. Anyway, you'll have more stories to tell me when you return."

I stood up. "Thank you," I said, putting a hand on his shoulder.

"Nothing to thank me for."

I walked away again.

When I got back from University nothing was quite the same. The house seemed smaller, my mother seemed suddenly older, and I felt as if I didn't really fit in anymore. At College I had met Julie, my first real girlfriend, and a couple of other girls I hadn't really noticed yet, one of whom was called Andrea.

Joe was the only part of my home life that hadn't changed, and I was very glad to go and tell him the stories of my first term. He listened intently and smiled when I began to discuss Julie. "You love her a lot, don't you?"

"Yes."

He made a little sound under his breath, as if he were thinking about something and wondering whether to say it.

"What is it?" I asked.

"It's just I don't think she's right for you. From what you say, anyway. Now what was that other one you mentioned, the one in the play who played the faerie queen and looked great in her cocktail dress at the party?"

"Andrea."

"Yes, her. I liked her. I think you should spend more time with her."

Again, Joe was right, not that I actually did anything about it. Almost as soon as I got back I heard that Julie had decided to start sleeping with someone else, and Andrea was nearby when I wanted a shoulder to cry on. We started going out half-way through that term, and got engaged at the end of my second year, which was her third. Joe was both pleased and slightly smug.

"Told you."

"Yes, I know you did. So you're a good judge of character."

"There aren't that many types of people around, you know. Not that many at all."

I have no idea why I made the sudden jump from people to wishes, but during that conversation I started wondering about his third wish.

"Joe? You know you had three wishes?"

"Yes."

"Have you still got the third one?"

"Yes."

"What are you going to do with it?"

"That depends how cynical I feel when I next get bored. I was considering destroying the world, or maybe just dying. Who knows?"

"Why would you want to destroy the world?"

"I wouldn't. At least not destroying the world in the way you mean. I don't mean blowing it up, or anything like that. I mean making each and every person on the face of the planet think for themselves and realise their own responsibility for their situation, their government, and the world."

"And you think that would destroy it?"

"Most of it, yes. If enough people thought for themselves they'd realise how stupid everything was, and the whole system would collapse."

"So they'd create something else, better."

"I said think for themselves, not agree. There's no way two intellectuals could completely agree about the society they'd want, let alone a hundred, or a million, or the whole world. No, the whole place would fall apart."

"So why would you want to do it?"

"To prove a point. I don't like ignorance, and I don't like the way people walk about dead to the world, and the way they bring up children in the cities stopping them doing anything and shouting at them when they try to play anywhere. The people here are dead already. There's no sparkle. Look at the children over there, playing with the ball." He indicated a group of very young boys, playing a game of tag. "They've got some life in them, but their parents haven't."

"Those older children over there," he continued, pointing at a set of teenagers, "are probably about to go and steal something, or beat someone up. Where's the life gone? What happens to them to destroy that sparkle? I'll tell you.

They're told how awful the world is, and they're told they can't do anything about it, and they give up. Children believe they can change the world just by believing it will change. Why can't adults?"

"Because it isn't that simple to change things."

"Why not?"

"Because life is more complicated than you make out."

"Because people make it complicated. Come to think of it, that's probably the reason people have children. They want to try to remember that sparkle and feel its warmth again."

"I don't think it's reasonable to say that if everyone stayed childish the world would suddenly be better, though."

"I wasn't saying that. I was saying that people would be happier."

"And that's worth destroying the world for?"

"Most of those people are dead already."

We chatted about other things for a while, but stayed off his beliefs. To tell the truth I was shocked, as he'd never expressed strong opinions before, and now was saying he wanted to destroy the world.

I went away and thought about what he'd said, and decided I didn't believe a word of it. We didn't talk about it again. He did have a knack for knowing which subjects I didn't want to discuss.

My University career ended, and I went to work in a marketing company in London, so I didn't see Joe much for a few years. I did make a point of inviting him to my wedding, but he said he couldn't make it, which I think was probably just as well.

The day before my twenty-ninth birthday I formed my own company, and moved back here. It boomed right from day one. I was very lucky, admittedly, but also worked every hour God sent for the first six months. After that I went back to normal office hours, to Andrea's great relief. The company made huge profits, and I decided to buy my house outright and to treat myself to a new car. As I was signing the documents, I remembered Joe's prediction about my future, and wondered if he was still around. I'd been in town for nearly a year and hadn't gone to the park to check even once.

The car-dealer must have thought I was mad, because I suddenly began hurrying him along. Within about five minutes I was on the road in my new Jag, and driving, slightly too fast I must admit, to the park. I turned into the car park and skidded to a halt, having forgotten how difficult it is to brake on gravel. I got out of the car and pressed the little lock button on my remote-control thing, and looked over towards the corner of the park where he used to be. I ran some of the way, having seen a figure sitting in roughly the right place. People there probably thought I was mad, too.

"Joe!" I shouted, and then worried that it was not Joe, and that I was going to get arrested soon.

The man looked up, put down a small wooden carving, and waved.

I ran up to him and sat down. "Joe," I said again, out of breath. "You're still here."

"I said I would be. Now, what's been happening to you? Last I heard you'd got married and were working in London as a brain-dead office worker."

"I've got my own company up here now, and..." I was still out of breath, and sat panting for a while, trying to get enough breath to say the rest of my sentence.

"Everything I said you'd have. Good. I'd hate to be wrong. But are you happy, Jason? That's the question."

I nodded.

"Good. Happy already, and you haven't even had kids yet. You must be doing something right. Probably marrying Andrea was your best move."

I recovered my breath finally. "So how have you been?"

"Oh, not bad. I got arrested once, a year ago now, for loitering. They didn't think I had a right to be here. It took me some time to convince them. But I don't want to talk about me. What else have you been doing?"

I told him everything from the time I'd moved to London originally, through my founding a new company and moving, to my latest purchase of a car. I got a bit sidetracked into talking about marketing at one point, but Joe pretended to stay interested all the way through.

When I'd finished bringing him up to date it was getting into the late afternoon, and Andrea was going to be expecting me back, so I left Joe and went home. Andrea asked me why I'd taken so long, so I told her I'd been talking to Joe, and then had to explain who Joe was and why I was talking to him. She shook her head several times as I was telling her, and I knew she didn't believe him. That was when I realised that I did. I really did.

"She probably doesn't even exist," said Andrea, out of the blue.

"Who?"

"That woman, the archer."

"Come on, why would he make that up?"

"Why would he tell you such a pack of lies at all?"

"Look, I think he might be telling the truth."

"About being three-thousand? You can't tell me you believe that?"

"What's he got to gain from lying about it?"

"Nothing, but he's mad anyway. Why does he need a reason?"

"Okay, I'll find the woman, and we'll see."

"Even if she does exist, that's no proof. Just because he saw some attractive woman once doesn't mean he's three-thousand."

"Right, I'll find out who he is, as well. Isn't your tennis friend a private detective or something?"

"Ian works for a firm of investigators, yes."

"Well we'll get him to find out who Joe really is, then?"

"They charge a fortune."

"Oh, come on. We've got a fortune. And I want to know, once and for all, who Joe is."

"Okay. Go ahead."

I spoke to Ian about it, and he agreed to make every effort to find the woman and to find out who Joe really was. He suspected that the woman would be very easy to locate, as I had the location and rough date of the archery competition, as Joe had told me once, and she was actually one of the competitors. Joe himself could be followed to find out where he lived, and the house then checked.

* * *

It took two weeks before we heard anything back at all. They gave us the woman's name and address. Her name was Helen Wells. They hadn't found anything useful about Joe himself, though, as he'd been living in a disused hut. He had a large pile of cash in there, hidden, which he used for his living expenses. The days he didn't spend at the park he spent reading second-hand books, which he bought from the local Oxfam shop.

The only useful thing they had discovered about Joe was that his name, as written in each and every one of his books, was "David". There was no surname, and nothing further to help the investigators. They apologised profusely, and said that they would continue hunting for any clue as to his identity. I thanked them and settled the bill for the first half of the investigation.

Helen Wells lived in Dudley, just outside Birmingham. The investigators had provided me with a photograph of her, which I had to admit made her out to be extremely pretty. She fitted Joe's description perfectly.

"Okay, so she exists," said Andrea, half-way through the washing up. "What now?"

"Well, Ian might find out something else useful."

"Then again he might not. This guy's just your regular tramp."

"He's got a lot of money for a tramp."

"So he's robbed someone."

I stopped talking, because I have always disliked arguing with women holding carving knives, and Andrea was just washing up the huge great knife we always use on our Sunday roasts.

Part-way through making the coffee there was a telephone call from Ian's agency.

"Jason, I'm sorry, there's something we forgot to tell you about Ms Wells. If it's relevant, she used to be called Webster. She got married ten years ago, two months after that competition you were interested in. Her husband actually proposed to her that day, according to one of their close friends."

"Thank you."

"Sorry to disturb you, but we thought you might want to know."

"Yes, thanks. Bye."

I went back into the kitchen and told Andrea.

"So?" she said, stirring the coffee and handing me the mug with Animal from the Muppet show on it.

"So it was his wish that made them get married."

"Come again?"

"He wished for her to fall in love with him, so she got a proposal that day, so even if she is in love with him she can't marry him unless she gets a divorce first, and if she's not that kind of person she might never get a divorce and he'll have to wait until her husband dies."

"Okay, come again, again."

"Look, it's simple. Joe wishes for Helen to fall in love with him..."

"Yes, I understand what you said. I just don't understand how you can believe it, even for a moment. Fine, okay, it's a nice theory, and it fits together, but it doesn't mean anything. Coincidence, Jason."

"Add it to all the other things, like him knowing I'd be successful."

"Look, I could have told you that. You're that kind of person from that kind of background. In fact I think I did tell you that. Look, dear, you're being stupid, and I think you should forget about Joe completely."

"Well I ought to tell him about Helen, don't you think?"

"If you want to."

I went to the park that morning and was amazed to see Joe sitting upright on a little folding chair, wearing a suit, with a short haircut. He was obviously waiting to see me, and raised a hand as soon as I stepped out of my car.

"Good day, Jason, my friend," he said, agitated about something.

"What? Oh, hello. Why are you dressed like that?"

"I needed a change."

"Why? What's happened?"

"No, no. Wait. Your news first."

I stood open-mouthed, trying to work out how he knew something was up. "The archer."

"Yes. Her name?" He looked down, frowning.

"Helen. Helen Wells."

"Helen. A fine name."

"She's married. Her husband proposed on the day you

first saw her."

"Then my dream makes sense."

"What dream?" I asked, annoyed that he wasn't even slightly surprised by my news.

"Her husband. She loves him very much, I think. For my wish to be granted they must split, by death or his design. One way or another her heart must be broken." He looked up at me, his eyes wide, the puzzled look gone, and then spoke again, very carefully and slowly.

"My friend, you must find out something else for me, please. You must find out whether she does love him, as I dreamt she does. For if that much is true, I cannot allow my dream—perhaps I should call it a nightmare—to come true." He looked away again but continued speaking. "She would love me, you see, but she would always be sad. Her beauty was not meant for sadness, my friend. Find out for me." He had never before spoken with emotion—always with his cold, knowing, tone, and I was struck by his sincerity. Whatever else this man believed or knew, I was certain that he needed to know the answer to the one question he asked.

"Of course," I said. "I'll go and find out."

"Yes," he replied, already looking off into the distance. "Thank you."

I rang Ian that afternoon, and asked him to check the state of Mrs. Wells's marriage. He was confused, but I told him that it was vital, and he said he'd find out as soon as he could. It took him less than a day to find a variety of Helen's friends, and her husband's, all of whom said they had a very close marriage indeed, and no one he spoke to thought that anything could ever come between them.

I sat by the phone for a good half-hour before I resolved to go to see Joe again. He would still be there, I knew, and I felt I owed it to him to tell him immediately.

When I got there, he was sitting on the same folding chair as before, in much the same posture. He nodded to me, but said nothing, waiting for me to speak. I told him, simply and plainly, that Mrs. Wells was believed to have a near-perfect marriage.

Joe leant backwards, and I thought he was going to fall off his chair. He began laughing hysterically, and looked upwards and said "You bastards" quietly. He carried on laughing, despite my efforts to see if he was all right, and I think I heard him say "Well, that's that then."

"Do you feel like a drink or something?" I couldn't think of anything else to offer.

"No, I'm okay, thanks. I just need some time to think, that's all, if you wouldn't mind. Thank you, though, for everything."

"You're sure you'll be okay?"

"Of course. I'll be here tomorrow, if you want to stop by. Yes. Stop by tomorrow."

I left, puzzling over his change of looks and personality. Andrea asked me about it, and I summarised for her. She said, "Told you he was mad" and fortunately left it at that.

At eleven that night we got a phone call from Ian, this time sounding quite distraught. "Jason? We've found out something about David."

"What?"

"His real name, according to our latest findings, is David O'Donnell. His money was inherited from his father, who died during the war. He is fifty-eight. We have no records of a mother, or any record of his birth. The only clue that he ever existed apart from the inheritance document is a house in his name that he's been seen entering, and that he bought for cash twenty-five years ago. He stays there every few months. I got inside to check things out, and found over half a million pounds in cash, and a collection of antiques that rivals a museum, just sitting around, some of it thrown in the basement. Old swords, vases, armour, paintings, everything. A treasure trove. I checked a couple of the paintings, and they're unknown. Never stolen, never even believed to exist. Every one of them priceless. Who is this guy? Or who was his father?"

"Have you any records of his father?"

"No. None at all."

"Thank you. Thank you very much."

I didn't tell Andrea anything about it and tried to get some sleep. I slept very badly and kept wondering what Joe was doing. Eventually I gave up and went downstairs to read for a while. I found myself reading through a section about Michelangelo in my encyclopaedia, which sent me to sleep quite quickly.

I woke up in the morning with a stiff neck and Andrea standing over me. "What's wrong?" she asked.

"Nothing. I just couldn't sleep, so I came down here, and, well, fell asleep. What time is it?"

"Eight."

"I've got to go to the park."

I ran past her and up to get dressed. Two minutes later I ran out of the house, got into the car and drove off. I pulled into the park three minutes after that, having nearly destroyed the car's gearbox on the way.

There was a police cordon around the area in which I expected to find Joe. Three policemen watched me getting out of the car and running over. "What's happened?"

"Did you know a Mr David O'Donnell, sir?"

"Yes. What's happened? What's going on?"

"Are you friend or family, sir?"

"Just a friend. We've spoken off and on for years."

I stepped sideways and looked past, and saw David lying on his back, legs straight, arms folded on his chest. He looked very relaxed. For a moment I felt jealous, that I could never lie like that without my chest going up and down, and then I realised he was dead.

"What happened?"

"We don't know that, yet, sir, but there are no signs of injury, so I suspect he died of exposure. He was found lying here this morning by a jogger."

The police didn't need me for anything, as I wasn't good enough for formal identification, even though no one else was, but they were very good about keeping me informed. The autopsy couldn't find a cause of death, and the inquest recorded an open verdict. I found out during the inquest that he'd been carrying a forged passport with the name David O'Donnell. The police still called him that, as there was no other clue to his real identity.

As soon as I left the park, I rang Ian and asked for the address of David's house. "Sorry, Jason," came the reply. "There was an arson attack last night. The whole place was doused in petrol and set alight. As was the disused hut. Sorry."

"Damn." I slammed the phone down, walked back to the car, and drove round the block a couple of times to get my head straight before I went home. Andrea was waiting for me and asked me about what had happened. I told her. She gave me a hug.

***

A week later Andrea and I were the only people at his funeral. As the vicar read the service, I spent the whole time trying to make up my mind, but I couldn't. And I still haven't. It annoys me that whenever I think of Joe now I'm annoyed at him for leaving the question mark. I'm going on holiday next week with Andrea, as she'll be having a baby in June and we're getting some holidays on our own while we can. Hopefully when I get back from that I'll be able to forget, and stop ringing Ian in the hope of more information, or writing down the facts on a blackboard and trying to make sense of them. Hopefully.

―――

Robert lives to the west of London and is an active member of the Slough Writers Group. He is abnormally upset about the lack of a single Russian oligarch with a preference for recreating zeppelins over buying football teams. Aside from a few short story successes, he has written a novella, The Girl in the Wave, *a modern gothic horror set on the beautiful Cornish coastline. Find him on Twitter @r_kibble.*

ALI

Liz Fyne

The first thing I noticed about Ali, what everyone noticed, was a horrible scar that cut his face vertically through the middle. Soon after he began working at the campus crêperie, rumors circulated regarding the mysteries of its origin. My favorite was that he'd been in a knife fight in the street—that before he became Ali the crêpe maker, he was part of a notorious gang, maybe the Crips. Such a fun story, he changed an *i* for an *e*, he switched his switchblade for an apron and hot griddle. Then one day he looked up from crêpe making, he caught an undergrad poetry major (that would be me) watching him from the sidelines, and just like that Cupid shot him straight through the heart.

Suddenly when I ordered the the banana-Nutella crêpe, it had extra Nutella. Once he added actual hazelnuts. There was an unexpected crunch; for a moment I thought I'd broken a tooth.

When I stood in line to order, a new game emerged: we took turns, Ali and I, looking at each other and then away. In those moments when the looking was mine, I'd admire his body, lean and dark with olive-colored skin. Always, however, the dining experience was less than it should have been, encumbered by my best friend's nattering voice at our table. Her own theory was that Ali was ex-Special Forces. She said she'd happened upon him several times outside of work, and he always wore a camouflage T-shirt. She imagined he was a man marked from bravery, ambushed by ISIS militants and left to die in a bed of hot sand.

I found the Special Forces idea unlikely. Just because he wore camouflage—

But he was a puzzle, an alluring one at that. The obvious and undisguisable history of violence was so at odds with the gentle passion of his work: beholden to the creation of the perfect crêpe. Each order was a thing of beauty, then delivered to tables peopled by academics and bohemians. Their own, non-hazardous indoor lives were absent warring and street/sand/battle-fighting. Ali seemed utterly beyond such experiences, himself, when he cooked, arranged, drizzled chocolate or raspberry syrup on round white porcelain. When it was me who ordered, the syrup arrived in the form of a large, gracious flower. I wondered if he was too bashful to make a heart. Maybe deep down he was too hardened from years of unknown savagery.

* * *

He spoke no English; I learned this one day from the cashier. She was a small woman with a guarded smile and a childish lisp. I inquired about the symbols she drew on the order sheets. They bore no obvious resemblance to language.

"He only speaks Arabic," she said.

This news was unexpected.

"So how does he work here?"

"He's a refugee."

"He's what?"

"A refugee."

I turned my eyes to the griddle area. Ignorant of our conversation, Ali was occupied cutting strawberries. He was delicate about it, making thin, even slices.

"You're writing Arabic then?" I asked.

"No, it's made up, but he gets the idea."

"How long has he been here?"

"In the US?" she said.

"Yes."

"Two months."

It was in this way I realized my friend's story might be closer than expected: a man slashed in the face, retrieved from sand red with blood. But what had followed was no military hospital, no homebound trip to Mom and apple pie. Rather he was dragged, kicked, pulled to a truck bed filled with other men's bodies.

Locked in filthy prison. Hated and beaten for pleasure. Maybe.

At the crêperie, Ali looked up from slicing. He caught my gaze and this time I held it instead of turning away. I let my eyes wander his scar like before I'd wanted to but hadn't. It was an injury long healed and darkened from the pink of raw flesh. Still, the experience might be fresh in his mind; a memory of fear not triumph.

All this time whatever silly adventures we'd imagined — myself, my friends, and others — always they'd been his choice.

We'd all been so wrong.

* * *

I grew up on Long Island. My family vacationed in the Hamptons. We had a yacht and spent afternoons sunning ourselves in deckchairs accompanied by two spotted Welsh Corgis.

"The Queen's dogs," my mother always said.

Strife and hardship were far away; they were the misfortunes of other people.

But recently world news arrested my attention: bombs in Iraq, combat in Afghanistan. I went online and for the first time researched the history of endless proxy war in Syria. Tens of millions (*tens*?) of people displaced. Where did they go?

Next time I went to the crêperie, I went alone—this was a first, also. I stood in line and when Ali saw me, I didn't look away. He did, blushing through the dark tan of his skin. But when I received my order, I was surprised to find the flower drizzle continued to the edge of the plate, taking the form of a long question mark. I looked up one more; he made a smile that was inquisitive but bashful, and I wondered at this punctuation, where he'd learned it and what he meant. I wondered at his age; he was older than me, but could have been anywhere between twenty-five and thirty-five. In almost every way we were opposites and strangers, just that we incredibly overlapped within the tiny sphere of a campus crêperie.

That day I took my plate to one of the outdoor tables, where I pulled a chair woven from wrought iron. I traced the chocolate question mark with my finger. When I'd finished eating I kept my seat, asking myself how it could possibly work out, taking this path forward.

Time passed, and I retrieved my phone and reviewed the headlines. The news was newly depressing, so instead I scrolled through photos of the corgis: Porgy and Bess. Weekdays like this they spent with my mother in her antiques store, listening to Gershwin and shedding all over the merchandise.

When Ali finally emerged, a day done with work, I had red crisscross marks on my forearms where I'd leaned into the gridded table surface. I sat straight and he stared at my arms, like for just a moment we shared some common history after all.

I stood and he stayed where he was. Facing him like this it hit me how truly difficult it was, being with a person who couldn't understand anything you said and vice-versa. Words piled up inside me, they had nowhere to go. I gestured to him to approach, which he did. When I turned and began walking, he walked with me.

He had an easy stride, longer than my own, but he accommodated my naturally slower pace. He smelled of cooking oils and butter from the griddle. His fingers drew near mine, engaged in tentative exploration. I took his hand, which was cool but not soft. As we walked, I lifted it to get a better look. His skin was callused and worn like I hadn't seen with anyone else. He had a scar here also, but much smaller. It could have been a cut that occurred incidentally: sloppy childhood cooking or scissors that slipped while wrapping birthday gifts.

I turned to see him watching me as I rubbed the unfamiliar texture of his hand. He rubbed mine in return, which was smooth and free of calluses or cuts of any kind.

He was a strong person, I could tell through his clothes, but it seemed more the wiry build of lifelong physical labor than the bulk of weightlifting at a gym. Despite an obvious power of body, he was careful with himself, with my own hand, with that sharp knife at the crêperie.

Had I been with anyone else, I would have made small talk already, but we passed in silence and with no clear destination until Ali deviated from my path. As our arms strained apart I stopped and he did, too. I located the source of his distraction: long streamers out in front of the art museum. They were rich with color, billowing in a soft breeze and promoting a temporary show of Caravaggio paintings on loan from Italy. Ali seemed entranced and I wondered if there were art museums where he came from, if they'd been bombed years ago, if he'd had the opportunity to go even before then. Maybe he'd lived in a tiny village, hauling water and sowing crops while dreaming of another life far away.

Our own museum closed at five-thirty. You could enter until four, which was just ten minutes away. I tugged Ali by the hand, pulling him up the concrete steps, past the outsized lion sculptures. He followed them with his eyes, then craned his head backward until he almost stumbled.

Inside he looked every which way as I paid for both of us. Audio tours were available in a variety of languages, and I nudged him to the register, pointed to the long list of options. He smiled, radiantly pleased at finding this Arabic selection in an American museum. The staff provided a handheld player and headphones that he adjusted carefully.

On the third floor we entered a room packed with Caravaggio, master of chiaroscuro. Several of these paintings I'd seen previously on family trips to Rome, to Florence at the Ufizzi. But this could be Ali's first time seeing Western art up close, maybe any art at all — including that of his own country — and he froze quite suddenly in place.

* * *

There's a curious phenomenon called Stendhal syndrome, in which persons exposed to great beauty become dizzy, sometimes even faint. And now I felt Ali's formerly tight grip go loose. I turned to see his face grown pale, his body nodding in an unsteady lean, and I thought with astonishment he might be physically overcome by splendor. We moved to a bench in the center of the room where he sat with head down, elbows perched on knees, until steadiness gradually returned. His fingers, which had abandoned mine in crisis, returned slowly and with a question. I took them in my hand, rubbing again the strange texture of his skin. When he appeared restored I pointed to my watch, meaning to communicate time was short. He nodded, made a sheepish grin and his face, even with that curling scar, seemed a thing more wondrous than Caravaggio or paintings of any other kind. My own face felt unsettled as suddenly it was him pulling me, first to a standing position, then to the wall. He gestured to my audio player, and I forced my gaze from him to the device. I sensed his eyes on me as I took the player in hand, searched for the relevant painting number. I helped him do the same. When I pressed *play*, a man's s voice flooded my hearing and embarked on its educational narrative.

The Crucifixion of Saint Peter was completed in 1601. As portrayed here by Caravaggio, Saint Peter requested to be suspended upside down on the cross, so he wouldn't rival Christ's own crucifixion. The painting is understated, Saint Peter's —

Ali and I stood near together, and I was aware of my previous experience of soul eating, of wordless love communion. For a moment I felt unsteady, myself. He looked at me, his eyes wide and keen and incredible.

"Ah," he said.

His voice, this first time I'd ever heard it, was dulcet and smooth.

He dropped my hand and ran his fingers through my hair. The audio voice-over continued as from a distance.

— the cross is depicted in a very convincing way —

And I wondered, Was this painting disturbing for him? For this beautiful man escaped from violence and war? But I had no answers. I just followed as he walked from one painting to the next, each time pressing *play*. Tour words ran through my hearing; they were a blur with no significance. Then important words did arrive, via the intercom, that the museum was closing. Ali looked toward the ceiling with a puzzled expression. It was much too soon, this closing. Really a lifetime of exploration remained, but not here or now or in this place. I pointed to my watch, and he removed his headphones with an air of mournful acceptance.

"Ah," he said, again.

"We can come back," I said, hoping he'd the gist if not the details.

When he smiled then I thought maybe he did, and I smiled in return.

* * *

When I brought him to my apartment that night, I was surprised at myself. I was surprised at the world for presenting this odd bit of circumstance. I was surprised at Ali, that he followed me through the outside door to my building after just a momentary hesitation. Maybe I shouldn't have wondered at that last part, but he'd looked surprised, himself, as I held the door open and waited with anxious expectation.

For sure he'd imagined this moment, even if he hadn't thought it would arrive in real life. For myself, I actually hadn't thought of *this* moment, although I'd thought of others, like kissing and rolling up his sleeves to search his bare arms for further tales of woe.

Now we stood in my bedroom. We faced each other, each in our own worlds of wordless thrall. He reached down and pulled his shirt over his head, dropped it to the floor. He waited then, maybe wanting to be sure he had the right idea after all. And as he did so, I observed his body was marked as I'd guessed, at least one more sad story etched in the template of flesh. It ran the length of his right upper arm, wound round his shoulder to his back where it escaped my view. I stepped near, reached my hand. With my touch I sought to extract everything he couldn't speak, much as I'd questioned that question mark, caress of his soul, drizzled to my plate with such artful precision.

At this contact he took a sharp breath in. He leaned down, he kissed me — tentatively at first, then with all the hunger he'd kept locked inside so long.

***

He was a tender man, a generous lover. He seemed amused by the idea of safe sex, but was amenable. As we made love, I felt as if I were a great painting; he held me in a way that was secure but fragile, awed, mindful that sometimes in life events go atrociously wrong. Horror swells and propagates when really the world should be a place of peace and loving kindness—

Life so stunning we can't help but faint at the view.

***

He stayed the night but woke early. He pointed at my watch that lay sideways on the bed stand. It was time to get cooking, crêping. Another day of pressing his spirit into batter, dispersing of himself to strangers in some act of crazy, defiant world love. He stood and smiled and blew me a kiss goodbye.

Later that morning I pulled myself from bed, also. I dressed in a fashion that was languid and distracted. Outside I dawdled, walking slowly, tripping on a crack in the sidewalk so raised and obvious and easily avoided that afterward I laughed. Because in this new life nothing mattered but Ali. I knew that as, closing time approached, I'd arrive at the crêperie once more. I would be slow there, too, luxuriating in the fresh glow of carnal knowledge. He would raise his eyes, he'd catch in the moment because the idea that I'd return, that he'd return, that such moments of unspeakable joy could transpire over and forever without interruption, without fear or restriction—

***

It was strange to me when I did arrive and another man manned the griddle, instead. I'd seen this person before; he was more of a boy than a man. Other days he'd waited tables and delivered cappuccinos with hearts swirled in froth, but now he occupied this place not his own. When I appeared in line he turned away, appearing vexed and hurried and confused.

The woman with a guarded smile was at the cash register as always, but today she wasn't smiling. When I reached her, she turned away, also.

I followed her gaze to the wall, like somehow Ali had been standing there all this time and been hidden from view. But he wasn't hidden, at least not there. And I wondered, Was he on break? Of course he'd take breaks. He might leave for the back, put his feet up and wipe sweat from his face. It was reasonable to think he was gone for just few minutes, that he'd reappear and life would continue as planned. Even so, something inside me was going stiff and hard because there was a tension here, an obvious running from my presence.

"Where—"

I stopped.

Again I told myself this was nothing, how silly to ask. But the cashier had red eyes. Just a moment ago they'd been normal. When she replied her voice came thick and low.

"He's gone," she said.

No, how could that be? Gone where?

"Gone home?" I asked.

"Sort of."

I stood mute, unsure what this could possibly mean. As I did so, she reached below the counter and, in an unexpected move, handed me a Post-It note. On its surface was the outline, done in what looked like black ballpoint pen, of a single flower. The drawing was strong and smooth but for the tail end that veered off the paper in an unnatural way.

It was unquestionably done by Ali.

"He left this for you," she said.

I didn't understand this, either. I turned the note over; the back side was blank.

"He didn't have much time," she said.

Why on earth not? My mind formed questions; so many they seemed to cancel and leave a crushing blank. The cashier shifted her weight, looked round the room, then gestured me aside and began to explain, slowly: Ali, she said, had been deported, at least he *would be* deported—

"But—" I said.

She continued through my interruption: He was here pending approval of his asylum application. If the application was denied—

"Did they see his *body*?" I interrupted, once more.

These things are complicated, that's what she said. She was trembling now, her words choked. I fell back in space and time: He was in my bed, he made love to me until I'd thought I'd cry from the experience I'd known before but never like that.

My fingers behind his shoulders had found more hard lines of raised flesh. In a moment of paradox, he'd smiled.

"No worry," he'd said.

So he knew some English after all.

"We've had refugees here before," said the cashier. "This happens."

No, I thought. That's not true, something like this never really happens.

* * *

I didn't see him again. I've always tried not to imagine what his life became.

I have the Post-It, still. When it seemed certain he was really gone, I had it framed. The size seemed so horribly diminutive, I requested wide squares of white matting and a wide white frame. In the end, the note resembled a small yellow sun within a bright light sky.

I've never known anyone else like that, I suppose I never will.

It was just one day of many, that we spent together, but no else loves like that, no one else can be loved like that —

Beautiful Ali.

———

Liz Fyne is thrilled to have a story in this, as well as two previous anthologies published by S & H Publishing. Additional stories are published in 34th Parallel, Literary Orphans, Intima: A Journal of Narrative Fiction, *and* Anastomos. *Learn more about her at lizfyne.com. Follow her @lizfyne*

DID YOU ENJOY THE BOOK?

MAKE THE AUTHORS HAPPY

LEAVE A REVIEW!

S & H Publishing, Inc. is proud to publish this and other books by many of these very talented authors. Visit us at http://sandhpublishing.com